MOVING TARGETS

SPIDER SHEPHERD: SAS

Dead Men
Live Fire
Rough Justice
Fair Game
False Friends
True Colours
White Lies
Black Ops
Dark Forces
Light Touch

Spider Shepherd: SAS thrillers :
The Sandpit

Jack Nightingale supernatural thrillers:
Nightfall
Midnight
Nightmare
Nightshade
Lastnight
San Francisco Night
New York Night

PRAISE FOR STEPHEN LEATHER

'A master of the thriller genre'

Irish Times

'Let Spider draw you into his web, you won't regret it'

The Sun

'The sheer impetus of his storytelling is damned hard to resist'

Daily Express

'Written with panache, and a fine ear for dialogue, Leather manages the collision between the real and the occult with exceptional skill, adding a superb time-shift twist at the end'

Daily Mail on *Nightmare*

'A wicked read'

Anthony Horowitz on *Nightfall*

MOVING TARGETS

SPIDER SHEPHERD: SAS

STEPHEN LEATHER

CHAPTER 1

S abit Kusen trudged wearily along the dusty street, heading home from the market where he had spent all day squatting in the dirt, trying to sell the cooking pots and water jars that his father pounded into shape in the tiny forge alongside their house. There had been only one customer all day and he had beaten Sabit down in price, twice walking off in apparent disgust before returning to grudgingly buy a pot for a price that would barely pay for the family's bread.

Once a welcome refuge from the desert, a bustling, prosperous oasis and resting place, the modern town of Turguan now had little to offer travellers. Most of the buildings were one or two storey mudbrick houses, separated by crumbling alleyways. There were a few drab concrete apartment and office blocks close to the town centre, but they were shoddily designed and even more shoddily built, corrupt government officials and contractors having siphoned off much of the money to construct them. There were a few cars and diesel-belching lorries

1

on the streets but also carts pulled by donkeys and buffaloes, while strings of scrawny camels plodded along, laden with bales of the traditional fabrics that had long been the pride of Sabit's people and their principal export.

High on its windswept plateau, it was a place of extremes, burning hot by day with summer temperatures of over 40°C, though even then it was bitterly cold at night. In winter, it could be 20°C below freezing, and the biting north winds howling over the desert brought flurries of ice and gritty sand that stung the skin like hornets.

The isolated town was surrounded by mountains and deserts. To the west and north-west the jagged, snow-laden peaks seemed to pierce the sky. To the north and east the dunes began, a desert so vast that even the nomads roamed only the fringes of it. The sun-bleached bones of animals – and men – in the million square miles of burning sands showed that none could survive in that wasteland. A modern highway crossed the fringes of the desert, a straight line ruled across the landscape like a Roman road. Outside the town, the only man-made structures were the steel skeletons of 'nodding donkey' pumps extracting the oil that was both the blessing and the curse of this remote region, bringing a few much-needed jobs, but also ensuring that the government would fight to the death to defeat any campaign for independence.

Even in his short lifetime, Sabit could remember farmers coaxing crops from the dry, stony fields that surrounded the town, the dust from their ploughs drifting like smoke through the streets. Now the dunes had advanced right up to the edge of the town and drifts of shifting sand were spilling into the streets, threatening to engulf it altogether. An ancient road bisected the town from east to west, a trade route that had been used beyond the memories of men. For five days that road had been blocked by protesters, among them Sabit's father, uncle and brothers. It was an all-male household, for Sabit's mother had died giving birth to him.

Sabit's father, Rebiya Kusen, was one of the town elders. They gathered every Friday to drink green tea and discuss the town's affairs, though their discussions and conclusions were merely symbolic, for all power was concentrated in the capital, Beijing, a thousand miles away. Only rarely in their history had Sabit's people governed themselves. Down the centuries a succession of warlords and tyrants had conquered the region and ruled it with blood and iron.

Already cowed by decades of repression, the people had reacted with sullen, resentful acquiescence to the ever-growing number of petty restrictions upon them. However, a small spark – the arrest of an imam for 'anti-state activities' – had ignited a blaze of protest. The town's young men took to the streets, shouting anti-government slogans, throwing rocks and bottles. The police responded with clubs, tear gas and water cannons, and 150 youths were arrested. Stripped of their coats and jackets, beaten and tortured, they were held for a week in freezing conditions, made worse by being doused daily with cold water. By the end of the week, fifty of them had died and many of the survivors were suffering from frostbite.

As news of the atrocity spread, popular outrage outweighed the fear of reprisals and protests flared again, growing into open rebellion. The protesters marched on the central police station, demanding the release of the remaining captives, and when that was refused they stormed the building, smashing the windows, battering down the doors, freeing the prisoners and attacking their tormentors – the state police. They wrecked the building and made a bonfire of all the files and documents they found there, including the intelligence files held on every citizen. Having ransacked the building, the protesters overturned police and government vehicles and erected barricades on the main road, then banners began appearing, demanding self-rule and independence from the hated regime. Most of the protesters were relatively peaceful, but a handful, more passionate or more reckless than the rest, began beating ethnic Chinese immigrants and looting and burning their houses. Before long, the smell of oily smoke hung heavily in the air.

Sabit's father and the other elders grew increasingly concerned at the escalation of events. 'It will not succeed,' Rebiya said to his son. 'It will bring repression and terrible suffering upon us.' But because he was a proud member of his race, he continued to speak for the community, even when he disagreed with them.

After several days of rioting, an uneasy silence had settled over the town. The banners with their defiant messages still fluttered above the barricades and the young hotheads still patrolled the streets, attacking any immigrants foolish enough to show their faces. The older, wiser heads, led by Rebiya, talked quietly together, their gazes flickering constantly to the east, beyond the town's outskirts, where the concrete ribbon of the highway, grey against the red-gold dunes that flanked it, lost itself in the desert haze.

As darkness fell that night, Rebiya, his face etched with worry, began to dig in the dry, stony soil of the walled yard behind their house. He carefully scraped off the top layer with his shovel and piled it to one side, then dug down into the darker earth beneath. When Sabit asked him what he was doing, his father merely put a finger to his lips.

'But is it a grave?' Sabit said, looking down into the deep, narrow trench his father was excavating.

A brief flicker of a smile crossed his father's face. 'Let us hope not, my son.'

When he had finished digging, he took a length of rusting iron water pipe and drove it into the side of the trench near the top, at an angle that meant it broke ground a few feet from the trench. He buried it under a heap of stones and rubble, so it was invisible to anyone searching the yard. He disposed of the earth he had excavated by scattering it the length of the winding back lane behind the house. He broke up the old wooden store chest that had stood in their house since his grandfather's time and used the wood and a piece of battered corrugated iron to roof over the trench he had made, leaving a narrow gap at one end that would be filled by the last piece of wood. He lowered an earthenware water jar, a metal container with a hinged lid and a bucket into the trench, then scattered the topsoil he had removed over the corrugated iron. He sprinkled water on it and trod it down until it was indistinguishable from the trampled earth in the rest of the yard.

He turned to face his young son. 'Now do you understand?' he said.

The boy shook his head.

'These are dangerous times, my son. Bad men are coming. I will be put in prison and if they find you, they will take you too. When I tell you it is time, you must not hesitate for a second. You must climb down into the trench and stay there while I cover the top. Do not be frightened, there will be air to breathe from the pipe, and there is water and a little food. It will be dark but by day there will be a little light through the pipe. Whatever sounds you hear, even if footsteps come very close, you must remain absolutely still and silent. When it is safe, I will come and get you. If I do not, you must count the days and nights – the brightening and fading of the light from the pipe will help you count them – and wait at least four days before you come out. You will have to push hard on the wooden plank, and eventually the soil will give way. Do it at night, come out very carefully and tiptoe to the lane. Do not go back into the house because bad people may be waiting there. Keep to the back ways, do not speak to anyone, and make your way to the edge of town, then take the road west. Hide by day and walk only at night, until you reach my cousin Rahman's village – you remember him?'

The boy nodded.

'Tell him what has happened here, and say that I am entrusting you to him. He is a good man and he will be like a father until I come for you.'

The boy started to protest but his father held up his hand to silence him. 'You must obey me. It is my command. You must get away from here, far enough to be safe. The state's spies are everywhere, so be careful always to whom you speak and what you say. But in your heart, never forget who you are and where you are from, and never forget the people who have taken our land, our country from us, and forced us to live and die on our knees.' He paused. 'And my son? If I do not return, then promise me that when you become a man, you will swear revenge against the killers of your father.'

That night passed without alarm but the following night, Sabit was woken by his father shaking him. 'It is time,' he said. He led him out of the darkened house and as they crossed the yard, Sabit could hear the low rumble of truck engines and a metallic clanking and grinding noise that he did not recognise but which filled him with fear. Rebiya crushed him in his arms as tears wetted his hair, and then helped him down into the trench. Sabit saw his father's face for the last time, dimly lit by the waning moon, and then the last plank was put in place. He heard the noise of Rebiya scattering a layer of soil onto it and tramping it down, and then his whispered 'Goodbye, my son, may Allah protect you.' There was the soft scuffing sound of his footsteps as he walked back across the yard and then Sabit was alone in the darkness and silence.

He stayed there throughout the night, occasionally sipping a little water and nibbling at a piece of naan bread. From the street beyond the house, muffled by the soil above him, he could hear the sound of explosions and the bursts of gunfire. About the middle of the next day he heard footsteps crossing the yard and voices speaking in an accent he did not recognise. The footsteps paused almost overhead. Numb with fear, he waited with his ear pressed to the mouth of the pipe and his heart pounding. There was a brief silence, then he heard the faint scratch and flare of a match and, a few moments later, smelled a faint whiff of cigarette smoke through the pipe. Five minutes later there was a gritty sound as the unseen searcher threw down his cigarette end and ground it out with the heel of his boot before turning and walking away. There was a shouted command and then a terrifying rumble close at hand that made the walls of his refuge shake and sent fine sand drifting down onto him.

As his father had ordered, Sabit remained in his hiding place until the fourth night. His father had still not returned and Sabit tried to still the dread in his heart at what might have happened to him. Well after dark that evening, straining his ears for any sound, Sabit eased up the wood and iron roof of his refuge and crept out. His family's house, like every other house in the street, had been demolished by a bulldozer or a tank, and the yard now lay open to the deserted town square. Hearing the sound of an approaching vehicle, Sabit hid among the rubble of his home and was forced to stay there, his hair, skin and clothes so dust-laden they were indistinguishable from the ground on which he lay as Chinese soldiers disembarked from a lorry and began to patrol the square.

At first light the next morning, Sabit saw rank upon rank of captive men, perhaps a hundred in all, marched into the town square, hands and feet bound, shuffling and stumbling along, jabbed onwards by Chinese soldiers with bayonets. He recognised many of them. Almost the last to be brought out was his father with his hands tied behind his back. He was barely recognisable, his face battered and bloodied, a purple swelling almost closing one eye, and the marks of cuts and burns on his exposed arms and chest. Like all the others, he was forced to his knees.

A silent crowd of women and older men lined the square, dragged from their houses at gunpoint and forced to watch the unfolding spectacle. They were told that anyone who tried to avoid it or look away would meet the same fate as the prisoners. Soldiers with rifles took up position behind each man.

There was to be no real trial. The charges were read out by the chief of police, a small man with a neatly clipped moustache and a uniform that appeared to be several sizes too big for him. 'These men are guilty of criminal acts, anti-state activities conspiracy to commit acts of terrorism and attempting to split the motherland.' He turned to face the sullen crowd. 'Let this be a warning to you all. Any who conspire against the state will face the same pitiless fate.' He raised his arm, held it aloft for a dramatic pause and then let it fall.

A succession of shots rang out. The soldiers standing behind the prisoners shot each of them through the back of the head with their rifles. The town elders were the last to die. Rebiya was forced to watch as his three eldest sons — Sabit's grown-up brothers – were shot in front of him. Then he too was killed by a bullet to the back of the head. Gnawing on his fist to stop himself crying out, Sabit watched as his father pitched forward and sprawled in the dirt, his face blown away, the last of his lifeblood spilling into the sand. Sabit's father, his three brothers, his uncle and his grandfather had all been killed. He was the only male in his family to survive.

The gunshots ceased soon afterwards, but the ululating cries of grief from the wives and mothers of the dead continued throughout the day and far into the night. Sabit remained in hiding among the rubble all day and escaped in the dead hours of the following night, taking with him only a goatskin water bottle and his last piece of stale naan. He dodged the patrols of soldiers enforcing the curfew and slipped away, past the last of the mud-brick houses on the outskirts of the town, and began the long, exhausting walk to the west, making for the village where his father's cousin lived. He plodded through the edge of the desert, keeping to the rock outcrops and stony terrain that would hide his footprints from anyone following, but always with the highway in sight. Without it, he would soon have been lost in the vastness of the dunes. As he walked, he swore a vow that he would never rest until the killers of his father, his brothers and so many others had been brought to justice – not only the men who had pulled the triggers, but those who had given the orders for the executions.

CHAPTER 2

'You know, if it weren't for the dust, the flies and the fact that people keep trying to kill us, this wouldn't be a bad place for a holiday.' Jock McIntyre's voice, cured by decades of cigarette smoke and whisky, could have made him a fortune in voice-over work had his thick Glasgow accent not made him virtually unintelligible to anyone born south of Hadrian's Wall. He was several years older than the other members of his SAS patrol, his hair tinged with grey. His round face and broad features gave him a simple, uncomplicated look, but people who under-estimated him were making a serious mistake. He had a keen intellect – the SAS rumour mill claimed he could read *The Iliad* in the original Greek, though his patrol mates suspected the rumour might have been started by Jock himself – but it was his prowess as a fighter that had earned him their unconditional respect. Whether in a firefight in the Afghan moun-tains or a knife fight in one of the rugged bars of his Scottish home city, there was no man they would rather have had alongside them.

His patrol leader, Dan 'Spider' Shepherd, propped himself up on one elbow and glanced around. Even in late summer, the towering peaks of the Hindu Kush – 'Hindu Killer' was the literal translation, though those forbidding mountains had also claimed their share of Buddhists, Sikhs, Christians, Jews, Muslims and followers of almost every other religion – were still capped with snow, gleaming white against the deep blue of the eastern sky. The surrounding terrain was mostly bare rock, desert sand and scrub burned brown by the long Afghan summer, but closer to the fast-flowing river running through the valley there were stands of larches, pines and cedars. The riverbanks were lined with poplars, their golden leaves shimmering in the bright sunlight. In the fields alongside the river the crops were ripe and ready to be harvested, including the number-one cash crop, here as elsewhere in the country – the opium poppy.

'You're not wrong, Jock,' Shepherd said. 'Tell you what, if you take some leave, you could stay on for a few weeks at the end of this op and really get to know the place. Geordie'll join you, won't you mate?'

Geordie Mitchell, his thinning hair plastered to his scalp by the heat, paused in the middle of making yet another brew on the primus stove. 'Don't talk shite, man,' he said. 'When we finally get out of this shithole, I'll be on the beach at Whitley Bay.'

'That won't be much different from here then,' Jimbo Shortt said, yawning and stretching his six foot two inch frame. 'Because Whitley Bay's another bloody desert: lousy beer, crap food and the women all look like Soviet shot-putters.' He ducked as Geordie flicked a used teabag at his head.

'No, that's just Geordie's missus,' Jock said.

Geordie grinned at Jock as he handed him his mug of tea. 'I'm afraid yours has got a horsefly in it, Jock. I was going to have that one myself but after what you said about my missus ...'

Jock scowled, then scooped out the fly with the tip of his combat knife and flicked it onto the ground.

'That's a waste of good protein,' Jimbo said. 'Spider would have eaten that.' Years before, when they were on jungle training in Belize, Shepherd had eaten a tarantula for a bet, earning himself a nickname that he'd never been able to shake off.

Jock gave a weary smile. Army banter was nothing if not predictable, pandering to every British stereotype going. Scots were invariably 'Jocks', Welshmen were 'Taffys', Irishmen were 'Micks', north-easterners were 'Geordies' and officers were 'Ruperts', though never to their faces. Jock was a Scot, therefore Jock was a tightwad, QED. Just as any Premier League footballer with a GCSE in woodwork was automatically nicknamed 'Brains' or 'Professor' by his teammates, so any SAS man taller than the Regiment's average height of five foot nine was usually christened 'Lofty'. Some squadrons had as many as four or five, because somehow, Jimbo excepted, no one ever got around to thinking up a different nickname for any of them.

There was only one 'Spider', however. Nicknames were used not because they were usually shorter than the real ones, but because for security reasons SAS men, just like spooks, never used their real names when on operations and the habit was maintained even when back at base and off duty.

There was an unbreakable bond between the four members of Shepherd's patrol, forged in numerous contacts and incidents over the years. They had not long crossed back into Afghanistan after the latest one, a highly successful covert op deep into Iran, and they had all been hoping that their success might at least have earned them a bit of leave and the chance for some long-overdue R & R back in 'the Big H' – Hereford. However, their superiors had had other ideas and they had at once been reassigned as part of the Quick Reaction Force operating out of Bagram Airfield, fifty kilometres north of Kabul.

Five thousand feet up on a plateau among the western mountains of the Hindu Kush, Bagram had been built in the 1950s as part of the Great Powers' rivalry over Afghanistan, which had been going on since the 'Great Game' in the nineteenth century. American money had funded the construction of Bagram, but it had become a Soviet base during 'Russia's Vietnam' – the Soviet war against the Afghan mujahideen. After the Soviets' humiliating defeat and withdrawal, Bagram had been the scene of ferocious fighting between the Taliban and Shah Masood's Western-backed Northern Alliance, both of whose forces occupied opposite ends of the airfield at times and shelled each other relentlessly.

The Taliban had eventually prevailed but now that their brutal, fundamentalist regime had been overthrown by the US-led invasion, Bagram had become the major American base in the country, with scores of giant Hercules and C-5 Galaxy transport aircraft landing daily, adding yet more military supplies to the mountains that had already been shipped in. It was more than fifteen years since the Soviet withdrawal, but rusting wrecks of destroyed Soviet and Afghan air force aircraft, helicopters, tanks and military vehicles still lined the runway. They had simply been bulldozed out of the way and then left where they were to rot. In the dry Afghan air that would be a very slow process. The runway also bore the faint outlines of hundreds of overlapping craters that had been repaired countless times. Every building was also still pocked with bullet holes and the blast and scorch marks from mortar rounds, RPGs and artillery shells.

The plateau surrounding Bagram was scarred with the scorched outlines of the Taliban's bombed-out camps, destroyed in the ferocious air assault that had preceded the US-led invasion. Risking their lives to cross the minefields surrounding the base, looters had quickly stripped the ruined camps of anything valuable, even robbing and defiling the corpses of the dead. But earthenware water jars, rotting clothes, filthy mattresses studded with bullet holes and stained with blood, and even human bones still lay around the bomb craters and blackened sites of missile strikes, all within sight of the base's perimeter fence.

US troops from the 82nd Airborne Division at Fort Bragg, the 10th Mountain Division, and Special Operations Command from MacDill Air Force Base in Florida now occupied the base. The SAS had been allocated a small corner, separated from the rest of the airfield by razor-wire fences and some hastily bull-dozed berms shielding it from IEDs, RPGs, snipers and suicide bombers. The battle for Bagram might have been over, but the war with the Taliban showed no signs of going away. The only other British troops there were a unit of Royal Marine Commandos who kept themselves to themselves, which, given the tra-ditional hostility between the competing arms of the British forces, suited Shepherd and his patrol mates just fine.

Being assigned as part of the QRF required the SAS men to maintain an extremely high level of fitness. That meant a daily workout, which, in line with their unofficial motto of 'Train hard, fight easy', included long runs wearing boots and carry-ing heavy Bergens over the forbidding Afghan ter-rain, coupled with weight-training and martial arts to build strength and agility. Their kit and weapons were always kept close at hand, ready for action at a moment's notice for whatever might be operationally required: rescuing a hostage, kidnapping a Taliban commander, ambushing a suicide bomber, target marking for a retaliatory air strike, or anything else that the Allied commanders could dream up.

Shepherd's team had been on QRF duty for three weeks, but so far the only alarms had been false ones. Apart from the stand-to an hour either side of dawn and dusk, which they always carried out when on ops, hyper alert for any threats from the rugged terrain surrounding the base, they spent the long late-summer days training and practising with their weapons on the Close Quarter Battle range they had dug out of the side of one of the berms. With the exception of Geordie, whose milk-bottle complexion had only two shades, white and bright red, they were all bronzed from the sun. They wore a mixture of army kit and local Afghan clothing, making them look more like brigands than British Army soldiers, and all had a heavy growth of beard. While other troops shaved every day and used camouflage cream to break up the shape of their faces, the SAS troopers did not shave and so didn't need to use cam cream.

The only items in their equipment that were immaculately clean were the AK-47s they carried and lovingly tended with the extensive weapon-cleaning kits they all had. They had chosen those particular weapons not only because they were utterly reliable and not prone to the jams that could affect most other similar rifles, but also because their near-universal use by regular and irregular forces around the world meant that wherever the SAS were fighting, they could always obtain spare ammunition. On QRF or other 'official' postings, they could draw ammunition from the stores on their base, and when on covert ops, they simply collected it from the bodies of their dead enemies.

Their AK-47s had all been lightly oiled and the only sign of wear on them was around the change lever, where they had used emery paper to rub away the metal until the lever would slip from safe to auto and semi-auto fire with the least resistance. All of them knew from experience that this would give them a potentially crucial edge in a contact with the enemy. The power of their weapons and the phenomenal accuracy of their shooting meant that even a few milliseconds' advantage would be enough to guarantee their survival and their enemies' deaths. The downside was that the change lever had to be kept firmly in the safe position on patrol, and over time this had caused each of them to develop callouses on their right thumbs and the beginnings of 'trigger finger' – the inflammation of the hand's flexor tendons that caused it to form a claw-like shape. As a result, long-term SAS men were always flexing their fingers when at rest in an effort to ease the symptoms.

Earlier that day, bored with army rations, Jock had bought a young goat from one of the Afghan farmers who were always clustered as close to the gates as the base guards would allow. There could have been Taliban spies among them too, so they were closely watched. Jock was relaxed as he haggled with the farmer, then eventually he strolled back into the base, leading the goat on a piece of cord.

'You're never going to kill that are you?' Jimbo asked.

Jock gave him an incredulous look. 'Directly or indirectly you've been responsible for the deaths of scores of men in your SAS career and now you're worried about the fate of a goat?'

'That's different,' Jimbo said. 'I've never seen a goat toting an AK47.'

Jock shrugged. 'I take it you'll not be wanting your share of the goat curry tonight then? Anyway,' he said, pulling out his combat knife, 'if you don't want to see it having its throat cut, this might be a good time to go for a stroll.'

Jock killed, skinned and jointed the goat with practised ease. He tossed some of the meat into a mess tin and began cooking it with some onions he had liberated from the American PX and a generous dollop of the curry powder he always carried with him in a closely sealed plastic bag. Jock had eaten dog, cat, rat and a few other even less appetising things over the years, and with enough curry powder, they all tasted OK.

CHAPTER 3

Hamid sat cross-legged on the dirt floor, finishing his simple meal of rice and lentils, then wiped his bowl with the last scrap of naan. He was seventeen but despite his wispy beard, he looked much younger. He sipped a mouthful of green tea, the last he would ever drink, and paused for a moment, lost in thought, before rising to his feet. All day he had watched the line of sunlight streaming through the tiny, high window as it inched down the wall and across the floor, but now night was falling; it would soon be time.

In the last of the light, he took a creased and heavily thumbed photograph from his pocket and gazed once more at the familiar image. It was a group portrait of him and his father, mother and brothers, all squinting into the low sun in front of a canvas backdrop of an idealised landscape, erected by the itinerant photographer who had stopped at their remote village some years before. It was Hamid's only link with his family and his home, for there were no phone lines to their village, and even if he had been able to write them a letter, they could not have read it. They were all illiterate. As he took a last look at the picture he felt a momentary pang of regret and a faint hesitation, but then he squared his shoulders. He was ready. He carefully placed the photograph face down on the upturned wooden crate that served as a table, and poured some water from an earthenware jug into a battered metal bowl.

He completed his ritual wash with care, unfolded his prayer mat and, as he heard the muezzin calling the faithful of Kabul to prayer from the minaret of the Grand Mosque a few streets away, began his own devotions. He added what fragments he could recall of the prayers before dying that the mullah had performed at the deathbeds of his grandparents. 'There is no God except Allah, and Muhammad, peace be upon Him, is the messenger of Allah. O Allah, forgive the bad deeds of your servant Hamid, make those who are guided aware of my sacrifice, grant benefits to those whom I have left behind, and forgive me, O Lord of Worlds. Make my grave wide for me and light the way for me. Grant me paradise, protect me from hellfire and help my family to endure their sorrow.'

At last he straightened up and folded away his prayer mat. Under the barks and yelps of the feral dogs that infested the streets he could hear the sound of generators starting up in the distance in response to the capital's usual evening power cut. However, in this poor district almost no one had electric lights and there were no generators. He lit a candle as the last of the dusk light faded into night.

He heard the sound of footsteps scuffing through the gritty dust of the street outside and a moment later Mullah Omar pushed aside the torn curtain that separated the room from the other end of the mud-brick house. '*Salaam Alaikum*, Hamid,' he said. 'It is almost time. I will help you prepare.' The mullah was in his late sixties, his skin black and wrinkled from years of exposure to the unrelenting Afghan sun. He was tall and thin and bent forward from the waist as if a huge weight was pressing down on him. There was a massive wart on the side of his nose from which sprouted half a dozen long black hairs.

Two men had followed the mullah into the room. They had kohl-rimmed eyes and were dressed in black robes with long black scarves wound around their heads, the forked tails of the scarves trailing down their backs. They did not speak to Hamid, nor look at him, but simply stationed themselves on either side of the door. Their rifles – the newer AK-74s, rather than the traditional AK-47s – marked them out as trusted, senior figures in the Taliban hierarchy.

Mullah Omar was carrying a large, heavy bag, which he placed on the floor before carefully lifting out the contents. Hamid swallowed nervously when he saw the bulky 'waistcoat' – a cotton vest covered with a series of grey packs bound together with tape. The ends of two detonators were visible, protruding from the packs, electric wires linking them to a small black plastic box, featureless except for the round button on its upper surface. Inside the box was a battery and a simple electric circuit that would be completed when pressure was applied to the button on the outside.

Hamid murmured a prayer under his breath but kept his gaze steady as the mullah gave him a questioning look. He held out his arms to help the mullah place the waistcoat on him. Mullah Omar adjusted it and then overlaid it with another improvised garment, a shalwar kameez to which the wife of one of his followers had sewn a score of fabric flaps like oversized pockets, all of which were now stuffed with nails, screws, fragments of sharp metal and shards of glass.

When he was happy with it, the mullah taped the black plastic box to Hamid's right side, just above the waistband. 'You remember your instructions?' he said.

Hamid nodded. 'As well as I remember my own name.'

The mullah produced a white flag from his bag – white was a holy colour to the Taliban – unfurled it and draped it over two rusty nails protruding from the wall. It was far from the first time they had been used for this purpose and it would not be the last. He positioned Hamid in front of it, put an AK-47 in his hands and then produced a small Sony video camera. 'Remember the lines we rehearsed?' he said. He began to film Hamid as he made his last declaration. It was a message to his family but also to the wider world, a call to arms ending with *Allahu Akbar*– 'God is great'.

Mullah Omar nodded with satisfaction, switched off the camera and replaced it in his bag, wrapped in the Taliban flag. 'Now for the rest of your disguise,' he said, pulling a shapeless black bundle from the bag.

As the mullah unfolded it, Hamid stared incredulously at the garment he was being offered. 'Surely I cannot become a martyr dressed like this?'

'It is the only way to be sure of success. And the gatekeepers of paradise will not care how you are dressed, they will only wish to know how many kaffir unbelievers you have killed.' He watched Hamid narrowly for a few more seconds. 'In paradise you will have the finest silk robes decorated with golden threads, and beautiful virgins will surround you. But now you must wear this. It is the will of Allah, blessed be His name.'

After a moment's hesitation, Hamid bowed his head and put on the garment. He pulled the hood over, muffling all sounds and reducing his vision to the small opening, half obscured by a fabric mesh, directly in front of him. 'One more thing,' the mullah said, handing Hamid a bundle. 'Carry this, it will make your disguise more convincing.'

'Surely they will see that it is false?' Hamid said.

'Only when they are close enough to touch and by then it will be too late.' Mullah Omar shot a glance up at the now darkened window and nodded to himself. 'Are you ready, Hamid? It is time. Remember in the final moment that as your mouth closes here, it will open in paradise with a shout of joy! Allah be with you.'

He gave Hamid a careful embrace, keeping his arms well clear of the boy's right side, then crossed to the doorway, pulled the curtain and stood aside. Hamid moved past him without another word. Tracked by his two Taliban minders, the mullah slipped out of the house into the narrow, twisting street. At once they were swallowed up by the darkness, the sound of their footsteps fading like whispers in the dark.

CHAPTER 4

Eric Kirkland stared morosely out through the plate-glass window of the lobby. Like most of the hotel's security guards, he was ex-military. He'd grown up in a sleepy village in Devon and had served a combat-free, twenty-two-year full term in the Royal Engineers. He had then found himself in his early forties, unemployed and only offered menial work like stacking supermarket shelves, which didn't stretch him physically or mentally and was also badly paid. He had his Army pension but that wasn't enough for a decent standard of living and in the end, like many ex-soldiers before him, he went 'on the Circuit' – the informal network of ex-forces members who passed on details of bodyguarding, close-protection work and mercenary soldiering for more dubious overseas contractors.

When Eric heard on the grapevine about the chance of a security job at the Inter-Continental hotel in Kabul, he jumped at the chance. But having acted in haste, he now had ample chance to repent at leisure, for while the work was relatively well paid, it was both tedious and perilous. The hotel guests either ignored him altogether or, if they did deign to notice him, treated him with contempt. He was much older than the majority of the other hotel staff and out of step with them, and he felt a gnawing sense of insecurity and threat in almost every interaction with ordinary Afghans. As a result, when he was off duty, his social life, such as it was, consisted mainly of drinking in the staffroom with a couple of other, older security staff. Off-duty employees were not allowed in the cocktail bar used by the hotel guests, and the streets of Kabul were too dangerous for *faranji* – foreigners – to wander by day, never mind at night. He had signed a twelve-month contract and had only been in Kabul for six weeks, but he was already counting down the days till he could leave.

Tonight he was working the graveyard shift – eight in the evening till six in the morning. He shot a look across the lobby towards the receptionist, Jasmine, but she looked away as soon as she felt his gaze on her.

The lobby was deserted apart from Eric and the other security guards, for all the guests were in the bar or at dinner in the restaurant. Jasmine stifled a yawn. A beautiful, almond-eyed Australian of Anglo-Asian descent, she had applied to work as a receptionist in Kabul partly out of curiosity to see what was left of the country her father had eulogised after taking the 'hippy trail' through Afghanistan in the 1960s. The other reason was that in Sydney's overheated property market, the double pay and substantial bonus for completing twelve months in Kabul, which the hotel chain had been forced to offer to persuade staff to work there, had seemed like her only hope of ever raising the deposit on an apartment back home.

A movement in the corner of her eye caught her attention and through the glass walls at the front of the lobby she watched a line of three Toyota Land Cruisers driving up the road towards the hotel. There was nothing unusual in that, for one in every two vehicles in the country seemed to be a Land Cruiser. They slowed as they drove up to the checkpoint where the security guards halted all visitors to examine their documents before letting them approach the hotel.

The hotel security guards were all ex-military, boosting their service pensions – or satisfying their wanderlust and thirst for the adrenaline of risk they missed – by providing security for the businessmen, wheeler-dealers and carpetbaggers who, like maggots drawn to a festering wound, flooded into war-torn countries almost as soon as the guns had stopped firing.

After an earlier terrorist incident in which a van loaded with explosives had been rammed into the hotel and then detonated, a row of massive concrete blocks now protected the approaches. The only gap wide enough to admit a vehicle was a chicane in front of the checkpoint that forced everyone to slow to a crawl.

A group of Afghan civilians were squatting in the dust near the checkpoint: taxi drivers hoping for fares, and people looking for work at the hotel or hoping for baksheesh from any passing Westerners, though there were precious few of them in daylight, let alone after dark. Jasmine could make out clusters of figures holding weapons in the back of each Land Cruiser and felt a momentary frisson of fear. The risk of attack on the hotel was sufficient for every staff member to know the emergency drills, escape routes and locations of safe havens by heart, and almost unaware that she was doing so, she began to move away from the counter and towards the reinforced door leading to an office that doubled as a panic room. However, as the Land Cruisers drove into the pool of bright light around the checkpoint that was powered by the hotel's own generators, she saw that they were wearing Afghan Army uniforms and breathed a sigh of relief.

She watched disinterestedly as the driver of the lead vehicle began to speak to the guards at the checkpoint, and then turned away to finish filing the arrival cards from today's batch of guests. They included a Briton and an American, who, from the size of their entourages and the bowing and scraping that had preceded them, must have been very big wheels indeed.

The next moment she heard a sound like a series of dry coughs. She looked up to see three of the four guards at the checkpoint sprawled on the ground, and the other one crouching behind one of the concrete barriers, firing his weapon as the Afghan Army soldiers – if that was really what they were – spilled from the Land Cruisers and began running towards the hotel, firing as they ran.

There were another half-dozen security guards inside the lobby and they began to return fire as she turned to make a dash for the panic room, but a shot passed close enough for the bullet to pluck at her sleeve, and a burst of fire from an automatic weapon then shredded the mahogany counter, creating a blizzard of needle-sharp splinters that tore at her face. She threw herself down, wormed her way under the counter and huddled there, sobbing with fright, her heart beating so wildly it felt as though it was bursting out of her chest, while blood from her cuts trickled onto the marble floor.

CHAPTER 5

By the time the goat was cooked, Jimbo had managed to overcome his qualms and settled down to eat with the rest of his patrol mates. They stood to for an hour either side of sunset, as much out of habit as necessity. In theory, the US troops guarding the perimeter were providing security for the whole of the base, but the SAS men had learned from bitter experience never to trust their safety to less highly skilled, trained and dedicated soldiers, least of all infantry privates for whom sentry duty was a tedious, much resented quasi-punishment.

The SAS men sat around the embers of their fire as the sky darkened into night. The stars filled the heavens above them, but Jimbo was in no mood to wax poetical. 'God I'm bored,' he said. 'Three weeks on QRF and the only action we've seen is Jock killing that goat.'

Barely were the words out of his mouth when the QRF alert began to sound: first the rising and falling note of the wailing siren, and then the tannoy crackled into life and a code word was repeated several times. There was a series of code words, such as 'Topcat' and 'Ants Nest', for different situations; this one was 'Tempest', denoting a Taliban attack.

'Someone up there is obviously listening,' Jimbo said as they scrambled for their kit.

'Yeah,' Shepherd said. 'Probably GCHQ via a satellite.'

'Know why they chose Tempest to mean a Taliban attack?' Jock said.

Geordie gave a weary sigh., 'No, but I'm betting you're going to tell me.'

'Cockney rhyming slang for Shakespeare scholars: "Caliban" equals "Taliban".'

Geordie frowned. 'What the fuck is a Caliban?' he asked.

Jock grinned but didn't reply. There was nothing he enjoyed more than winding up his patrol mates.

While they were bantering with each other, Shepherd had activated the satphone at his shoulder and was in almost instant contact with the Head Sheds in Hereford. Not for the first time he reflected on the absurdity of having to contact SAS commanders thousands of miles away to be given orders about an incident that was probably taking place almost within earshot of where he stood. Back in the day, SAS patrols were often out of comms with their officers in-country, let alone back in Hereford, for days or weeks on end, and they'd made their own decisions. The officers hadn't liked that, of course, but there was nothing they could do about it at the time. Now

the development of satellite communications meant
that no SAS patrol anywhere in the world need ever
be out of contact with the Head Sheds. As a result,
all decisions were made in the UK, and the major
ones were made in Downing Street, or occasionally at
Joint Force Command Headquarters at Northwood.
Everyone down the line was under the cosh, with the
politicians controlling the news output through a few
tame journalists.

Shepherd spoke little, listened more and then
broke the connection and turned to the others.
'There's an attack on the Inter-Con, here said.
The Hotel Inter-Continental was the only five-star,
indeed the only surviving hotel of any quality, in
Kabul. Its concrete facade was scarred with bullet marks, two of its four public rooms were unus-
able and its swimming pool was full of rubble and
war debris, but it was still the place where visiting
Western businessmen, politicians and journalists
tended to stay. It offered as secure accommodation
as the city could provide – which in war-torn Kabul
was still not very secure at all. It had been attacked
repeatedly during the civil war and afterwards, and
the American-led invasion was unlikely to alter that
state of affairs.

'Another attack?' Geordie said. 'So what's new,
that place gets targeted at least once a month.'

'Not on this scale,' Shepherd said. 'This one
has three Landcruisers worth of presumed Taliban
fighters wearing Afghan Army uniforms, eighteen to

twenty men in all, armed with AKs, RPGs, grenades and satchel bombs.'

Jock frowned as he exchanged a look with Jimbo. Packed with PE – plastic explosive – satchel bombs were a crude but deadly weapon, particularly useful in confined areas where the terrorists couldn't fire RPGs because the backblast would kill them as well as their targets. As the name suggested, a satchel bomb looked like a schoolkid's satchel, with a pull handle on the outside to arm it as the attacker approached his target, and a time fuse usually set to five seconds. Swinging it by its long strap, the attacker could launch it in an arc thirty or forty metres over rough ground, but he could also slide it across a polished surface – like the marble floor of a hotel lobby.

'They drove up to the checkpoint,' Shepherd said. 'Then opened fire and detonated a couple of bombs when challenged. The security guards were targeted but there was the usual cluster of Afghans, so there are several civilians down as well as the security personnel. And probably by no coincidence whatsoever, a heavy-duty delegation of Yank and Brit politicians, spooks and civil servants arrived at the hotel today.'

'The Taliban'll have been tipped off by someone,' Jock said. 'Afghan army or police, or one of the hotel staff, you can count on that.'

Geordie nodded. 'Probably all of them. This country leaks like a sieve.'

'Right, let's go!' Shepherd said, and within seconds they had gathered the rest of their kit and were sprinting for a Chinook on the hard standing near the end of the runway just outside their base. The pilot had also been alerted and the rotors were already turning. They ran up the ramp, squeezing past a soft-skinned 'Pinkie' Land Rover positioned facing outwards. It was still in the desert camouflage paint that gave the Pinkies their nickname.

Jock gave the vehicle a sour look as he squeezed past it. Pinkies were long-wheelbase vehicles, making them cumbersome and awkward to manoeuvre, and despite their V8 engines they were very underpowered. The main reason for that was the weight of the fuel they carried. The petrol tank filling the floor space behind the driver and passenger had a 100-gallon capacity, giving the Pinkie a 1000-mile range. The weight of the fuel made the vehicle even more ponderous, but the size of the tank created another problem. For entirely understandable reasons the RAF was not a fan of having petrol vapour inside its aircraft, so whenever Pinkies were transported by air, RAF rules required that either the fuel tanks had to have been emptied and washed out to remove any remaining vapour, or the tanks were brimful of liquid fuel. Since a vehicle with no fuel was not going to be much use when they landed, the patrol's Pinkie was full of petrol, making it even more cumbersome and even less manoeuvrable.

'A range of a thousand miles and we won't be doing more than ten,' Jock said. 'Regulations will be the death of us one day, you can count on it.'

'With all that petrol for company,' Jimbo said, 'if we take an armour-piercing round, we'll all be fried like KFC.'

Shepherd shrugged. The Pinkie was yet another piece of obsolete kit that the SAS were forced to hang on to because budget cuts and MoD dithering and procurement cock-ups meant there weren't any replacements on order. But he knew there was no point in complaining; they had no choice other than to make the best of what they had.

They settled themselves on the helicopter's steel floor as the ramp was raised and the tempo of the rotors accelerated to a scream. A moment later the Chinook lurched skywards and swung around to the south, making for Kabul. The rest of the briefing took place during the few minutes' flight. 'The attackers are fighting their way towards the lobby,' Shepherd said. Even though they were wearing headsets, the thunder of the Chinook's engines and the relentless chop of its rotors made his words difficult to hear even when he shouted. 'The security guards inside have taken some casualties but the rest are holding off the Taliban for the moment, though I doubt if they'll be able to do that for too much longer.'

As the Chinook swept in towards the Temporary Landing Zone – a patch of level ground on the edge of the city – the four SAS men were already filing back down the ramp and clambering into the Pinkie. Jimbo squeezed his lanky frame behind the wheel, with Shepherd alongside him in the front and the other two in the back, all sitting with weapons at the ready.

As the pilot began counting them down – 'One minute to landing... Thirty seconds...' – Jimbo started the engine and took up the pressure on the handbrake. The Chinook was pumping out a snowstorm of chaff and flares to draw off any shoulder-launched missiles, including the deadly American-made Stingers. The Taliban were known to possess a store of them, a legacy of the mujahideen's war against the Soviets when the CIA had supplied them with hundreds. The Americans had since offered a very substantial bounty for the return of the unused missiles from that conflict, but none had appeared and the stocks were thought to be still hidden in Taliban armouries in caves and tunnels throughout Afghanistan.

The city below them was in darkness, not through any terrorist action, just from the nightly blackouts caused by Kabul's creaking power generation system. It worked by day when there was minimal demand, but regular as clockwork, as soon as Kabul's citizens got home from work, turned on their lights and began preparing their evening meals, the power went off. In the capital's wealthier districts the nightly blackout was greeted with a chorus of hundreds of Honda generators firing up and the lights flickered back on, but in the poorer districts only the glimmer of candles and kerosene lamps and the glow of open-air cooking fires pierced the darkness.

The Chinook did not make a vertical descent but came in like a fixed-wing aircraft and made a rolling landing. As soon as its wheels touched the concrete, almost lost from sight among the dust storm stirred up by the downwash from the giant helicopter's twin rotors, the ramp swung down, scraping along the ground in a shower of sparks. The thunder of helicopter rotors was even louder now, battering their ears and drowning out every other sound.

Jimbo gunned the Pinkie's engine, sped down the ramp and hit the ground with a teeth-rattling thump. They roared off towards the city as the Chinook lumbered back into the air, its track marked by the showers of chaff and flares still spilling from its dispensers, fierce white against the night sky.

The thunder of helicopter rotors was now lost beneath the roar of the Land Rover's engine. It was a cold, black night with not a trace of moonlight and the streets were in total darkness. There had never been many street lights in Kabul in any case, but they had all been smashed long ago and the electric cables looted. Even if they'd worked, the nightly power cuts would have blacked them out. The road surface was littered with broken glass, rocks, ashes and cinders, while an oily black patch on the ground marked the outline of a hijacked car that had been torched. The smell of smoke still hung in the air. The streets were almost deserted and the few figures that were visible hugged the walls, every one a potential enemy.

Jimbo rubbed his face with his hand. 'Here we go then: another perfect day in paradise.'

The glare of headlights from an American Hummer heading in the opposite direction cast the dark rings under his eyes into even deeper shadow. 'Bloody typical, isn't it?' he said, fighting the wheel as he slewed the Pinkie around a blind corner and accelerated up the hill towards the Inter-Continental. 'The Yanks go into battle in armoured Humvees and all we've got is a Land Rover protected by the British Army equivalent of deckchair fabric.'

The Pinkie had fearsome armaments, with a general-purpose machine gun mounted on the bonnet in front of Shepherd and two more at the rear, but its lack of armour made it very vulnerable to RPGs and IEDs.

'And you know what's even more typical?' Jock said with his trademark cynicism. 'The Yanks were heading away from the scene of the action, not towards it.'

They sped through one of the poorest districts, where almost all of the buildings were in partial or total ruins from the decades of civil war. Most were in darkness but here and there the flicker of flames or the faint glow of a lamp or candle showed where poor Afghan families were still living among the ruins. Beyond these ghettos of Kabul's poorest citizens was a district of crumbling concrete apartment blocks, built during the Soviet era. From a distance they might have seemed no different from similar blocks in the outer districts of Volgograd, Poznań or Karl-Marx-Stadt, but close up, their disintegrating walls bore the marks of decades of warfare. During the civil war the competing factions of Shah Massoud, Gulbuddin Hekmatyar and other warlords had occupied different parts of the heights surrounding the city and, when not firing at each other, they had subjected the district to an incessant barrage of rocket attacks. The Taliban takeover and the American invasion had led to further destruction and the flats, once coveted for their running water and electricity, now had neither and were in ruins. Flapping sheets of plastic had replaced some of the shattered windows, but the rest had been left gaping, even though most of the apartments, other than the burned-out ones on the upper floors, were still occupied.

As the Pinkie accelerated up a hill, they saw an Afghan Army jeep ahead of them, also apparently speeding towards the Inter-Continental. An instant later, a Toyota saloon shot out of a side street and ploughed into the jeep. There was a microsecond's pause and then both vehicles disappeared in a volcano of smoke and flame as a car bomb detonated.

The SAS men were some distance from it, but the force of the blast was still powerful enough to lift the Pinkie off the ground. As it thudded back down, bottoming the springs, Geordie whistled. 'Jesus H Christ,' he said. 'If we'd been ten seconds earlier, that could have been us.'

Jimbo merely twitched the wheel to swerve around the blazing wreckage and put his foot down a little harder, bumping over some debris and scraping the wall of the neighbouring building to get past in a shower of sparks, close enough to feel a brief flash of searing heat from the inferno.

As the Pinkie crested the last rise and the Inter-Continental came into view, the SAS men could hear the rattle of gunfire above the noise of the engine and saw dark figures outlined by their headlights and the handful of lights still burning in the hotel lobby. They could see the security guards inside the hotel and a few Afghan police outside trying to engage the terrorists. There were muzzle flashes from a score of weapons and they heard the whoosh as a rocket-propelled grenade was fired, followed instantly by the crump of the explosion as it detonated. Shepherd brought his GPMG to bear on the two terrorists who had fired the RPG, loosing off a short burst that ripped through them like a buzz saw.

The Pinkie screeched to a halt and Jock and Geordie, and then Jimbo, added their firepower to Shepherd's. There was a sudden slackening of the firing from the terrorists and they began to pull back, though whether this was in reaction to the SAS men's arrival or because they were making a planned, tactical withdrawal was not clear.

A moment later a figure in a burqa holding a baby in her arms ran out of the darkness towards the hotel. The Afghan police and the security guards in the hotel froze for a fatal instant, not sure if this was merely a frightened Afghan woman or something more sinister. There were shouts for her to stop, repeated in Pashtu and English, but by then she was already at the entrance to the lobby, stepping across the threshold over one of the bodies of the dead. The figure held up the bundle as if appealing for help for the baby, but in the next instant, the right arm swept down and there was a blinding flash as the suicide vest was detonated. The body disappeared, evaporated by the force of the blast, taking out at least three security guards. No one would ever know if the figure had been a man or a woman, nor whether he or she had really been carrying a baby or just a doll. Hamid had earned his martyrdom.

As the suicide bomber disintegrated, the blast was contained by the lobby's concrete walls and channelled out through the bullet-holed plate-glass windows at the front, creating an ice storm of glass fragments that sparkled in the Land Rover's headlights. It was a beautiful but deadly sight, a billowing cloud of murderous glass shards lacerating anything and anyone in its path.

The ground shook as the dull thud of the blast echoed from the walls of the darkened buildings. Dense clouds of black smoke and dust swirled around the SAS men, pierced by the glare of tongues of dull red and orange flames licking around the blown-out windows.

The terrorists emerged from the shadows again and renewed their attack with even greater ferocity.

Only a couple of security guards were still fighting back and had the SAS men not arrived, the terrorists would now have been running through the hotel corridors, hunting down any Westerners. Instead, while Jock and Geordie kept up suppressing fire from their GPMGs, Shepherd and Jimbo dived from the Pinkie and began to take out individual targets with their AK-47s, firing and moving, diving and rolling through the dust, using double taps and short, targeted bursts against the wild automatic fire coming from the terrorists.

Knowing that without armour to protect them they were sitting ducks for an RPG, their two patrol mates fired another burst from their GPMGs, then dived clear of the Pinkie and also began taking out Taliban targets with double taps. The noise of gunfire was deafening and the darkness and the swirling smoke and dust made identifying friend from foe even more difficult, but with a ruthless, clinical efficiency born of years of training and close-quarter combat, the SAS men picked off enemy after enemy. The Taliban were brave enough, emerging from cover to run straight at the guns of the SAS men, firing as they ran, but their rudimentary training made them no match for the most deadly fighting men in the world.

The firing eventually slowed and then stopped, all the visible terrorists having been eliminated. Shepherd waited another few seconds, scanning the area for movement, then wiped the cold sweat from his brow and shot a glance at the others.

Geordie was already on his feet, at once turning his attention to the casualties littering the hotel approaches. A gifted medic, he had applied for Selection to the SAS because the Regiment's constant involvement in ops and combat offered the best opportunities to develop his skills in his specialist area: battlefield trauma.

The nearest casualty was an Afghan, a woman whose bad luck it had been to be passing the hotel's security post as the Taliban launched their attack. Geordie felt for a pulse in her neck, then shook his head and prepared to move on to the next casualty. She was beyond help.

Scanning their surrounds and the roof above them, dimly outlined in a deeper black against the night sky, Jock and Jimbo stayed in defensive positions, alert for any suspicious shape or hint of movement that might herald a suicide bomber stepping out of the darkness, or a sniper preparing to take a shot.

A crowd had begun to form immediately the firing had ceased, as if that was the signal they had been awaiting, drawn by the bomb blast and the gunfire like moths to a flame. Many of their faces were contorted with hate, though whether that was directed at the Westerners or the Taliban bombers was not immediately clear. Most were probably just curiosity seekers or relatives of hotel employees anxiously waiting for news of them, but Shepherd and his team stayed alert – there might have been more suicide bombers or Taliban gunmen using the crowd for cover.

A truckload of infantry had now arrived, members of the Royal Anglian Regiment who were stationed on the outskirts of Kabul and had only just arrived in-country. From their youthful faces, nervous expressions and jittery movements it seemed they were experiencing their first posting to a war zone and were not enjoying the experience. Their NCOs shouted, cajoled and bullied them into some sort of defensive line and they then began to expand the perimeter, trying to push the crowd back, away from the casualties and the devastated hotel.

Afghan interpreters relayed the NCOs' orders to the crowd. There was no time for niceties. Any Afghan who showed any hesitation when told to move back would be shoved out of the way or flattened if he resisted. Anyone who looked even slightly suspicious, whether through his expression, his posture or even the drape of his clothes, was told to raise his hands above his head. And any movement of the hands towards the body, rather than up and away, would be interpreted as an attempt to reach a weapon or trigger a suicide vest and the man would be shot without warning.

Not altogether trusting the skills of the infantrymen, Jock and Jimbo kept a wary eye on the crowd while Geordie and Shepherd continued to tend to the wounded. In the flickering light from the fires they saw several men, their faces masked with blood, sprawling or staggering around. One had a neck wound from which blood was pouring. A security guard was rolling around on the ground, screaming in pain as blood spurted from his knee, another was rocking himself like a child, and a third dazedly crawled around on his hands and knees. The rest of the street was littered with bodies and severed limbs.

Shattered glass from the hotel lobby crunched underfoot as Geordie and Shepherd moved between the casualties. Blood drenched them as they tried to staunch the wounds, until their hands were slippery with it. As Shepherd moved from one casualty to the next, he stumbled and tripped on a severed limb that went skittering across the street with a hollow, rattling sound. He stooped to pick it up and found that he was holding a wooden leg. There seemed to be scores more, scattered across the street, among the bloodied limbs and body parts of genuine casualties.

Geordie had also picked up a wooden arm. 'What kind of fucking sick joke is this?' he said, throwing it down in disgust.

Shepherd pointed up the side street next to the hotel, where a ramshackle, mud-brick and corrugated-iron workshop had taken the full force of the blast from the lobby. 'They must have come from there,' he said. 'Afghanistan's only growth industry: prosthetic limbs for people crippled by landmines, IEDs, bombs and RPGs.'

There was a brutal pecking order for casualties, based on the speed at which they might die without treatment. Even though blood was still pumping from the security guard's severed leg, Geordie left him to Shepherd and went to the man with the neck wound first. A piece of glass from the bomb had ripped through the man's neck, tearing away the flesh, but miraculously it hadn't severed the arteries. 'You're going to be all right,' Geordie said to the man. 'Believe it or not, today was your lucky day, because if the wound had been a few millimetres deeper, you'd already be dead.' He pressed the flap of skin and flesh back into place and covered it with a shell dressing. 'Hold that in place until the army medics arrive,' he said, already running to the next victim.

The guard on the ground was still writhing and screaming in pain. His leg below the knee ended in a ragged stump from which blood was still spurting. Shepherd ripped the man's trouser leg to fully expose the wound, then clamped a tourniquet around his thigh, trying not to rush, even though there were still more casualties waiting. He was very conscious of his lack of cover and the continuing sound of gunfire as Jock and Jimbo engaged further Taliban fighters who kept emerging from the shadows. Fortunately, their fire was ragged and often unaimed, coming blind from behind low walls or around the corners of buildings, but it would only take one lucky shot.

Shepherd pushed that thought away and ran to the next victim, a security guard who had been blown off his feet and was wounded by shrapnel and badly burned by the suicide bomb. As Shepherd approached him, the man hauled himself to his feet and, still clutching his weapon, began staggering towards the crowd. The consequences of this badly wounded and disorientated man blundering into a hostile crowd while holding a loaded weapon did not bear thinking about. He had to be stopped. Shepherd sprinted towards him, ignoring catcalls and a couple of stones thrown from the crowd still pressing against the infantry cordon, despite all the threats and warnings that had been issued.

He grabbed the man's arm. 'You're all right. Let me have your rifle.' As he turned him away from the crowd he saw the scale of the burns to the man's face. He'd clearly been close enough to the blast to be flash blinded and deafened by the explosion, and his face and body had also been shredded by shrapnel and flying glass so that his uniform was soaked in blood. He stood there, staring wildly around him, the rifle still grasped in his hands, but he obviously had no idea what had happened to him or where he was. Shepherd shouted at him again, trying to make him understand, but the guard couldn't see Shepherd's face and his voice must have sounded as meaningless to his blast-ravaged ears as the buzzing of a wasp.

Shepherd moved closer and laid what he hoped was a reassuring hand on the guard's arm, then stretched slowly across him, watching his face all the time, and with the other hand clicked on the safety catch of the guard's rifle and then pulled it gently out of his hands. He turned the man around and began walking him back towards the hotel, away from the yelling crowd, then sat him down to wait for the army medics.

There was now only one remaining unexamined casualty – another security guard, who must have been the closest to the suicide bomber when he detonated his bomb. He had been blown out of the hotel entrance by the force of the blast. He lay sprawled on the ground immediately in front of the crowd.

Shepherd saw one Afghan man, and then another, lean forward between two of the hapless infantrymen and spit on the body before melting back into the crowd. A security guard emerged from the wreckage of the hotel and stood staring down at one of the dead with a look of horror on his face. Shepherd hurried over to him. 'What's your name?' he asked.

'Eric,' said the man, his voice a hoarse whisper. 'Eric Kirkland.'

'Are you OK?'

Eric nodded. 'I think so.'

'Give me a hand, will you? I think your mate there is past help, but I'm damned if I'm going to leave his body there for those bastards to spit on.'

When they reached the body, Shepherd waved the crowd back, reinforcing the message with the butt of his rifle. He turned to two of the infantrymen, who were staring at him open-mouthed. They might have been recent recruits, but they already knew enough of the army to suspect that this scruffy, bearded soldier must be part of the legendary SAS.

'Do whatever it takes to keep these fuckers away from the casualty while we get it out of here,' he said.

Either through an injection of courage or out of fear of him, the infantrymen began forcing the crowd back again. A glance at the casualty was enough to confirm that he was beyond all help. Both arms had been blown off in the blast – black flies were already clustering around the bloodied stumps – and the security guard's head was so charred by burns that even his own mother would not have recognised him. A smouldering flak jacket still encased the upper body, but although it had stopped the explosion from ripping the torso apart, it hadn't absorbed or deflected the blast and every bone and organ within had been destroyed.

Shepherd and Eric stooped to pick up the corpse. Lifting a body in which every bone is fractured and every organ ruptured was like trying to pick up a blancmange with a pair of pliers. Every time they tried to lift it, the weight lurched from side to side, like water in a waterbed, and they couldn't maintain their grip. Each time they dropped it there were laughs and jeers from the crowd.

Eventually Shepherd pulled a length of timber from among the rubble left by the blast to use as a precarious stretcher. By this time Eric looked close to passing out. He kept his head turned to the side, away from the body, and beneath the streaks of dirt and soot his face was the colour of candle wax, while a nerve was tugging at the corner of his eye.

He struggled to help Shepherd manhandle the body onto the makeshift stretcher, but eventually they succeeded. 'You take the front,' Shepherd said, reckoning that at least that way Eric would have his back to the body.

As they picked it up again and began to move away, towards the wreckage of the hotel lobby, the crowd bayed like football supporters taunting the opposition. Eric swung round to stare at the crowd, the tic now even more pronounced. 'Fucking animals,' he said. 'Fucking animals.'

Shepherd kept his voice quiet and level. 'Just ignore them,' he said. 'He's dead. He's beyond being upset by them. Don't let them get to you.'

Eric's mouth worked silently as he stared at the mob, but when Shepherd said 'Move!' he helped him carry the body into the lobby. Shepherd swept the broken glass and debris from a marble-topped coffee table with his arm and they laid the security guard's smouldering body on it, a thin spiral of smoke still rising from his flak jacket. They stepped back, wiping the blood and dirt from their hands.

Astonishingly, Shepherd saw that one of the hotel staff, a pretty Asian girl, was standing behind the reception desk in the middle of the wrecked lobby, apparently unmarked save for a trickle of blood from scratches on her forehead. When the firing stopped, she had waited a few more minutes and then emerged from her hiding place just as Shepherd and the guard came into the lobby with the body. The night wind was blowing through the gaping window frames and she was shivering from cold and fright.

'What's your name?' Shepherd said.

'It's Jasmine.'

'My mates call me Spider, Jasmine. OK, look, the worst is over now, but you're bound to be in shock. If there's anywhere in this wreck you can find some strong, sweet tea or coffee, now's the moment to get it. Then you need to find a place where you can sit down – ideally somewhere that isn't covered in blood and broken glass. All right?'

As he said it, he heard a faint crackling sound and the smell of scorching flesh again filled his nostrils. Jasmine gave a blood-chilling, hysterical scream, pointing a shaking finger behind him. He whipped around to find that the corpse they had laid on the coffee table was ablaze. The wind blowing through the lobby had reignited the dead man's flak jacket, which was now burning fiercely. Shepherd sprinted across the lobby, tore a shrapnel-shredded hanging from the wall and smothered the flames with it, the stink of burned wool merging with the smell of charred flesh.

Jasmine had stopped screaming but she and Eric were both standing there white-faced, mouths gaping open as they stared at the body.

Shepherd whipped around again at a noise from the rear of the lobby, his weapon following his gaze while his thumb nudged the change lever and his finger tightened on the trigger of the AK-47. He relaxed as he saw it was a bodyguard for one of the political or military bigwigs, peering around the corner, checking if it was safe for them to emerge from the bombproof incident room in the basement to which they'd retreated when the attack began.

'All clear,' Shepherd said. 'Your principals can come out and have their coffee and petits fours now, always assuming there's anyone left alive to serve them.'

He walked over to Jasmine, who was still ashen-faced and apparently unable to tear her eyes away from the body on the table. He took her gently by the shoulders and turned her around so that she could no longer see it. 'Forget the cup of tea,' he said. 'What you need is a very strong drink, and if you've a friend or someone here you feel you can talk to, let it all out to them. Sometimes it helps. I'd pour you a drink myself, but I can't leave here until the cavalry comes.' He paused, searching her expression. 'You all right now?'

She gave him a grateful smile. 'I think so. It's just... I've never seen anything like that before.'

'Believe me,' Shepherd said. 'I've been in plenty of firefights and seen plenty of blood and bodies, but that...-' He glanced at the body on the table. 'That was a first for me too.'

'You're very brave.'

'Not really, just well trained,' he said, with a rueful smile. He held her gaze for a moment, and then said, 'OK, Jasmine. You take care, and I hope we meet in happier circumstances one day.' He watched her slim figure as she made her way unsteadily towards the far end of the lobby.

'Penny for your thoughts?' Jimbo said, with an evil smile.

'You know me better than that, Jimbo,' he said. 'Sue's waiting for me back in Hereford and I'm strictly a one-woman guy.'

'One woman at a time anyway,' Jimbo said. He ducked under the mock haymaker that Shepherd threw at his head. 'Anyhoo, the US cavalry is arriving in a herd of Hummers, so we'll be good to go any minute now.'

A dozen armoured Humvees were already pulling up outside the hotel, their heavy armour and weapons making the SAS Pinkie look even more old-fashioned and vulnerable. 'Just like both world wars,' Jock said. 'The Yanks are always late to the party.'

The Hummers disgorged a troop of US infantry who began relieving the Brits. US Army medics had also now arrived, and the SAS men waited while the American troops established a secure perimeter. Geordie talked the medics through the casualties that he and Shepherd had treated, then they headed back to the TLZ.

They got back to their base just before dawn. Bone-weary, Shepherd stretched out on his camp bed but he lay like stone, unable to sleep, staring into the fading darkness. Every time he closed his eyes, he saw that hideously disfigured corpse, blazing on the marble table.

CHAPTER 6

In the aftermath of the executions of his father and brothers, hiding by day and moving only at night, Sabit had walked 100 miles through the desert to reach the house of his father's cousin, Gheni. Gheni had hidden him until Sabit had regained his strength, but he told the boy that it was not safe for him to remain there. Rebiya had been a well-known elder, a focal point for his people's nationalist aims, and in a village where gossip was the common currency and state informers were everywhere, word that Rebiya's youngest son had survived the massacre would inevitably reach the ears of the state government. So Gheni gave him what money he could spare, wished Allah's blessings upon him, and then sent him west with a smuggler from the village who used the perilous trails through the high mountains to carry contraband into and out of Tajikistan and Kyrgyzstan.

The boy eventually reached the Tajik capital of Dushanbe. Despite his youth, he found work there as a builder's labourer. The builder had strong Party connections and through a contact in the government – and a healthy bribe repaid by Sabit from his wages – secured Tajik citizenship papers for him. Tajikistan was a landlocked state, with Uzbekistan to the west, Kyrgyzstan to the north, China to the east and Afghanistan to the south, and access to Pakistan through the Wakhan Corridor. A civil war in the aftermath of the collapse of the Soviet Union had left 100,000 dead and the country devastated. Sabit stayed in Dunshanbe for a year and then moved on to the Gorno-Badakhshan region. He chose it because of the large Muslim population there, but just as in his homeland, they too suffered repression from the government.

As in post-Soviet Russia, criminal gangs controlled everything in Tajikistan. Many of the warlords and military leaders from the civil war had become the heads of gangs of organised criminals, looting millions through protection rackets, extortion, prostitution, gambling, drug dealing and arms smuggling. With a government awash in corruption and factionalism, even those officials and politicians not open to bribery and corruption were powerless to prevent it. The brand-new Mercedes and Jaguars on the streets of Dushanbe were all bought, directly or indirectly, with drug money. 'If you've got a big house or a new Mercedes, you're in the mafia,' Sabit's boss had told him. 'You can't buy those things on two dollars a month.'

One of the 'Big Five' mafia gangs was based in Gorno-Badakhshan and had a flourishing drug and arms trade with the Taliban and al-Qaeda, importing opium and heroin base from them, refining it and then trafficking it north into Russia, as well as to the former Soviet republics of Kazakhstan, Kyrgyzstan and Uzbekistan. Although they were fighting the *faranji* invaders in Afghanistan, very few of al-Qaeda's men were Afghans. A few were Chechens, but most were Arabs. They seemed to have an almost unlimited supply of funds, not just from the sale of drugs and the money they extorted in the areas they controlled, but from their Sunni Arab backers in the Middle East. Having noted that, Sabit began learning Arabic, paying an impoverished clerk in the Egyptian consulate in Dushanbe to teach him.

Sabit had grown into a strong and handsome young man. From behind their veils, many of the town's women cast glances in his direction, but he showed no interest in marriage, remaining a solemn, serious young man who spent his evenings studying. As well as Arabic, he learned English and Russian. All Tajiks had to serve as conscripts in the armed forces, but he did not wait to be conscripted and enlisted as soon as he was old enough. He kept himself aloof from his comrades, cool and unflappable, speaking little and listening more, and was marked out for rapid promotion. He volunteered for special forces training with the Tajik Spetsnaz, becoming a marksman and demolitions expert.

The army was as mired in corruption as the rest of Tajik society and his commanding officer had close connections with the mafia. He used Sabit as part of his personal protection force and sent him on several private missions, selling Soviet weapons from the armoury to his mafia connections. When several of the local mafia don's bodyguards were gunned down in an ambush after a turf war with a rival gang, Sabit's strength, fighting skills and ruthless edge, coupled with his reputation as a man who kept his mouth shut, saw him hand-picked as part of a new bodyguard team for the don. He walked out of the gates of his army base and never returned, but was not posted as AWOL or as a deserter, and his former CO made sure that any questions about him remained unanswered.

Sabit rose rapidly through the ranks of mafia bodyguards and enforcers. Intelligent, shrewd and calm in any situation, even when the bullets were flying, he was also an ice-cold killer when required. He became one of the mafia's principal intermediaries with the Taliban and al-Qaeda groups who supplied them with raw heroin and bought all the weapons, ammunition and explosives they could supply. Speaking passable Arabic and sharing the al-Qaeda men's Sunni faith made him even more valuable to his mob boss, who never had cause to doubt Sabit's loyalty.

One autumn evening he left on the regular run south with a shipment of weapons, explosives and ammunition to be traded for heroin. They were driving an ex-Soviet Army ZIL truck, with three other mafiosi riding shotgun. Sabit waited his moment as the truck rumbled south towards the Afghan border, knowing that it was a four-hour drive over rough and twisting back roads. Eventually he called a halt so they could relieve themselves on a deserted stretch of road passing through a sparse birch forest. Two men jumped down from the cab of the truck and strolled into the trees to urinate. The driver clambered down the other side and, like drivers the world over, began urinating against the tyre of his truck. He thought nothing of it as he heard Sabit jump down behind him, but it was to be the last sound he would ever hear, for a moment later Sabit pressed the muzzle of his silenced Makarov pistol against the back of the driver's neck and blew his head apart with a single round.

The other two men had heard nothing above the sound of the cold wind from the steppe whispering through the trees. Sabit waited until they returned to the truck, joking with each other as they emerged from the trees. The first one was still laughing as a round from Sabit's pistol hit him dead centre, sending him sprawling with blood pumping from the hole in his chest. The other man had time to let out a cry of surprise and began a frantic attempt to reach the pistol at his belt but before he could do so, there was another 'Phtttttt!' sound and he too was blown backwards, his arms outflung as a round drilled into his heart.

Sabit made sure with a single shot to each man's forehead, his face a blank mask. He returned to the truck to pull on a boiler suit from behind the seats, then dragged the bodies back to the truck and lifted them into the cab. They were, literally, dead weight, but he handled them as if they weighed no more than a bag of groceries. He climbed into the driver's seat and drove on towards the border. His al-Qaeda contacts were already waiting at the rendezvous. They greeted him with '*Salaam Alaikum*', touching their hands to their hearts in the traditional way, and embraced him. There were six of them in three Toyota Land Cruisers. In one of the vehicles was a captive, hooded and with his hands and feet bound.

While four of the al-Qaeda men began to transfer the weapons and ammunition from the truck to their Land Cruisers, the other two dragged their captive out of the vehicle and dumped him on the ground at Sabit's feet. 'As you asked, brother,' one said in Arabic. 'He is a spy for the *faranji* kafir. Normally we would have skinned him alive, cut off his manhood and stuffed it in his treacherous mouth, but you asked us for a man who would not be missed, so we have brought him to you.'

He ripped off the captive's hood, dragged him to his knees and then produced a wickedly sharp sword from his belt. He held it to the man's throat and gave Sabit a questioning look, but he shook his head. The al-Qaeda man frowned, then sheathed his sword and stepped back. The captive thought he had been saved and began to babble a stream of thanks to Sabit, calling down Allah's blessings upon him, but the words died on his lips as Sabit grabbed him by the hair, held his pistol to the man's head and without a flicker of emotion pulled the trigger. The round drilled a neat hole in the man's forehead and blew a jagged exit hole in the back of his head, taking most of his brains with it.

Sabit dragged the body over to the cab and man-handled it into position behind the steering wheel. He took off the bloodstained boiler suit and tossed it into the cab as well, then took from behind the seats his small shoulder bag containing $10,000 in cash and his only other worldly possessions: a copy of the Koran and a change of clothes. He took the jerry cans of spare fuel they carried as a necessary precaution in a territory where petrol stations were often hundreds of miles apart and doused the cab and its occupants with fuel. He emptied the remaining petrol into the back of the truck, then lit a petrol-soaked rag and tossed it into the cab. There was a momentary pause and then the fuel ignited.

Sabit turned his back, strolled to the lead Land Cruiser and jumped into the front seat. As they drove back towards the Afghan border, a pillar of oily black smoke and flames rose high into the night sky.

When Sabit and the others did not return, their mafia boss sent others to investigate. They found the torched truck a few miles from the border. Four blackened bodies were inside the car, each with a bullet hole in the forehead but burned beyond rec-ognition. There was no sign of the load of weapons they had been carrying nor the heroin they were to have traded them for. The mob boss put out word of a huge reward for any information but was met only with silence. Unsure if he was the victim of a double-cross by al-Qaeda or a hijack by a rival gang, he was eventually forced to swallow the loss, which, in any event, was only a drop in the ocean of money to be made from the heroin and arms trades. Shipments of weapons going south and heroin travelling north were soon resumed, and Sabit and his dead comrades were quickly forgotten.

CHAPTER 7

After the frenzy of the attack on the Inter-Continental, Shepherd and his mates were back in QRF routine for the next couple of days, but it was destined to be a brief respite. On the third morning, as they were sitting outside their tents in the sunlight, recovering from a punishing workout, a Land Rover came roaring around the perimeter of the Bagram runway and pulled up at the entrance to their compound. As the dust blew away on the breeze, they saw a familiar figure emerging from the passenger seat.

'Perfect,' Jock said. 'Here comes the CO to spoil a beautiful morning. Doesn't that lazy bastard ever walk anywhere?'

The CO was a portly figure with a bald spot like a monk's tonsure and, despite his forty years, the pink, scrubbed face of an overgrown schoolboy. While his men were all in their customary mix of well-worn army kit and local Afghan gear, he was as clean and pressed as if he was conducting a parade at Sandhurst.

'Good news,' he said, lowering himself onto a spare chair. 'We've got an op for you. The prime minister has demanded that British forces – which means us – be given an active and prominent role in the campaign against al-Qaeda and the Taliban. So we've been tasked with attacking a site being used as an al-Qaeda base and major opium storage facility. It's in the Registan Desert in Helmand Province, four hundred clicks south-west of Kandahar and fifteen from the southern border with Pakistan. It won't be a walk in the park because it is at the foot of a mountain that screens it on two sides, there are stone buildings but also caves inside the mountain of unknown size and length, and the whole target area is heavily fortified with sangars, bunkers and strongpoints, with between eighty and one hundred al-Qaeda fighters dug in around it. We believe it's being used as a regional HQ and a transit point for opium being shipped out to Pakistan, with weapons and ammunition making the journey in the opposite direction.'

'Sir, so why aren't the Americans using cruise missiles or bombs to flatten it from the air?' Shepherd said.

The CO's lips pursed at the interruption. 'Because our planners suspect that it will yield some high-value intelligence, and as you know, the only way to get that is to put boots on the ground and go in and get it. If the Yanks did it, as you say, they'd probably just bomb it to pieces, whereas we will have the opportunity to get our hands on some high-grade and maybe even priceless intelligence – our intel suggests that a very high-value enemy target may be based there, perhaps the highest-value one of all.'

Shepherd had listened to him with an expression of growing disbelief and he now interrupted him again, making no effort to hide his anger. 'With respect, sir, you're talking absolute bullshit. If the Yanks thought for one minute that there were any high value al-Qaeda or Taliban figures there, let alone Muj 1,' he said, using the codename for Osama bin Laden, 'the number one man on their Most Wanted list, do you really expect us to believe that they'd let us go in and get him?'

'Spider's right there, Sir,' Jock said. 'We all know that the Yanks keep the prime targets for their own units and all we get is the crumbs from the rich man's table, or the targets that are so hazardous they aren't willing to risk their own men to attack them. So this is obviously a target that Delta Force and all the other US elite units have turned up their noses at. And that's not surprising, because frankly, from what you've told us, sir, it stinks worse than Geordie's socks after a fifty-mile forced march.'

'Anyway, we know the real reason why we've been given this, don't we, sir? It's down to Tony Brown-Nose,' Shepherd said, using the caustic SAS nickname for a prime minister already famous for his determination to be closer to the US president than a second skin. 'He's desperate to have UK forces involved somehow, so he can crow about it to the press and the Yanks, with the full monty to back him up: soundbites, film clips, body counts – the works.'

'Aye,' Geordie said. 'Our great leader wants us to be there so he can show the man in the cowboy hat that he can wield a six-shooter too.'

'And if it comes to cocks on-the-table time,' Jimbo said, 'Tony wants to be able to whip his out without the Yanks laughing at him.'

By now the CO knew that he could not count on Shepherd and the others for support. Regimental protocol called for just one 'sir' or 'boss' at the beginning and end of any conversation. The fact he was being referred to as 'sir' in every sentence told him they were keeping him and his hare-brained scheme at arm's length. This would circulate on the grapevine throughout the Regiment and any respect he might once have had would be gone for ever.

The CO held up a hand to silence them all and his voice was icy as he spoke again. 'Nonetheless, whatever your personal opinions might be, that is the task we have been given and that is the task we shall carry out. Any further comments before we proceed?'

Shepherd and the others exchanged glances but remained silent. The CO waited a further moment and then resumed the briefing. 'Right. My orders are that the attack must take place as soon as possible, so it will proceed on the basis of the intelligence we already possess, without a detailed reconnaissance or close target surveillance.' There was another rumble of anger, but he ignored it and hurried on. 'Furthermore, in order to coordinate with the availability of US aircraft to carry out air strikes in support of the operation, the attack will be made between ten and eleven a.m.'

'For fuck's sake,' Jock said, unable to contain himself any longer. 'An attack on an elevated, fortified and heavily defended target in broad daylight, without any worthwhile intelligence and no humint, detailed reconnaissance or close target surveillance whatsoever, and with limited close air support? That isn't just dangerous, it's suicidal.'

'Nonetheless, those are our orders. I hear what you say, but the timelines have been imposed by CENTCOM – US Central Command – who are only able to provide us with one hour's on-call close air support. Two squadrons – yourselves and G Squadron – will be involved, flying in two waves in six Hercs.'

'Involving two squadrons is just not sustainable,' Shepherd said. 'In case you've forgotten, there are only four SAS squadrons. Given that one is permanently deployed on counter-terrorist duty and another on QRF, if you deploy the other two together, then when you rotate the first two, the others have to replace them, so there's no room for anyone to rest or retrain – and if we don't keep training, our skill levels drop, and they are what separates us from the rest.'

'Granted, granted,' the CO said, 'but the two squadrons will only be involved for the brief duration of the op. At its conclusion, G Squadron will return to their normal routine at Hereford. Right,' he said, hurrying on, 'I've talked it through at length with the Head Sheds in Hereford and Northwood, and this is the plan we've formulated. Air Troop will HALO jump into the desert to secure and mark out a Temporary Landing Zone for the Hercs. After landing, both squadrons – one hundred and twenty men using twenty-eight Pinkies, eight scout motorcycles and two ACMAT mother ships – will drive to the Forming-Up Point. G Squadron will set up a fire support base ready to engage the al-Qaeda defences from stand-off range and American aircraft will destroy the opium stores. Using the cover of the air strikes and the fire from the FSB, the other squadron – you – will assault the base, overwhelm the defenders, take prisoners for interrogation and then sweep the site for intelligence materials. Under continuing cover from the FSB, you will then withdraw from contact, followed by G Squadron.' He paused and began reading from his briefing sheet. 'Now, weaponry: the Fire Support Team will have the standard M2 Browning heavy machine guns and GPMGs on the Pinkies, plus 81mm mortars, MILAN anti-tank missiles and Mk 19 grenade launchers.'

'Hang on a minute,' Shepherd said. 'MILANs great. We're not going to be encountering any tanks but with a range of three kilometres and a joystick to guide them, a good crew will be able to put them right into those cave mouths. The Mk 19 grenade launchers are a great close support weapon too, up to

STEPHEN LEATHER

a range of eight hundred metres, but they fire at sixty rounds a minute on rapid fire so they need a shitload of ammo to feed them, which may be an issue. So that's all good, but the 81mm mortars? Sure, they've got a three kilometre range, but they go up thousands of feet – there's a time of flight of thirty seconds – and that means we can't fire them into caves, so why would we want to take them on this op?'

'Spider's right,' Jock said. 'And if there's an air-craft over the target you can't fire the mortars any-way, and in fact artillery and everything else has to stop as well. We can't even fire the GPMGs because although they have a very low trajectory, there's a danger from ricochets.'

'I've noted your comments,' the CO said, 'and of course you're free to choose your own personal weapons for the op, but G Squadron, not you, will be manning the fire support base and they will make the decisions about what weapons they'll deploy. Agreed?'

Shepherd shrugged. 'Agreed, though of course if it all goes tits up because the Fire Support hasn't done its job properly, it won't be G Squadron that has to face the consequences, will it?'

The CO made a fussy gesture with his hand, as if brushing Shepherd's awkward comments aside. 'Now, one final point. The aim, as always, is to mini-mise our own casualties and with that in mind, all troopers will be issued with Strike plate-carrier body armour and the new MSA TC-2000 US helmets.'

'To hell with that,' Shepherd said. 'We've tested both of those. The body armour weighs a ton and is uncomfortable to wear, slowing us down in the field, and while the helmets obviously provide protection to the head and neck, they also reduce vision and hearing to unacceptable levels. We need to be able to see our enemy and we need to be able to hear what's going on around us, so as far as we're all concerned, that's a non-starter.'

'It isn't up for negotiation,' the CO said. 'The decision has already been reached at a level well above my paygrade, never mind yours, so that is what will be happening and any man who does not wear his body armour and helmet will be RTU'd.' He paused, studying each man's face in turn. 'Any other questions? Then let's get going, because we don't have much time. The op is scheduled for the day after tomorrow.' That provoked a fresh outburst from Jock, but the CO was already heading out of the door.

They used the remaining twenty-four hours to prepare as well as they could for the op, putting in hours on their improvised firing range honing their close-quarter battle skills, and discussing and visualising every conceivable 'What if' so that whatever events might occur, their reaction would be swift and effective. Hopefully.

CHAPTER 8

The night before the op, the two squadrons assembled at Bagram for the final briefing, G Squadron having flown in from Hereford earlier that day. The men from Air Troop who would be making the High Altitude Low Opening insertion were all members of Shepherd's own squadron. Although they were usually away on specialised training or ops, they knew each other well enough to exchange greetings and banter, and Shepherd had actually been through SAS Selection with four of them. As with the rest of the Regiment, they were all known by nicknames: Lefty's was a reference to his left-handedness, not his political affiliations; Jeeves had briefly worked as a butler in civilian life; Abs's was a semi-sarcastic tribute to the six-pack he worked so hard to maintain; and Feral was named for his untameable hair and beard, and the way that even the smartest clothes looked scruffy as soon as he put them on.

There was a three-quarter moon that night, an uncomfortable light for a covert insertion, so Air Troop had to wait until the moon was setting before their Herc pilot took off from Bagram. By the time they reached the drop zone, the only light came from the stars dusting the sky above them. The aircraft was flying at over 20,000 feet and even at ground level the temperature was close to freezing, but when the green light signalling 'Go' came on, none of Air Troop's men hesitated for a second before launching themselves into the darkness where the slipstream pummelled and tore at them. Paras would normally jump one at a time to avoid the risk of becoming entangled in each other's harness and rigging, but the men of Air Troop were so confident and so supremely skilled that they hurled themselves out of the Herc simultaneously in a bomb-burst formation, giving them enough room to manoeuvre but with the certainty that they would land within close margins of each other.

They plummeted earthwards for 16,000 feet before their altitude sensors automatically triggered their chutes at 4,000 feet. However, one man's chute failed to open automatically and by the time he had used the manual control to deploy it, he was so close to the ground that he broke his ankle on landing. The troop's medic immobilised his foot and gave him a morphine shot while the others began checking the area.

The site had been chosen on the basis of air reconnaissance imaging that showed roughly level and solid-looking ground, but Air Troop immediately began testing the ground to make sure it was hard enough to withstand the impact of a succession of Hercules landing and taking off again. They then marked out the landing strip, an area of desert a little over 250 metres long and only twelve metres wide. It was far shorter than a conventional runway, but just long enough for the skilled pilots of the SF Squadron to make a successful landing and take-off.

Air Troop signalled that all was in readiness and within an hour the sound of aircraft engines – a bass rumble like distant thunder – announced the arrival of the first wave of the massive Hercules transports. Lefty and Abs guided them in using infrared torches. The Hercs took it in turn to make a rolling pass along the temporary runway, their loading ramps already lowered, allowing the SAS Pinkies they carried to speed down the ramps before the Hercs took off again.

As each patrol cleared the landing strip, they immediately went into all-round defence. They remained in their positions, alert for any sign that the mission had been compromised, until the Hercs returned from Bagram an hour later, bringing in the second wave of SAS men and their vehicles. Once the last group had deplaned, they formed up into two columns with four men on Kawasaki dirt bikes as lead scouts, roaming ahead of each column to prove the route and watch for any sign of enemy ambush. They were followed by the Pinkies, with the ACMAT trucks that were acting as 'mother ships' bringing up the rear. Piled high with fuel, water and mountains of ammunition, they were so heavily laden that they were bottoming on their springs.

'Bloody hell,' Jock said, impressed despite himself as he saw the column of vehicles stretching away in front and behind them. 'I bet there hasn't been an SAS op on this scale since the Second World War.'

Despite the darkness, made worse by the fine dust thrown up by the vehicles ahead of them, they drove over 100 kilometres across the desert to a pre-planned Lying-Up Point, screened from direct line of sight of the target by a low ridge. They set up a defensive perimeter and stationed observation points on the ridge to keep watch on the target, then remained in cover until the time to launch the attack. They shivered through the cold of the night, then sweated in the searing desert heat as the sun rose higher in the sky.

At ten o'clock that morning, the engines of the Pinkies roared into life almost as one, tearing apart the stillness of the day as they moved to the start line. They set out at once and as they cleared the ridge their target came into sight just over a mile away: a group of low stone buildings within a compound at the foot of a rocky, near-vertical cliff face. The compound was surrounded by defensive positions. Throughout the Middle East, instead of digging trenches in rocky terrain the inhabitants built drystone walled enclosures known as 'sangars' that would be manned by their defenders in the event of an attack. They punctuated every track and stood at the entrance to every village.

Al-Qaeda had brought the tradition with them to Afghanistan and built rings of reinforced sangars to provide cover for their fighters. Here, the cliff curved in an arc to either side of the compound's defences, protecting it from attack from the north-east, north and north-west; any approach from another direction had to be made up a steep slope strewn with scree and fallen boulders from the cliffs above. The only way in for vehicles was a dirt track winding between two huge boulders – an obvious ambush point and potential deathtrap.

As soon as they broke cover, the pall of dust thrown up by the vehicles marked them out to the enemy, who immediately began launching RPGs at them. G Squadron manoeuvred into position and began returning fire with their heavy weapons. Crews with M2 Browning heavy machine guns and GPMGs put down a barrage of fire while others launched MILAN missiles at the strongpoints and cave entrances, and still others fired the belt-fed Mark 19 grenade launchers that rained down grenades like hail. They kept pouring down suppressing fire onto the enemy, while SAS snipers armed with L82A1 Barrett rifles moved covertly to within a kilometre of the compound. The snipers began taking out individual targets whenever careless or overeager al-Qaeda fighters revealed themselves, some by their muzzle flashes, others rising from cover, ready to take aimed shots they were never to fire.

Meanwhile, the other SAS squadron, including Shepherd's patrol, was still roaring onwards to begin the ground assault. Jimbo had the accelerator floored as their Pinkie sped towards the target, sending it bucketing over the ruts with bone-jarring impact, while lurching and swerving from side to side to throw off the enemy's aim. One Pinkie was less lucky and suffered a direct hit from an RPG. It erupted in a fireball, but the others had no time to contemplate their comrades' fate as they roared onward. Shepherd was standing upright on the passenger side, firing the Pinkie's GPMG as they raced towards the foot of the steep slope leading to the compound. As they reached it, Jimbo braked to a savage halt. The vehicle slewed around, skidding in the sand and dust, but before it had even come to a stop, rocking on its springs, the patrol had spilled out into the dead ground. They began scrambling up the rocky, dusty slopes, using every scrap of cover and fire and movement to avoid the torrents of automatic fire from the al-Qaeda fighters in the strongpoints and sangars on the heights above them.

An instant later, a series of deafening blasts signalled the impact of Maverick missiles fired from a range of ten or twenty kilometres by US Navy F-18 Hornets flying from an aircraft carrier in the Gulf. The missiles turned the opium storage areas into infernos, with belching clouds of oily black smoke almost obscuring the fierce fires burning at their core. Even amongst the heat, smoke and dust of battle, Shepherd could smell the sickly-sweet aroma of burning opium on the wind.

Within a minute, the scream of fast jets filled the air. The Hornets flashed overhead, making low-level passes and strafing the defences with their rotary cannon. Shepherd's patrol had advanced rapidly up the east side of the slope and they were forced to dive for cover as one Hornet pilot either mistook their position for an enemy strongpoint or, more likely, as Shepherd thought in the aftermath, was too gung-ho with excitement to care much either way and unleashed a barrage of 20mm cannon shells that smashed into the rocks around them, filling the air with a murderous swarm of jagged rock splinters. Even above the din of combat, Shepherd heard Geordie's agonised cry as one of the rock splinters sliced his cheek open to the bone. He shouted 'Geordie! Are you okay?'

There was a heart-stopping pause before Geordie called out, 'I'm all right, a scratch is all.'

'Then physician heal thy fucking self,' Jock said. 'And be quick about it. In case you hadn't noticed, there's a firefight going on.' Jock kept giving cover while Geordie patched himself up and Shepherd and Jimbo advanced a few yards further up the slope. They then fired bursts to keep the al-Qaeda heads down as Jock and Geordie, now sporting a blood-soaked field dressing on his cheek, scrambled after them.

An al-Qaeda machine-gun nest – stationed in the gap between two boulders and further protected from frontal attack by a stone and concrete wall linking them – now had the SAS men pinned down, unleashing a hail of fire at any sign of movement. Shepherd and Jimbo tried to fire and move again, but as he broke cover, Shepherd felt a succession of savage blows to his body and was thrown backwards into the cover he had just left. He lay there gasping for breath for a moment, feeling fluid trickling down his thigh. He hurriedly checked himself for wounds and, to his relief, found that an enemy round had smashed into the steel water bottle on his belt. Had the bottle been empty, the bullet could easily have exited through the other side and given him a serious wound in his hip or groin, but it had been full of the water now running down his thigh and that had taken enough momentum off the round for it to do no more than pierce the other side of the bottle and become wedged there.

He also felt stabs of pain from his chest and ribs and as he examined those, he muttered a silent prayer of thanks for the clumsy body armour he hadn't wanted to wear but which had just saved his life. Two rounds from something like an AK-47 had smashed into it. The ceramic plates had been driven into his body with such force they had bruised his flesh and threatened to crack his ribs, but they had not been pierced.

'Fuck this for a game of soldiers,' Shepherd said. He spoke into his shoulder mic, giving their position and a sitrep. Within a minute, an American F-14 Tomcat providing close air support had obliterated the strongpoint. The bomb it dropped detonated so close to the SAS men's own position that they were rocked by the blast wave, but, forewarned, they had wormed their way into deep cover and blocked their ears with their fingers. 'Good thing it wasn't that Hornet that nearly wiped us out,' Jimbo said. 'He'd probably have bombed us and then dropped ammo and rations to the ragheads up there.'

Although one strongpoint had been eliminated, there was little let-up in the storm of fire from above and when the neighbouring patrol tried to advance, one trooper was hit by a round in his thigh, below the protection of his body armour, and was sent sprawling to the ground. Two other troopers sprinted forwards and half carried, half dragged him into cover.

The RSM in charge of the fire support base, whether concerned that the attack was losing momentum or just desperate for a taste of the action and perhaps a medal for himself, now abandoned the previous plan and led a group of his men forward to join the fighting. His reward was to be hit in the leg by an AK-47 round. Although the wound would increase his chances of a medal, it had been an ill-judged decision to advance, taken by a man famous in the Regiment for his arrogance.

As he was treated by a G Squadron medic, the close air support aircraft returned to the attack. They kept flying sorties until they had run out of ammunition. By then the volume of enemy firing was beginning to slacken a little under the impact of multiple assaults from the aircraft, the fire support base, the sniper teams and the ground troops who were steadily whittling away the numbers of defenders. MILAN missiles fired directly into the cave mouths had killed the fighters around the entrances and wounded or burst the eardrums of those a little further inside, and no further reinforcements were appearing to aid the hard-pressed defenders as the SAS vice closed around them.

Jock was first over the top of the slope, lobbing a grenade into an al-Qaeda sangar and then following it the last few feet up the slope. He appeared on the rim of the sangar a heartbeat after the grenade detonated, cleaning out the survivors with staccato double taps that followed so fast on each other they almost sounded like a continuous burst of automatic fire. Geordie was hot on his heels, and Shepherd and Jimbo then breached the next sangar, surprising two al-Qaeda men who scrambled to raise their weapons to meet the threat. Neither succeeded. A third man had thrown down his rifle and raised his right hand as if to surrender, but Shepherd saw his other hand jerk the pin from a grenade dangling from his belt. As he dived towards Shepherd, aiming to blow himself and his enemy to pieces in his final act, Shepherd drilled a double tap through the man's forehead. He was hurled backwards by the impacts while Shepherd and Jimbo dived over the far side of the trench. They heard the grenade detonate behind them, but, blocked by the thick wall of the sangar, it

only added fresh wounds to the body of the already
dead al-Qaeda fighter.

Fortunately for the attackers, the defensive positions had not been planned with any sophistication.
The dozens of sangars and other fire positions did
not have interlocking arcs of fire, and the heavy weapons did not have designated defensive fire targets.
Two other patrols had now breached the last ring of
defences and together the SAS men began eliminating the remaining visible resistance. The al-Qaeda
fighters still outside the caves emerged from cover
and began taking on the attackers in open combat.
That was not a wise move; they were outgunned and
facing men who were infinitely better trained and
more highly skilled, so the firefight was only ever
going to have one conclusion. However, the al-Qaeda
fighters continued to charge at the SAS, firing their
weapons until they ran out of ammunition. The last
two left alive ran at the nearest SAS men, brandish-
ing knives, until they too were cut down with precise
double taps. Shepherd couldn't decide if they were
incredibly brave or simply deluded and believed that
death in combat would earn them a place in heaven.

Using hand signals to communicate, Shepherd
and Jimbo then stationed themselves either side
of one of the cave entrances and switched on the
Maglite torches slung under the barrels of their AKs.
Shepherd counted down on his fingers while Jock
and Geordie unleashed a barrage of fire into the
cave. When he reached 'zero', the other two ceased

fire and in that same instant Shepherd and Jimbo sprinted into the cave entrance, diving and rolling to throw off the aim of any surviving defenders.

They found themselves in a chamber carved out of the solid rock. The entrance was littered with bodies, while carpets spread on the floor in the centre of the cave still bore traces of the meal the al-Qaeda fighters had been eating when the attack began. Shepherd took out one enemy, then dived into cover behind the body of another, killed earlier in a MILAN missile blast. As enemy rounds smacked into the corpse, Shepherd rolled to one side and double-tapped another shooter, whose AK-47 carved an arc of impacts upwards into the cave roof, sending ricochets whining in all directions as he fell back, stone-dead. Shepherd dropped back into cover as the ricochets and stone chips filled the air, then sprinted onwards. The echoes of a double tap to his left told him Jimbo had eliminated another fighter.

They barrelled down a long stone passageway and emerged into another chamber carved out of the mountain, this one lined with crates of weapons and ammunition piled up to the roof. Unbelievably, given the infernal noise of the firefight outside, they found deep in the cave three al-Qaeda fighters who had slept through the whole combat. Shepherd and Jimbo kicked them awake and they opened their eyes to find themselves looking down the wrong end of two AK-47 barrels. Shepherd kept them covered while Jimbo cable-tied their wrists and ankles. Jock and Geordie had now also arrived, having completed the mopping-up of the first cave, and they dragged the three captives outside, ready to be taken back to Bagram for interrogation.

Shepherd and Jimbo had meanwhile begun a sweep of the cave, gathering up two laptops and a sheaf of papers stacked on a weapons crate the al-Qaeda fighters had been using as a table. They then began searching the bodies of the dead for mobile phones and found three, which they added to their haul. They also checked the faces of the dead, but recognised none of the al-Qaeda and Taliban leaders they had seen in photographs circulated in intelligence briefings. 'Well Muj 1 definitely wasn't here,' Shepherd said. 'Nor any of his top echelon.'

'And given the lack of senior commanders here, I doubt if the intel from that little lot will justify the risks and casualties we took,' Jimbo said.

Shepherd nodded. 'But I tell you what, even if all this lot contains is their search history on Amazon, by the time Tony Brown-Nose's spin doctor has got hold of it, I'll bet this will be hailed as the greatest cache of intelligence material since the capture of an Enigma machine in World War Two.'

With the search complete, they joined their comrades in forming a defensive perimeter while SAS demolition experts entered the caves and laid charges of plastic explosive to destroy the arsenal of weapons and ammunition Shepherd and Jimbo had found. With the charges laid, they pulled back to the slopes below the cave entrance, shielded from the shock waves and any rocks dislodged by the blast. When the charges were detonated, there was a deep bass rumble and Shepherd felt the ground lurch beneath him. Smoke and flames jetted from the cave entrances and debris spattered down on the slopes around them. When the smoke cleared, the cave entrances had completely disappeared, replaced by a broken jumble of rocks.

They pulled back to their vehicles and moved out in a phased withdrawal. Some of the Pinkies had been destroyed or damaged in the firefight and those not fit to drive were completely destroyed by the SAS demolitions men, rendering even their parts unsalvageable by the Taliban. The remaining vehicles had SAS men clinging to the outside of the doors and the rear bumpers as they drove back towards the TLZ at a more leisurely pace than when they'd made the journey in the opposite direction.

Back at Bagram later that afternoon they carried out a debrief, a noisy and fractious process with many SAS troopers angry about an op that had brought so little tangible reward and cost them six casualties in addition to the two who had died when their Pinkie had been hit by an RPG. The CO remained imperturbable, describing the op as a triumph in the best traditions of the Regiment. I don't underplay our own casualties – even one is one too many – but when we compare that with enemy losses...' He paused and studied a sheet of paper he was clutching. 'We killed ninety-three terrorists and captured three more, together with a priceless cache of intelligence material.'

'Now I know you're talking bullshit,' Jock said, his face puce with anger. 'None of us were counting bodies before we pulled out, and if you've been hit by a Maverick or a MILAN missile there's precious little left to count anyway, so don't tell us "ninety-three enemy dead" and expect us to believe it. Don't make me laugh. It's like US bodycounts in Vietnam: exactly ninety-three dead and all of them terrorists, including the babies.'

'And where was Muj 1 and the other al-Qaeda and Taliban leaders in all this?' Geordie said, backing up his mate. 'Nowhere to be bloody seen, as we suspected. We didn't do this op for intel, or to take out terrorists leaders, or even for ninety-three dead terrorists. We did it because our prime minister wanted something – anything – that he could wave at his new best friend in the White House to show we were playing our part.'

The debrief broke up in acrimony soon afterwards. G Squadron flew out that night, heading back to Hereford, but for Shepherd's patrol it appeared there was to be no early exit from Afghanistan and to their disgust they found themselves back in their compound on the far side of the base, still on QRF duty. Shepherd explored his tender ribs with his fingers and then gingerly eased off his shirt and examined himself in the cracked mirror dangling from a rusty nail in the doorpost of their hut. There was a large purpling bruise on the right side of his ribs and another one directly over his heart. 'Too close for comfort that one,' Geordie said. 'If it hadn't been for the body armour, we'd have been inscribing a new name on the plinth of the regimental clock.'

The post-op debrief had taken place under conditions of maximum security – 'Top Secret: UK Eyes Only', the highest possible classification – yet within forty-eight hours the story of the raid had been plastered all over the pages of the newspapers. A copy of that day's front page of *The Sun* was faxed through to Bagram from Hereford and Jimbo brought it over to the others while they were sitting in the last rays of the afternoon sun, wondering what the night might bring.

'Take a look at that,' Jimbo said, tossing it down in front of Jock. He picked it up, his scowl deepening as he read the headline: VCs ALL ROUND FOR SAS HEROES. The story was sensationalised almost beyond recognition. It claimed that the HALO jump had been 'the first ever HALO jump into enemy territory by the SAS under combat conditions' – which, as Jock sourly noted, 'is perfectly true if you don't count the one the Regiment did into up-country Aden way back in 1965, and the further insertion into the Musandam Peninsula in Oman in the 1970s.'

'Blimey Jock, if you were in on those, you're even older than you look,' Geordie said, with a wink to the others.

'I heard it from the Old and Bold who were there,' Jock said, refusing to rise to the bait, 'but I guess dressing this one up as if it was the first is just part of the Whitehall sales pitch to the media.'

The *Sun* story ended by quoting the same ludicrous figure for terrorists killed and other details that only someone who had witnessed the debrief – or had read the report circulated only to the most senior military commanders and the prime minister – could have known. 'What a pile of bollocks,' Jock said, tossing it aside. 'The only true bit is where they said the op took place in Afghanistan.'

Shepherd picked it up and quickly scanned it. 'I notice the RSM gets a prominent mention,' he said, 'and that'll not hurt his medal chances, but for once I'm willing to give him the benefit of the doubt, because this has the fingerprints of the PM's spin doctor all over it.'

'You're right there,' Jock said. 'After all, like Geordie said in the debrief, what's the point of getting us to risk our lives attacking some low-grade target the Yanks could have flattened with a couple of cruise missiles, if you can't brag about it afterwards to your new Texan best friend?'

As its headline suggested, the *Sun* article was calling for Victoria Crosses and other medals to be dispensed liberally among the SAS men who had carried out the raid, but none of them believed that was ever likely to happen. Sure enough, when the CO announced the decorations for the raid, there was only a DSO for him and the Military Cross for the two squadron commanders. The other ranks – even the wounded RSM – got nothing, not even a mention in dispatches.

CHAPTER 9

Sabit Kusen had remained in Afghanistan for only a few months. Al-Qaeda was coming under increasing pressure from the Americans and their allies, who were bombing and rocketing them out of a succession of their former strongholds. At first the leaders and a group of battle-hardened fighters, including Sabit, were forced to take refuge in the White Mountains and the Tora Bora caves. There he was introduced to a tall, hook-nosed man known to his followers simply as 'The Leader', a devout, ascetic individual with a punishing personal regime of fasting and prayer. When the Americans began bombing and then attacking the Tora Bora caves too, Sabit was part of the small group of bodyguards that formed an escort for The Leader as he fled through the snows of the high mountain passes to a refuge in the tribal borderlands of Pakistan.

Once safely there, Sabit put a proposal to him. In return for a pledge of funding for his own particular aims, Sabit volunteered to pick up the torch of jihad and take the war once more to the great cities of the *faranji* imperialists. He would strike at some of the highest-profile targets in the world, planning and carrying out the attacks himself, but leaving The Leader and al-Qaeda to claim all the credit for them.

Two weeks later, armed with a letter of introduction from The Leader, Sabit left Pakistan using forged documents supplied by an al-Qaeda sympathiser in Pakistan's Inter-Services Intelligence agency. He flew to Saudi Arabia, where he was met by an al-Qaeda contact at the airport in Jeddah and then driven deep into the desert to a nomad encampment. It was so lavishly equipped and its black tents were surrounded by so many gleaming, top-of-the-range SUVs, it was clear that the occupants were no ordinary nomads.

Although they shared his religion, his hosts were at first suspicious, even hostile, and when he produced the letter from The Leader, even though it caused a noticeable thaw in the atmosphere, they remained dubious about Sabit's value to them.

'Allah be praised, we have our own army of fighters and martyrs,' their leader said. 'Why should we pay you and your men to fight for us?'

'The bravery and the success of you and your fighters has echoed around the world,' Sabit said, applying a generous coating of honey to his words. 'But your success has put the infidels on their guard. Arabs are the object of suspicion wherever they go, whereas our people are still seen merely as tourists or businessmen. I look like any other Chinese and no one sees me as a threat. I can go where you cannot and pass in a crowd without arousing a trace of suspicion. The Americans and their running dogs are stupid. They think all terrorists are Arabs. While they are searching men in Arab robes, we will be at work. And when the time is right, inshallah, we shall strike blows at the infidels from which they will not recover. We do not yet seek publicity for our own cause – quite the reverse. So, if you agree, we will carry out the actions, but you will claim the credit for al-Qaeda and the glory of Allah.'

Looking around the group, measuring the impact of his words, he knew he had them and a deal was soon agreed. Sabit would mount successive operations against two of the highest-profile targets in the West. In return, al-Qaeda's Saudi backers would provide him with funding for a further spectacular operation of his own, against another equally high-profile target, but with one important difference. This time the victims would not be Western capitalists and imperialists, but the cruel oppressors of his own people.

Sabit was already plugged into a network of exiles from his homeland, a worldwide web of contacts among whom were young men bent on avenging themselves against their persecutors, as well as older 'sleepers' apparently fully assimilated into their new countries' customs and ways of life, but also awaiting a call to action against their people's oppressors. Other menial recruits – cannon fodder – were supplied by his Saudi mentors. These young Muslims from a variety of countries, poor and ill-educated, were willing to martyr themselves for a combination of reasons: religious devotion, dreams of the seventy-two virgins awaiting them in paradise, and a more practical desire to provide their families with money they could never generate from a life of toil. The Saudi backers also provided Sabit with a desert training camp where he could prepare his troops for the first of the battles to come.

The training programme he devised – based on his own special forces training and the more unorthodox but equally effective methods of the mafia's enforcers – included enough physical-fitness work to sharpen their reactions and condition them to unquestioning obedience to his orders. There was no need for more fitness conditioning than that; they were not regular troops and would not be marching into battle or travelling long distances across country to reach their targets.

They were also trained in unarmed combat and the use of firearms, including close-range drills and the handling of explosives. Before going into action, each man would be issued with a necklace and wristbands of detonating cord; a handheld device activated by a 'dead man's hand' trigger would detonate the explosive when the pressure on it was released, whether voluntarily or involuntarily. Al-Qaeda did not care whether their men were recognised after death, but Sabit had powerful reasons for not revealing the identities of his own recruits. His plan depended on the oppressors of his people remaining unaware that they were his ultimate target until it was too late to do anything to stop him.

CHAPTER 10

In the aftermath of the raid on the al-Qaeda base in Afghanistan, Shepherd and his patrol mates were still stuck at Bagram, doing fitness training, practising their skills and counting down the days until the end of their period on QRF. 'Just six more days,' Jock said, 'and then they'll have to send us back to Hereford for some R & R. I've been away so long, I've forgotten what my missus looks like.'

'Believe me, Jock,' Geordie said. 'That's a good thing.'

Jimbo's laughter turned into a groan as he saw the OC – Officer Commanding – walking across the compound towards them. 'Great,' he said. 'Just when you think things can't get any worse.'

They answered in monosyllables as the OC made uneasy small talk about the weather and the state of the campaign against the Taliban and al-Qaeda, waiting for him to reveal the real purpose of his visit. 'You men have already gone above and beyond on this posting,' he said, 'and you're certainly overdue for some leave.'

'But?' Shepherd said, after waiting in vain for the OC to come to the point.

The OC gave a nervous smile. 'There's always a but, isn't there?'

'There is with you,' Jock growled. 'So spit it out.'

'Well... the departing general in command of British forces in Afghanistan has planned a large-scale sweep-and-search operation south-west of Herat, near the Iranian border. The area has supposedly long been pacified and so has not been visited by troops for several months. The op is the general's pet project, if you like, his own last hurrah before heading home as well as a welcome present for his successor.'

'Or possibly he's jealous of the kudos and publicity generated by our raid on that al-Qaeda base,' Geordie said, 'and wants a bit of publicity for himself.'

'Be that as it may,' the OC said, his forced smile beginning to crumble around the edges, 'the general has insisted that every available man should be rounded up for the operation, even if it means that the patrol bases are left undermanned.'

'Great,' Jock said. 'So he's going to round up anyone capable of standing upright and holding a rifle, which means half the soldiers drafted into the op are going to be from rear echelon units with minimal infantry skills and little or no battle experience.'

The OC gave a tight smile. 'The general is also insistent that all the special forces in country must take part in the operation.'

'Why?' Shepherd said. 'As we all know, he's an infantry man himself and he bloody hates Special Forces.'

'Nonetheless, that's his order. Your task will be to man early-warning positions on the high ground above the infantry troops carrying out the sweep and search.' He paused and made an effort to soften his tone. 'I'm sorry, guys, this is none of my doing. If it were down to me, you would already be on a flight back to the UK, but I'm outranked on this. So just do the op and I promise I'll get you on the first flight out afterwards.'

They spent the next couple of days on preparations for the op, then on the third day the order duly came down that it was 'Time for the Big Push'. As Jock drily observed, 'the last time a British general used that phrase was at the start of the Battle of the Somme.'

'Yeah,' Shepherd said, 'and we know how well that turned out, don't we?'

An imposing-looking force had been assembled for the general's big show, with ground troops – an entire infantry battalion – supported by artillery, mortars, fast jets, attack helicopters and armoured vehicles. Two of the French military's multi-role ACMAT trucks had again been co-opted to act as mother ships for the operation, carrying spare fuel and water and prodigious quantities of ammunition, together with a couple of GAZ-66s, the Soviet infantry's 4x4 military trucks. Captured from the Soviets by the mujahideen, they were still going strong years later.

The night before the launch of the op, Shepherd and his team, along with an infantry GPMG crew, were dropped off by a Puma helicopter on a spot high above the place where the operation was due to start the following morning. Learning from previous operations in Afghanistan, the infantry battalion had wisely ditched the Minimi machine gun preferred by other units for the heavier-calibre GPMG, which could put down fire and churn up the ground at a much greater range. That made the heavier weight of the gun and ammo a price well worth paying.

However, the two-man gun crew were showing some signs of nerves at being so far from their comrades. They were used to working in large groups and would have liked to have been down on the low ground with the main body of troops. By contrast, Shepherd's team actively preferred to be on their own, although on this op their designated role within the general's master plan made them little more than ammunition carriers for the machine-gun crew.

Each of them had an SA80 over their shoulder, the standard-issue British Army rifle. They were carrying them because the brass had insisted that everyone on the op should carry the same weapons. Although this was contrary to the SAS doctrine that every man carried his own weapon of choice, the regimental hierarchy in country had bowed to the general's wishes, even though they knew it would cause considerable controversy in the ranks. The weapons they had were not even the latest version; no one in the Regiment would willingly carry the SA 80 because of doubts about its reliability in combat and its tendency to jam, so none were held in the unit's own armoury and they had had to be borrowed from the base armoury, where they were kept in reserve.

Having set up their OP during the night, the patrol stood to around dawn and then spent the early part of the day watching the build-up. First, fast jets strafed the chosen landing zone. That was followed by an artillery barrage and then Chinook and Puma helicopters brought in the main force. Finally, when everybody else was in position, the two generals – 'Sunrays' in army code – arrived in their own Lynx command helicopter, their Redcap bodyguards in an escorting Chinook, the ground wash stirring up fresh dust storms as they landed.

Shepherd watched through his binoculars as the two generals emerged from the Lynx. 'They both look as if they've come straight from central casting,' he said. 'Immaculately tailored camo kit, lightly tanned and firm-jawed – they look like a Hollywood director's wet dream of fighting soldiers.'

'Yeah?' Jock said, focussing his own binoculars on them. 'Just goes to show that looks can be deceptive. The senior general's even carrying a holstered pistol as his personal weapon, though the junior one has clearly got slightly more smarts, he's worked out that he'll be making himself a target by looking like an officer, so he's at least the sense to carry a rifle.'

Both generals had followed a similar career path, attending the same public school a couple of years apart, followed by Sandhurst military college. They had seen a little action in Northern Ireland as sub-alterns, and then done various staff jobs around the army, making sure they were close enough to any action to share a little reflected glory without actually being part of it. That meant they were able to pick up a variety of medals without exposing themselves to any danger. Now that they had one foot on the pinnacle, nothing was going to stop them from attaining the ultimate prize: a place on the General Staff in Whitehall. To any outside observer, they were exactly what the military needed: brave, decorated, steady and stable officers. The fact that the troops under their command regarded them both with varying degrees of contempt counted for nothing.

As he squinted at them through his binoculars, Jock's expression showed that, as usual, he was taking senior officers' promotions, medals, gold braid and expensively tailored uniforms as personal affronts. 'Bet they both "married well", as well,' he growled. 'Because in the modern army that's essential too. Back in the day, generals were almost always aristos, but now they can be from almost any background.' 'Except yours,' Geordie said.

Jock ignored the interruption. 'So they need something else to help them fit in, including a wife who knows which fork to use and how to make small talk.'

Geordie grinned. 'And who doesn't have tattoos or work in a lap-dancing club,' he added, determined to have the last word, 'which rules out your missus for a start.'

The senior general was loathed throughout the ranks. He was nicknamed 'the Count', which, as Geordie noted, 'is the closest anyone can get to calling him a cunt without ending up in a military jail.' His officious and equally arrogant military police bodyguards were likewise detested, and their misuse of their boss's power was legendary.

Geordie whistled through his teeth. 'Look at all the high-tech kit down there though, just for the general's fancy dress parade. It's bloody ridiculous. There's millions of quids worth of kit lined up, probably more than the GDP of the entire sodding country. We've got the capability to fight day and night, 24/7/365 against the most sophisticated enemies, and yet we're using it against a bunch of ragged-arse peasant farmers who are just the meat in the sandwich between foreigners like us and the local warlords. We don't or won't understand what motivates them, because it's easier just to blame everything on their religion, though the real reason is probably that they are being forced to fight by one side or the other.'

'That's Commie talk, you pinko sonofabitch,' Jimbo said, putting on his best Texan accent. 'You'd better shape up or ship out, 'cos we don't like your kind around here.'

'Would you ladies mind finishing the discussion group later and focusing on the task at hand?' Shepherd said. 'Looks like it's showtime.'

While the SAS men maintained their watch on the high ground, scanning every ridgeline and hillside for suspicious movement, the infantry sweep began, the troops advancing steadily over the terrain but meeting no armed resistance at all. For about forty minutes everything appeared to be going fine, until they reached the fields full of ripe crops surrounding the local village. Then there was a sudden burst of fire and a couple of soldiers in the leading section of infantry fell down wounded as their comrades scrambled for cover.

The whole of the operation now became focused on this incident, with medics tending to the wounded and Forward Air Control Officers calling up casevac choppers and fast-jet strikes. The infantrymen found cover wherever they could; meanwhile, the whole advance ground to an inglorious halt. In the melee, the senior general stood out from everyone around him both because he was still standing upright and because of his lack of a weapon other than the pistol at his hip. As a result, he became the main target for the Afghan fighters.

His lack of combat experience was apparent to everybody around him. Uncertain of what to do, he remained standing until he finally hit the ground in a cloud of dust when a burst of fire passed millimetres over his head. His resulting head-first impact with the ground caused a tremendous nosebleed and the medic from his BG team, thinking the general had been hit, risked his life to get to him and tend his wounds, only to be violently pushed aside as the general realised the indignity of his position. As he looked around, he became aware that the troops nearby were sniggering and muttering among themselves. The realisation did nothing to improve his temper. With his grand farewell now in danger of falling apart at the seams right in front of his successor, the general at once began casting around for something – or someone – to blame.

Just then, when everyone was distracted and their guard down, Jock spotted movement further along the ridge. Shepherd at once tried to call up their Head Shed to check if there were other friendly units in the area, but he found the radio net swamped with administrative traffic so that it was impossible to verify if the movement was friend or foe.

'Who put together the comms plan?' he said. 'Any idiot knows to keep operational and administrative traffic on different channels.'

Jimbo shrugged. 'Must have been the Brigade Signals Officer, because any other signals guy would have known not to do it that way. The problem is, those senior guys never get out into the field, so they know the theory, but not the practice.'

Leaving the other two in charge of the gun crew, Shepherd and Jock changed position, crawling along the ridge to a point where they could get a better view. After moving only a few yards, they were startled to see a force of a couple of hundred Afghans taking up positions, ready to engage the troops down in the valley. From their clothes and weapons, they appeared to be mostly local tribesmen, stiffened by a few Taliban fighters. Without firing, the two SAS men pulled back again, quickly briefed the others, and then all of them, including the GPMG crew, moved to a point from where they could attack the enemy. They wormed their way forward, using every scrap of cover provided by the scrubby vegetation, loose rocks and boulders, and crept into firing positions in a broad arc, two SAS men on either side of the GPMG crew. On Shepherd's signal, he, Jock and Jimbo opened up with their SA80s while Geordie directed the fire from the GPMG. As ever with the SAS, their rate of fire and the way they constantly changed firing positions gave the enemy the impression that they were facing a far larger force than just half a dozen men. Several of the enemy were cut down by the initial burst, but the others swung round to face their attackers and began returning fire.

The sudden explosion of firing from the ridge caused consternation among the already jumpy main force on the valley floor. From their reaction, they appeared to be unaware that there were friendly forces above them, but before anyone could make sense of what was happening, fresh bursts of fire came from enemy fighters on the high ground all around them, wreaking havoc and panic among the troops below.

Shepherd's patrol could now do nothing to help the main force, because they were in desperate straits themselves. They were heavily outnumbered by the enemy, who were trying to outflank them, a few of them creeping through the rocks and scrub. Meanwhile, the rest of the enemy fighters tried to keep the SAS men pinned down with a few RPGs and a barrage of automatic fire. Most of the enemy carried AK-47s, but some of the senior Taliban were using the more modern version, the AK-74.

Faced with those kinds of numbers and that weight of fire, the SAS patrol had little choice but to 'pepper-pot' backwards, with two men giving covering fire while the other two fired and moved, then switching roles to provide cover while the other two withdrew. However, they were far from beaten and whenever the Afghans thought they had them on the run and broke cover to push home their attack, the SAS men at once counter-attacked, each time killing several enemies and driving back the rest.

Although the locals still outnumbered the patrol many times over, their heavy losses had given them food for thought, and since they showed little appetite for fighting at close quarters, the SAS men were still able to hold them off. The fight went backwards and forwards until late in the afternoon, when the

GPMG took an indirect hit from an RPG rocket that bounced off the ground before hitting the machine gun, completely destroying it, wounding the two members of the gun crew and wrecking the patrol radio. Fortunately, the GPMG and the radio absorbed most of the force of the blast and shrapnel and the crew suffered relatively minor wounds. Although both of them lost a lot of blood, they were still able to walk.

'This is getting serious,' Shepherd said, seizing the chance to talk offered by a brief lull in the fighting. 'We're down on ammo, we've got two wounded men and no comms. If we stay where we are, we'll eventually run out of ammo and then we'll be overrun and I don't have to tell you what that means – we all know what Afghan fighters tend to do to any prisoners they take. I don't know about you, but being castrated and skinned alive is not high on my list of priorities.'

His patrol mates nodded in agreement.

'I'm not going to sit around and wait for that to happen, so unless anyone's got any better ideas, here's what we'll do,' Shepherd continued. 'Geordie will take the two wounded guys down the hillside to the nearest sub-unit. We will cover them until they are out of sight and then we'll use our remaining ammo to charge the bastards, the last thing they'll be expecting. If we survive, as we go through them we'll each pick up one of their AKs and as much ammo as we can carry. There'll be no point in trying to back-track to link up with the rest of the force after that, because we'll have to run the same gauntlet of hostiles. Since we haven't got a radio, even if we manage to get through them again, when we try to link up with the main force we'll stand every chance of being mistaken for the enemy, and targeted by the infantry and the close air support. So our best option is to go deeper into country and then try to link up with the Army either in one of their outlying bases or if necessary, we can walk all the way back to Bagram.'

Jock and Jimbo had already reached similar conclusions, so the only dissent came from Geordie. 'There's only one problem with that plan,' he said. 'You bastards can't leave me out of this. I know that after a contact our SOP would be to move out at top speed and put a lot of distance between the enemy and us, so there's risk in you hanging fire to RV with me. However, there's a greater risk for me in taking those guys down to a subunit and then coming back up to the ridge and picking my way round the enemy to RV with you. If I'm willing to take that chance, so should you, because we're a patrol, we're mates, and we stand or fall together. So unless anyone has any objections?' He paused and eyeballed each of them in turn. 'No? Good. So we'll make a visual RV point now that we can all find. I'll take these guys down and then we'll meet at the RV at 23.59 when it's nice and dark. If there are any problems for any of us in making that RV, then we'll meet up twenty-four hours later at the War RV we were given at the patrol briefing. If I'm not there either, then I won't ever be making an RV again. And if you lot don't make it, I'll know that none of you beat the clock this time.'

That drew a grimace from Jock. 'Beating the clock' was the SAS euphemism for staying alive. The names of SAS men who had died in training or on active service were always engraved on the base of the regimental clock at Stirling Lines, the SAS base in Hereford.

Shepherd was hesitant about agreeing to Geordie's plan but, against his better judgement, allowed himself to be persuaded. Unwilling to give voice to any forebodings, the remaining three just nodded to Geordie as he set off down the hillside with the wounded men. Picking their way among the rocks, they were all crouching low or crawling whenever they had to cross open ground, presenting the smallest possible target to any watching Afghan fighters.

The three SAS men watched them until they disappeared from sight and then Shepherd took a deep breath. OK, guys,' he said. 'I'll see you on the other side. No time like the present, so on the count of three, here goes fuck all ... One ... two ... three ... Go! Go! Go!'

The Afghan fighters were astonished when three ragged British soldiers suddenly rose from among the rocks and, instead of retreating, charged fearlessly towards them, unleashing a torrent of fire as they ran. Several of the farmers conscripted by the Taliban simply threw down their weapons and ran. Others snatched up their rifles but were cut down before they could bring them to bear, and the fire that was returned by the others was mostly high and wild.

With Jock and Jimbo at his heels, Shepherd kept sprinting and swerving across the open ground in front of the enemy, keeping up a stream of fire as he ran. He vaulted over a rock, drilling a double tap into an Afghan fighter crouching behind it, and shot two others who tried to bar his way. He dived and rolled to change magazines – his last one – double-tapped another enemy crouching in a dip in the ground, and then loosed off a last burst from the SA80 to keep enemy heads down as he dived into the same dip. Ditching his own weapon, he snatched the AK-47 from the dying man's grasp, his fingers slippery with the blood spouting from the fatal wounds. Shepherd tore the ammunition belts from the man as well and then burst from cover, still firing double taps and short bursts as he ran on through the last of the enemy. The whip-crack sound of AKs firing behind him showed that Jock and Jimbo had also switched weapons and were still taking a heavy toll of the enemy. Shepherd paused twice more to scoop up magazines and another ammunition belt and then was out beyond the last Taliban fighter, though still dodging and weaving to throw off the aim of any enemy targeting his fleeing figure. He dived into cover, twisted around and laid down covering fire as Jock and Jimbo sprinted towards him, then flattened themselves in cover alongside him.

'Both OK?' Shepherd said, shouting to make himself understood above the rattle of enemy gunfire and the ringing in their ears from their own firing. 'Scratches, nothing more,' Jock said, his face speckled with spots of blood where rock splinters had needled his skin.

Jimbo nodded. 'I'm good too.'

They remained in cover for another twenty minutes, moving constantly and keeping up a targeted fire whenever any of the enemy so much as raised his head to peer between the rocks. For at least one of them it was the last thing he ever did – Shepherd put a round through the man's forehead in the split-second he was visible. He was thrown backwards, arms splayed, his weapon spiralling from his grasp and although the second shot of the double-tap did no more than part the man's hair, a fine mist of blood droplets hanging in the air for a moment showed that the first one had already done its work. The enemy firing now ceased altogether and there was clearly little appetite for any further pursuit of the SAS men. Peering through his binoculars, Shepherd caught fleeting glimpses of some of the Afghan fighters crouching as they began to move off in the opposite direction, away from the patrol. As they began preparing to move out themselves, Shepherd suddenly said: 'Cover me, I'm going back. I forgot something.'

The other two exchanged puzzled glances but without attempting to question him or talk him out of it, they took up firing positions facing the enemy.

Using the rough ground to give him body cover, Shepherd slipped away among the rocks and made his way back to the site of the fire-fight. He disappeared from Jock and Jimbo's sight for a few seconds, but then reappeared and began making his way back. This time, he was not only carrying another enemy weapon and an ammunition waistcoat, but also a pair of the locally made flip-flops, the soles cut from a worn-out Dunlop tyre tread, which he had stripped from one of the Afghan dead.

'What the fuck was that about?' Jock said.

'We need a spare rifle and an ammunition waistcoat for Geordie, if he makes it.'

'And the flip-flops?'

'Will come in very handy over the coming days. Trust me. Now let's go,' he said. Before Jock could say anything else, Shepherd led them down the far side of the ridge, away from both the enemy and the main force of infantry in the adjoining valley. They found good cover in a place where they could ambush their track if any Taliban attempted to follow them, and then lay up for the rest of the daylight hours. After dark they moved again, close to the RV site that Geordie had identified.

Even though the RV system was as close to foolproof as it was possible to make it, none of them were ever comfortable using RVs. It was a regrettable fact of military life in Afghanistan that interpreters and the West's allies in the Afghan Army would often betray Allied plans almost as soon as they had been formed, or a captured soldier might be tortured to yield information. As a result, any prearranged RV was only approached after careful surveillance and using enormous caution.

Under their SOPs, as the time of the rendezvous had been set at midnight by Geordie, he had to be at the RV one minute before that time and the others had to make contact with him within five minutes. If that did not happen, the RV was abandoned and they had to move to the next one, the War RV, exactly twenty-four hours later. However, having made a thorough scan of the surrounding area to make sure no enemies were lying in wait, the three of them were delighted to see a pale-skinned, slightly balding figure emerge out of the darkness bang on time. Geordie broke into a huge grin as he saw all three of his patrol mates waiting for him.

'Bloody hell, I'm glad to see you all, even you, Jock,' he said, since even in a moment of huge relief, he was unable to resist the urge to wind him up. 'I was sure at least one of you was going to have copped it.'

'No such luck for you, you Geordie prick,' Jock said. 'And you seem to have come through all right as well.'

'I got down off the ridge with the gun crew OK, but then we had an anxious couple of hours looking for a friendly subunit, all the time praying we weren't going to be misidentified as enemy by some idiot who would then call in an airstrike to wipe us out. Anyway, in the end we found a subunit and I managed to get rid of the wounded on to them, and then came back up the hillside and across the ridge. I didn't see any live enemy up on the ridge – I think they might have had enough action for one day and pulled out – but I did see a lot of dead ones. Anyhoo, here I am, ready to roll.'

They moved out at once, still anxious to put distance between themselves and the enemy. Travelling quickly but tactically, they disappeared in a direction that the enemy would never have expected, going away from the valley where the main force was still fighting and deeper and deeper into Afghanistan, heading towards Mazar-e Sharif.

Although moving at speed, they were constantly alert. Shepherd, at the head of the patrol, scanned the terrain ahead, while Geordie and Jimbo watched the ground to either side and Jock kept an eye on the area behind them. They kept going until the pre-dawn light began to grey the night sky, then circled back on their tracks and found a Lying-Up Position surrounded by bushes and a group of boulders. Here they would be sheltered from watchers and the wind and could lie up during the daylight hours.

The patrol had approached their chosen spot by a circuitous route, always careful to place their feet on rocks only, so as to leave no sign of their passing in the dust and soil, then backtracking before entering the LUP. By doing this they were able to ambush their own tracks to check if they were being followed.

The trick had been developed by the insurgents in the Malayan Emergency in the 1950s, but had since been adapted and refined by the SAS and the patrol had used it on numerous operations in jungles and other dense cover around the world.

They watched the track into the LUP until the sun was high enough in the morning sky to bring some warmth into their weary bones. They took it in turns to clean and lightly oil their weapons, then settled in, trying to make themselves comfortable on the rocky earth. Even at rest they never dropped their guard, with at least one and often two men on watch so that the others were able to relax slightly. They were dog-tired after a night of physical and mental activity, but they were surrounded by potential enemies, both military and civilian, and there would be no relief or complete relaxation of their guard until they were able to link up with friendly troops. They had successfully disengaged from the enemy. All they had to do now was to re-engage with their own forces.

'Right,' Shepherd said. 'We had better get our heads together and come up with some sort of plan of action.'

After a "Chinese Parliament" in which each man added his own ideas to the mix, Shepherd summarised what they would try to achieve. 'Okay, we'll move only at night, taking on targets of opportunity if they present themselves and try to find a place where we can link up with a heli lift back to Bagram. That'll be easier said than done because for obvious security reasons, we don't have maps showing the locations of any British or American bases. So we'll need to use our wits to find one, and ideally it should be a Fire Support Base rather than an Infantry Patrol Base, because it'll be easier to make contact with rear echelon troops rather than guys who are out patrolling from their base and being fired on every day and night, who tend to be very trigger-happy, obviously. The last thing we want is a spot of friendly fire.'

'Yeah, makes sense,' Geordie said. 'The brass only visit the Patrol Bases for a couple of days every few months. They gee up the troops, stir things up with the locals and try to get among the medals, but once the pot is fermenting nicely they piss off back to Bagram for a few G & T's and fresh rations in the mess, and leave the poor saps in the Patrol Base to cop the retaliation from the locals and the Taliban. So the Patrol Bases stir up trouble whereas the Fire Support Bases are usually in relatively safe areas, so their troops are used to a quieter life and are less jumpy as a result.'

'Some of the locals quite like having the bases there,' Jock said. 'They can pick up shell cases and other scrap metal which they can sell on, and there are a few casual jobs from time to time as well, filling sandbags or washing clothes, or whatever.'

'But there's an obvious downside to that,' Jimbo said. 'The enemy can get access to as much intelligence as they want, including the ranges to targets, the number of troops on the base, the routines and the response plans if attacked, so we may be stepping out of the frying pan and into the fire.'

Jock shrugged. 'Nothing's risk-free, but it's the best available plan.'

'Agreed,' Shepherd said. 'We'll move out as soon as it's dark.'

Their LUP was halfway down the side of a ridge leading down from the high mountains of the Hindu Kush towards the fertile Afghan plains. Perched on a tiny ledge surrounded by bushes and rocks, they were totally invisible even from a few feet away. The place was carefully chosen; only animals move along the sides of ridges, men walk either along the ridge tops or through the valley bottoms.

It was an almost perfect place to rest, giving them the options of fight or flight. If discovered, they had the choices of either running uphill to the top of the ridge from where they would have a range of escape routes, or going steeply downhill into the valley bottom where the going would be easier and again would offer them a choice of routes to follow. If they were left with absolutely no other choice, they could stand and fight with their backs to the wall.

Close by they could hear the sound of a torrent of pure, ice-cold water, thundering down towards the bottom of the valley, cutting its way through rocks and boulders millions of years old. It was one of thousands of similar streams, fed by meltwater from the glaciers and winter snows in the high mountains. As they reached the valley floor, the streams merged into one of the fast-flowing rivers that made the plains of Afghanistan the bread basket of the country. The fertile soil fed the inhabitants with the staples of life – bread, vegetables and fruit – that were sold in the many markets and sooqs dotted around the towns on the plains, but it also nurtured the thousands of acres of poppies that fed the addicts of the great cities of the West with their drug of choice: heroin.

When the SAS men were on the run, they were only really conscious of the pangs of hunger when they were resting. They never felt hungry when they were on the march, because there were so many things to do. Each of them was carrying a couple of days patrol rations as part of their escape kit on their belts but it never entered any of their heads to start breaking into them. Instead, before settling into the LUP, they spent some time by the swiftly flowing stream, drinking copious amounts of the icy mountain water, refilling their water bottles and washing away the accumulated sweat and grime from the previous night's exertions.

They drank so much water that their bellies became distended and slowly over the course of the day they urinated away the toxins that would otherwise have accumulated in their bodies. Survival was all about "The Rule of Three" – a man could survive three minutes without air, three days without water but three weeks without food, so they were hanging on to their rations until they were really needed.

They were following the standard SAS escape and evasion routine of walking at night and resting during daylight hours. The long late summer days and short nights were frustrating, but any movement in daylight would lead to almost certain discovery. The routine in the LUP was relaxed but alert and they followed the cardinal rules at all times: no smoke, no fire, no noise and minimum movement. Shepherd had not laid down a fixed time for each man's sentry duty and downtime, as would have been normal in the rest of the army. Instead he allowed the patrol to set its own parameters, as long as they ensured that there was always at least one man awake and alert. This allowed the ones who needed more sleep to get it and the others who could get by on less sleep to take up the slack for the rest. It inevitably led to banter among them because, for whatever reason, Jock always got by on very little sleep. Geordie, who could never resist another dig at his Scots mate, said it was because 'You're a good few years older than us and old men are so decrepit they don't really need any sleep'.

It was just after midday and they were all rested and impatient to be on the move, but Shepherd knew that to set out before darkness would be suicidal. The afternoon lay ahead of them, with the long hours having to be filled somehow, so they whiled away the rest of the daylight hours dozing or talking in whispers, their heads close together like conspirators. Shepherd leopard-crawled back to the others from where he had just been taking a piss. Using his combat knife, he had dug a small deep hole into the rocky earth before emptying his bladder while still lying prone on his side. He waited until the liquid had seeped away into the ground before carefully refilling the hole. Without that precaution, the flies would have been all over them in seconds, making rest impossible with the added threat that they might be carrying disease.

Shepherd crawled back past Jimbo, who was taking his turn on stag, peering out through the scrub with a pair of binoculars to hand, his head covered with a piece of the camouflaged, fine mesh scrim netting that they preferred to the cam cream most soldiers used. Shepherd lay down next to Jock and Geordie, who were in classic LUP pose, flat on their backs on the ground, using their belt kits as pillows and with their weapons snug along the right side of their bodies, the butt under the armpit with the muzzle pointing down away from their feet. The backs of their heads were almost touching, allowing them to communicate in the tiniest whispers.

Shepherd was just settling his head on his belt, the third man in the triangle, when Jock's belly rumbled and he let out a fart. 'For fuck's sake, Jock,' Geordie whispered, 'you almost blew us off the mountain. If there were any enemy within half a mile, they'd not only have heard you, they'd have smelled you as well.'

Jock patted his stomach and then pinched some skin between his thumb and forefinger. 'Would you look at that,' he said. 'I'm fading away. I could do with a decent meal in there.'

Geordie smiled. 'Number One: the rest of us will have starved to death weeks before you've wasting away, you fat Scots gannet. And Number Two: you wouldn't know a decent meal from a pile of roadkill. You're always first in the scoff queue and you'll eat anything put in front of you – dead or alive.'

'And you're Marco Pierre Fucking White are you? Let me tell you something. I have eaten the finest, with the finest, and in the most surprising places.'

'Such as where, you Caledonian cretin?'

'A few years ago I was involved in a task on the other side of the Gulf. We were training on the edge of the Empty Quarter, living in tents and feeding on patrol rations for no better reason than that the Quartermaster's Department was too idle to organise fresh ones for us. The boss was a pedant and a keep-clean nut, the other guys not much better. The training was boring and something I had done a hundred times before. So one day I took the Land Rover and drove to the nearest sooq down on the coast where I bought a load of fruit, vegetables and fish, which I then drove back to the boys on the hill. This became a habit and every few days I would repeat the exercise until on the third or fourth trip, as I was dropping down the escarpment, I saw in the distance what looked like a mirage shimmering in the heat. I was so intrigued I drove the few miles from the graded track I was on, to what turned out to be a temporary village, with each building made from an enormous wooden box of about thirty cubic feet, probably used as transit cases for JCBs.'

Jock paused and rolled onto his stomach and Shepherd and Geordie did the same, glad of the distraction of Jock's tale, even if it turned out to be bullshit, as many of them did. Even Jimbo was not totally focused on his sentry duties, keeping half an ear on Jock. 'As I pulled up in a cloud of dust, an Asian guy came out of the nearest box and offered me tea in a mug filled from an aluminium kettle; there was nothing inside the box but an ancient Primus stove. He then asked if I was hungry and brought me a goat meat curry with some rice and roti in a chipped enamel washing-up bowl. The food was so delicious I devoured it at once, sitting in the sand, and when I asked how much I owed him, he just said "As you wish, Sahib".

'I gave him what I thought was far too much and said "Thanks, I'll be calling in again soon". By the time I did so, a few days later, he had acquired a couple of small wooden crates from somewhere and was using them as tables inside the big box. The curry he gave me was even better than the first one and he told me that he'd used some of the money I'd given him to invest in a greater variety of herbs and spices. When I said "How much?" the reply was the same: "As you wish, Sahib".

'This developed into something of a routine. I called in every few days and each time he had made some other improvement to make his box worthy of "a British sahib". So the next time I called there was a sheet of clear plastic tacked around the front of the box to keep out the dust and flies, and over the next few weeks scraps of oilcloth appeared as covers for the tables, a couple of chairs were rescued from the local dump, then there were tin plates and a couple of spoons and forks, and then the finishing touch: a waiter's napkin draped over the owner's forearm. The final upgrade was a Heath Robinson contraption of valves, taps and hosepipe to provide a trickle of running water for the restaurant box so that honoured patrons, which at the time, as far as I could ascertain was only me, could wash off the dust from the journey before sitting down to eat. All the time the curries, usually goat but occasionally chicken, were getting more and more delicious.

'Well, I couldn't get away with it much longer. The guys at the training camp were getting pissed off because I was spending more and more time away, and while they were losing weight because of the crappy rations, I was putting on weight, so they knew something was up. Eventually the Boss took me to one side and demanded to know what was going on. He was convinced that I had found myself a lady friend down in the town who was feeding me up, and when I explained about the wooden box restaurant, he didn't believe me and insisted that he would come with me on the next trip. The more I tried to talk him out of it, the more he insisted on coming with me. Like I said, he was a pedant and a keep clean fetishist who hated the dust and dirt of the desert, and I was sure he'd rather die than eat anything in the wooden box restaurant.

'We set off the next day and all the time the Boss kept giving me funny looks, convinced that I was trying to con him. When we arrived at the box restaurant and he saw the condition it was in his eyes nearly popped out of his head, but he gamely went in with me and I introduced him as "Officer Sahib".

'The owner was ecstatic, he'd been around the Raj long enough to know a proper officer when he saw one, and he went into his by now, familiar routine, overseeing us while we washed away the dust from our journey, and then guided us to a crate masquerading as a table. He polished a couple of spoons and forks on his sleeve before serving us with two curries, one goat and one chicken. By now the boss had a rictus grin but he gamely took a tentative mouthful. There was a pause and then his face lit up and he proceeded to demolish more than his share of the food on the table, though that was only fair as, unlike me, he hadn't had a decent meal in weeks.

'From then on, there was a different routine. The boss and I would drive down during the week and the rest of the guys at the week-end, on Thursday afternoon or Friday. The décor in the box restaurant kept evolving; there were now pictures cut out of magazines on the wall and even a strip of threadbare carpet on the floor. Then of course the inevitable happened; trouble flared up somewhere in the Gulf and we were packed off to deal with it at a rate of knots.'

Jock rolled onto his back again and let out a sigh. 'I've never been back to that part of the world since then, but I'd love to, because those were some of the best meals of my life. And you know what? If I did go back, I bet I'd find that the box restaurant has expanded into a chain of them by now, called something like "Big JCB Box Restaurants – By Appointment to the British Army".' He glanced at his audience and suppressed a burst of laughter.

'You lying bastard,' Geordie said. 'You made all that up, didn't you?'

'No, no, I swear it's all true. I was only laughing because when I was telling you about the food, you were all drooling down your chins.'

'Anyway,' Shepherd said. 'Change the record, will you? I can take having nothing to eat, but I can't stand Delia Smith here talking about what we could be eating.'

They fell silent and were soon once again dozing, recharging their batteries for the coming night. They remained in cover, unseen, throughout the day while all around them the whole country seemed to be up in arms. In the distance they could hear the faint sounds of artillery and heavy mortars echoing around the mountains, and high in the sky, they could see the con-trails of patrolling B 52s flying from Diego Garcia in the Indian Ocean, waiting for orders to release their payloads. They could also hear the sound of fast jets stacking up, waiting to be called down for a strike, and the dull concussions from exploding ordnance when they did so. From past experience, the SAS men knew that some of those bomb and missile strikes would not be hitting enemy targets, but areas chosen almost at random. Not wanting to return to base without releasing their deadly cargos – bomb loads had been known to detonate when combat aircraft crashed on landing – the pilots would often dump their bombs and rockets into supposedly empty areas, regardless of whether this caused collateral damage.

'I don't know what has caused all this to happen, but someone has really kicked over the anthill,' Geordie said.

'It's obvious isn't it?' Shepherd said. 'It's because that fucking idiot of a general directed his operation through the locals' opium crop. They'll have thought he'd laid on the op just to destroy the crop that is their main source of income, and for many of them their only one. So the word has gone round and the whole area is going to hell in a hand-cart, which shouldn't surprise any of us one little bit. And it's all down to the General wanting to go out in a bit of glory and collect his gallantry medal before getting himself a cushy number in the MOD.'

'The bastard,' Jimbo said, with feeling.

'And you know what, my friends?' Jock said. 'I'm afraid it probably means that we are up shit creek, in the proverbial barbed wire canoe, without a paddle, because you can bet the blame game for this cock-up has already begun and we all know from bitter experience that Rule One is that nothing is ever a general's fault. He'll be looking for scapegoats and we'll be right in the frame.'

'But bloody hell,' Geordie said, 'when it comes down to it, we're all on the same side and fighting the same enemy, aren't we?'

Jock, the eternal pessimist, shook his head. 'When the brass get their hands on us, they'll throw the book at us. We should all expect to be doing some time in the slammer.'

'Blimey, Jock,' Jimbo said. 'I'm all for a bit of Caledonian gloom, but that's a bit much, isn't it?'

'Is it? Army rules dictate that we should have attempted to link up with the main force again, not E and E'd across country. So if they're looking for scapegoats – and they will be – we'll be serving ourselves up, trussed, seasoned and ready for the oven. A hundred years ago the top brass used to break men on the wheel in this part of the world. Why? Because they could. And you know what? Not much has changed since then.'

'We do have rather more pressing problems right now than what's going to happen to us when we get back,' said Shepherd. 'We still have no comms, no rations and no way of getting back to Bagram, other than on foot. Shit, creek and paddle, lack of, comes to mind.'

CHAPTER 11

By early evening, the reddening sun was dropping swiftly towards the western horizon. Unlike the fierce heat earlier in the day, it was now spreading a kindly warmth, aided by the rocks around the LUP releasing the energy they had soaked up during the long daylight hours. None of the patrol were fooled by that, they knew that before dawn the air would be so cold that the water in their canteens would freeze and the only reason the streams and rivers did not ice up was that they flowed at too fast a rate. Even so, the backwaters and eddies would still be frozen by dawn.

They waited a while longer, watching dust devils chasing each other across the plain, until only the snowy tips of the mountains around the patrol were visible in a blue mist, then got ready to move out. There was no long period of dusk where they were; it lasted for only a few minutes before darkness as black and unbroken as a mineshaft at midnight settled on the land.

They had already been on full alert for a couple of hours, squatting behind the scrub, wearing their full equipment and camouflaged scrim nets. Weapons to hand, they were scanning the area around the LUP with fierce concentration. Shepherd was paired with Geordie, and Jimbo with Jock. As Geordie was going to lead the patrol down the ridge from the LUP, he and Shepherd were doing a visual reconnaissance of all possible routes down. They wouldn't use the route that had brought them into the LUP for fear of ambush, so they were minutely scrutinising all the other available options, because to take the wrong one could add miles to their journey.

Jimbo and Jock were quartering the countryside around them in general, looking for anything that was not natural and did not blend in. Starting close to the LUP, they gradually moved their gaze further and further outwards, before starting again in the next sector. They did this tirelessly, knowing that once they were on the move, their areas of observation would be very much reduced. Each of them had a set of binoculars but they were careful to have them inside the scrim net before raising them to their eyes, conscious that any sun-glare reflecting from the lenses could be spotted from dozens of miles away.

As the sky darkened, they heard the faint, distant howl of a pye-dog. Similar to the hyenas of Africa, they were related to the semi-domesticated dogs found in every settlement in Afghanistan, scavenging on anything edible that the inhabitants discarded. Pye-dogs lived on carrion and the weak and wounded of the rest of the animal kingdom, and it was not unknown for packs to take down a lone shepherd or another vulnerable human. They were also a constant source of annoyance to the army, because with their hyper-sensitive hearing, they would start howling and bark-ing long before the troops got close to them. In some cases, larger bodies of troops issued a couple of their marksmen with silenced weapons purely for the pur-pose of shooting a pye-dog so that the others in the pack would turn on it and devour it, buying a few minutes of silence.

The patrol waited until night had fallen and it was too dark to see more than three or four yards. Then one by one they stood up and settled their equipment more comfortably on their shoulders and waists, while resisting the automatic instinct of ground troops the world over to stamp their feet to get their footwear more comfortable. Their boots of choice were US Army jungle boots with rubber soles and partial black leather uppers, but with dark green canvas tops that allowed the feet to breathe and keep cool. They were also virtually invisible after dark, whereas on a moonlit night, the light brown British army issue desert boots could often be seen from hundreds of yards away.

At a signal from Shepherd they moved off and quickly fell into the familiar patrol routine, travel-ling tactically in single file, with Geordie leading, Shepherd and Jock next, and Jimbo bringing up the rear, shuffling along, wearing the local Dunlop flip-flops that Shepherd had liberated from the scene of the fire-fight, to obliterate the bootprints left by the other guys in front. After rehydrating at a stream early in the march they headed in the approximate direction they wanted, using strict march routine. This meant that they never moved farther than they could see in one bound, with Shepherd using binoculars to select the route and indicating to Geordie the direction he wanted them to travel. Communication was by finger or mouth clicks and then hand signals. Shepherd signalled forward to Geordie, and Jock signalled rearwards to Jimbo. Except when looking to Shepherd for instructions, Geordie kept his gaze fixed ahead while Jimbo watched the rear and the other two kept watch to either side. It was an extremely laborious, frustrating and slow way to travel, but it was safe. They could have travelled much farther and faster, but to do so would risk hitting trouble, whereas this way would take longer but with a little luck would get them safely out of danger.

By day they lay up in fissures in the rocks on the side of the hills away from the tracks along the ridge tops and valley bottoms. They now adopted a fifty percent alert strategy where alternately, two of them were awake throughout the day while the others rested. Although this routine was very tiring, Shepherd felt it was necessary for their security. Initially they headed north-east before gradually doing a half-circle and then travelling almost due south towards Bagram. Although they saw a lot of air activity and a few Afghan tribespeople at a distance, they did not come across any British or American army patrols.

Physically they were all already thin to the point of gauntness. In Bagram as part of the Force QRF they had had to be at an extremely high level of fitness and the daily regime of runs, gym work and agility had stripped the reserves of fat from their bodies. With one op hot following upon the heels of another since then, there had been no opportunity to regain weight, and now, trekking across difficult terrain with no food other than their emergency belt rations, they were losing weight at an alarming rate.

They continued to ignore the couple of day's rations on their belts, choosing not to use them until it was absolutely necessary. Even in their gaunt state, although they could cheerfully have eaten a horse, hooves, saddle and bridle included, they knew they could comfortably survive without any food at all for at least a couple of weeks. The major issue was always finding water, because without that, survival was measured in days or even hours. Fortunately in these mountains, even in the driest season of the year, water was never a problem. Before first light every morning they filled their water bottles and bags from one of the many streams that cascaded down the mountains and during the day, the liquid they drank helped to alleviate their hunger pangs.

As they moved on across the country, they occasionally came to a cultivated area where they were able to help themselves to a few bits of fruit and vegetables, though always being careful to leave no trace of their visit. However, they kept such foraging to a minimum because living off the land was very time-consuming and delayed their movement across country; better to be hungry but covering ground.

Perversely when on ops or E and E, with minimal rations and bellies rumbling they would spend much of their resting time talking about food. Jock had already treated them to his tale of the Big Box restaurant, and Geordie now took his turn. After his spell on watch on the fourth day, he was lying prone, talking quietly, almost to himself, so the others had to strain to hear what he was saying. 'I love my food, me,' he said. 'I don't mean on Ops, I don't care if I eat or not when I'm on operations and there's lots of other stuff going on, but I do like a bit of food when I'm in base or back in camp in the big H.

'First day back, I'll start breakfast with porridge, not the salty crap you Jocks eat,' he said, giving Jock a challenging look, 'but real porridge with sugar and lots of milk. Then I'll have a full fry-up: eggs – two – bacon, sausage, beans, fried bread, followed by toast and jam and a mug of tea. That'll be about 0730, then at ten I'll go to the mess and have a steak pie or a sandwich and a mug of tea.

'At dinner time, half-twelvish, I'll have three courses: soup, a roast dinner, meat and veg, followed by plum duff and custard and a mug of tea. That'll keep me going until about three in the afternoon when I'll have my usual wad of cake and a mug of tea,

STEPHEN LEATHER

then at five-thirtyish I'll have my tea, four courses
this time: soup, roast dinner or it might be a steak or
chops with chips and veg, followed by more duff and
custard, then bread and cheese or whatever else the
chefs have knocked out. Then I'll be out at night for
a few beers and on my way back I'll have a curry or a
Chinese to keep me going till breakfast.'

Jock shook his head. 'And you lot call me greedy!
Tell me, you fat bastard, have you ever thought for a
second about how all the food you shove down your
neck happens to be available in whatever mess hall
you park your arse? No? I thought not! The reason
the Regiment has almost unlimited supplies of food-
stuffs is down to a little known Scotsman, who to protect the innocent I shall call Joe B.'

'I knew it would be a bloody Scotsman,' Jimbo
said. 'Is there anything you lot don't claim credit for?'

'Yeah, the English,' Jock said with a grin. 'Anyway,
Joe B arrived in Hereford as a Corporal from a
Highland regiment. No one knew why he had been
sent to H, because he was far too overweight to even
start let alone finish Selection and he was only an
infantryman, not a trained administrator, but there
he was. In those days the Regiment lived to fight.
There was no fat on the bones to run the admin side,
so everyone chipped in. The guys accepted shortcom-
ings in the supply chain, and as long as the campaign
results were good, nobody got too fazed.

'One day, someone had a flash of genius and
installed Joe as ration storeman. In those days most

132

of the food was supplied by the NAAFI and anything they couldn't supply was bought on the open market. There were very strict guidelines on how much could be spent on each soldier but nobody thought to inform Joe, so when food ran short he just ordered more. He was so efficient that the only thing he kept in reserve were six cans of corned beef, but in the various Messes, everyone sang his praises. Every week his ration store was checked by the Duty Officer and every week there was the regimental reserve of six cans of "corned dog", so everything was in order.

'It lasted for a few years until a proper administrative officer was posted to the big H. This guy was like a dervish, sticking his nose in everywhere it wasn't wanted. He eventually got around to checking on Joe and was astounded to find out how he was operating. So he seized Joe's ledgers and requisitioning books and placed him under open arrest. He would have put him in the jail but the Regiment didn't even have such a luxury, since the guard block was being used as a store for spare mattresses.

'Joe was marched in front of the CO, a minor member of the Scottish aristocracy who had just returned from visiting a squadron fighting a particularly nasty little war in the Middle East. He could scarcely be bothered but was intrigued as to what had been going on in his regiment while his back was turned. The proceedings were opened by the Adjutant, a grizzled ex-NCO, who suggested that they took evidence from the prosecuting officer first and then stood him down. Although this was highly unusual, the CO agreed. So after reading out the charges: misappropriation, theft, false accounting and several others, the officer was told that he could stand down as he wouldn't be required again.

'Trying to be firm, the CO then asked Joe why he had requisitioned things like turkey, venison and salmon, when none of it ended up in the various messes. Joe looks him in the eye and says that they were special items requested by the CO's wife so that she could host a dinner for the wives of the squadron who had low morale because their husbands had been away on ops so long. It stopped the CO in his tracks, obviously. There was a pregnant pause and then the CO dropped the charges and sent Joe back to the ration store. So then the CO asks the Adjutant how he could stop it happening. Not the ordering, but the fact that it had become general knowledge. So the Adjutant suggests that in future all the Regiments orders are covered by the Official Secrets Act. And that's what happened and that is why greedy buggers like you can still eat five men's rations every day.'

He waited, impassive, while Geordie's suspicion battled with his curiosity. 'So what happened to Joe?' he eventually said.

'He retired to the fair city of Glasgow on a corporal's pension, and as you know, that isn't a lot, but strangely enough, he managed to buy a house in one of the more salubrious parts of the city, and whenever he was asked where he'd got his money he always replied "From legacies". After a couple of years he applied to join the Residents Association, signing his application "Joe B, Cpl Retd.," but putting a faint cross over the upstroke of the "l" so the locals would interpret it as being "Joe B, Captain, Retired". Somehow they heard he had been in Special Forces, so he was feted around the area. The dear old ladies did not object even when he brought a mail-order bride from the Philippines.

'Of course I wasn't yet in the Regiment when it was all taking place, but I was told it first hand by a guy who was there. And in the Sergeants Mess every Hogmanay they still raise a glass with the toast "Joe B, God Bless Him". And that is a true story, so help me God.'

There was a brief silence and then Shepherd burst out laughing. 'You know what they say, Jock: never bullshit a bullshitter and you've got three of them surrounding you here.'

Jock just gave an enigmatic smile, lay back and closed his eyes. 'Next time you're in Glasgow, I'll show you the house.'

'That's a pretty safe offer,' Geordie said. 'Because you know the next time I'll be in Glasgow is when hell freezes over.'

CHAPTER 12

On the fifth night, anxious to cover more ground, Shepherd took a slight risk and they moved out just before last light. There was a village on the lower slopes far below them, but the only potential obstacle in their path was an outlying, ramshackle mud-brick building just below the flank of the ridge that they were following. It was so decrepit-looking that they were more than half-convinced that it had been abandoned years before, but as they moved cautiously towards it, communicating by hand-signals, they heard a blood-curdling, high-pitched scream. Conditioned by years of training and combat, the patrol at once fanned out into a broad arc and went to ground, making them harder targets and giving them a greater field of fire.

Shepherd caught sight of a young boy who had been herding a goat and its kids into the dry stone-walled compound next to the building. The boy was frozen in panic, staring down at a snake, which was curled in a figure of eight on the ground in front of him. Shepherd could see it coiling, its scales rubbing together with a rasping noise that sounded like water drops sizzling on a skillet. An instant later there was a blur of movement as the snake struck. The boy shrieked in fear and pain, and a moment later a man who must have been the boy's father burst out of the building. He saw the snake coiling itself to strike again, snatched up a machete that was propped against the wall of the building and brought it down on the snake, severing its head with one stroke.

Geordie gave Shepherd a questioning look and at his nod of approval, broke cover and, followed by Shepherd, while Jock and Jimbo covered them, ran down to where the man was cradling the boy in his arms. The man flinched as he caught sight of them – despite their beards, sunburned skin and the largely Afghan clothes they were wearing, there was no concealing that they were *faranji*. Shepherd saw the man's gaze shift to the door of the building where, no doubt, he had left the rifle that all Afghan men carried. Shepherd made eye contact with him and held up one hand, palm outwards in the universal gesture of peace, though his left hand still held his own weapon. Lost in his world of pain and fear, the boy barely seemed aware of them.

Geordie was already crouching to examine the dead snake. Its rough-looking scales seemed grey in the fading light and there was a darker zig-zag pattern on its back. Shepherd saw a fleeting grimace cross Geordie's face. 'Do you recognise it?' Shepherd asked. 'Is it poisonous?'

'As poisonous as they come,' Geordie said. He pointed to the spear-shaped mark on its head. '*Echis carinatus* – the saw-toothed viper, Afghanistan's deadliest snake. It's responsible for more deaths than all the other snakes put together. They're bad-tempered, hyper-aggressive and will strike without provocation or warning – a bit like Jock, really. Most snakes will try to get away when they encounter people but I've seen reports of these bad boys actually chasing victims and striking them repeatedly. Their venom is a hemotoxin, which means it destroys the red blood cells and disrupts blood clotting, but it also causes general tissue damage and organ failure. It's powerful enough to kill a grown man with a single bite, and so would obviously kill a child. We need to move fast. If he's going to survive he needs anti-venom therapy pronto.' He held Shepherd's gaze. 'I've got anti-venom in my med kit, but it's the only one I've got. If I give it to him and any of us gets bitten by a viper, it'll be curtains.'

Shepherd shrugged. 'We'll take our chances. Give it to the boy.'

Still cradling his son in his arms, and endlessly repeating '*Allahu akbar*', the Afghan man's face showed his fear and suspicion as he stared at them

Geordie was already on his knees in the dust alongside the boy. 'Spider, take hold of him, keep his heart higher than his legs and do what you can to keep him calm. The less agitated and excited he is, the slower the blood will be pumped around his body, driving the venom towards the heart.'

Shepherd at once gestured to the father to allow him to hold the boy, and after a moment's hesitation, he did so, though he still kept hold of his son's hand. Shepherd took his place, holding the boy upright in a firm grasp with one arm. The boy's father continued to pray loudly and Shepherd put his finger to his lips to quieten him.

The boy's eyes darted wildly around at first and shudders kept running through his body, but gradually he became calmer and quieter. Geordie was working fast but every movement was calm and measured. He first used his belt as a tourniquet around the boy's thigh and jerked it tight. The boy winced but made no sound as the belt bit into his flesh. Geordie then switched his attention to the lower leg. 'Viper bites always cause rapid swelling and his ankle's already pretty swollen,' he said. 'But if we don't deal with it at once, the blood vessels in his leg will be blocked and his tissues will necrose and that will lead to gangrene.'

His voice was low, almost talking to himself, reminding himself of the course of action to follow. While he was talking, he began opening up the puncture marks on the boy's ankle with the point of his razor-sharp combat knife. The boy moved slightly in Shepherd's grip and his lips tightened, but he still made no sound or other show of pain. 'Like fathers, like sons,' Shepherd said. 'Love them or hate them, you've got to admit these Afghans are brave bastards, even the children.'

Geordie merely grunted in reply, entirely focused on his work. He pulled the water bottle from his belt and poured it over the puncture marks, sluicing away any residual venom. He filled the wound with antibiotic powder from his med kit and then began winding bandages around the boy's leg as tightly as possible, working downwards from the thigh. Shepherd could see the white gauze bite into the boy's flesh as Geordie drew it tight, compressing the veins and arteries. He was working so fast that a stream of sweat was dripping from his brow and splashing into the dust.

While he was still bandaging the leg, he called out 'Jock! Find me a couple of pieces of wood or something that I can use as splints.'

Leaving Jimbo on stag, Jock ran to the side of the building and began rummaging through a stack of wood used for the shepherd's cooking fires. He pulled out a reasonably straight branch, snapped it across his knee and gave the two pieces to Geordie, who began to splint the boy's leg with them.

'Why the splints?' Shepherd asked.

'If you keep the leg immobile, it stops muscle action driving the blood around his body.' When he had finished splinting the leg, he pulled a series of ampoules from his med kit, cracked them open and injected the boy with them. 'I've given him anti-venom, anti-histamine, hydrocortisone and antibiotics,' he said. 'He should have intravenous hydration as well, but we're not going to find a drip around here, so we'll have to do without that. Now let's get him under cover so he can keep warm. You take his head and keep his heart well above the level of his legs.'

With the father still walking alongside them, holding his son's hand, they carried the boy into the building. Its disrepair and the lack of anything beyond some bedding and the most basic utensils showed it was only used in the summer grazing season and would soon be abandoned for the year as men and goats retreated to the lowlands before the onset of the ferocious Afghan winter.

'And now?' Shepherd said.

Geordie shrugged. 'All that's left to do now is hope and pray.'

Shepherd looked out of the doorway at the darkening sky, now pricked with stars. 'We need to move on before long,' he said.

Geordie grimaced. 'But give me time to make sure he's stable, yeah?'

Shepherd nodded then moved back to where the other two were covering them and brought them up to speed. 'All right then,' Jock rasped. 'but if we come across any more waifs and strays, we're going to have to leave them to fend for themselves. We're the SAS, not *Medecins Sans Frontieres*.' His Glasgow accent made the English part of the sentence almost as incomprehensible as the French one.

Jimbo gave a mock sorrowful shake of his head. 'Come on now, Jock. Whatever happened to Hearts and Minds?'

'Well, in your case, it's been replaced by farts and whines.'

An hour later, Geordie made a final careful examination of his patient and then in a mixture of sign language and their few words of pidgin Pushtu, he and Shepherd managed to get the boy's father to understand what he needed to do. Geordie gave him a blister pack of painkillers, held up two and pointed to the moon, then used his finger to trace the line of an arc across the sky to the horizon and then held up two more painkillers. The Afghan man nodded.

'Will he be okay?' Shepherd said.

'I think so, yes.'

'And do you think can we trust his father not to betray us?'

'We saved his son's life,' said Geordie.

'That doesn't answer the question.'

'It does for me … and if not, we'll deal with whatever or whoever comes after us. What's the alternative. Spider? Save the son and kill the father?'

'Yeah, fair enough.'

They ruffled the boy's hair and then said their farewells to the father in the Afghan way, touching their hands to their hearts. He did the same and then made a short speech in Pushtu, hardly any of which they understood. He stood in the doorway with his arm raised in farewell until they had disappeared into the darkness. 'So what did he say?' Geordie said.

'I'd like to think it was "Thank you from the bottom of my heart and I promise not to dob you in to the Taliban",' Shepherd said. 'But just in case, we'll set off to the east till we're well out of sight, and then loop around on to our previous course.'

They linked up again with Jock and Jimbo and moved out, using the starlight to pick their way among the rocks.

CHAPTER 13

The following night, their sixth on E and E, the SAS men heard the faint sound of gunfire in the distance as they were moving along the flank of a ridge. There were single shots followed by short bursts, then a long gap before another few shots and another short burst. 'That sounds like harassing fire,' Shepherd said. 'Let's go take a look.'

They made their way carefully towards the sound of firing, keeping to the high ground as much as possible. As dawn broke, they found themselves looking down from the ridge on to an army base a couple of thousand metres below them, on the floor of a valley surrounded by low hills.

From their vantage point they could also see a couple of tribesmen, well hidden from the base, firing unaimed shots towards the troops, poking their AK 47s above the rocks that they were hiding behind and firing off a burst in the general direction of the base. Almost every time it provoked a reply, either a burst of .50 Browning fire or the occasional 81 mm mortar shot.

'The locals are not trying to do much damage, are they?' Jock said. 'They're just making the troops on the base stay alert, keeping them awake and playing on their nerves. Eventually it gets you down and you start to make mistakes. The same tactics have worked for centuries. They used to use fire-damp arrows the same way when they were putting castles under siege in the Middle Ages.'

'Always good to get a history lesson,' said Jimbo. 'Makes me wish I'd stayed longer at school.'

'I think there is also something bigger going on here,' Shepherd said, ignoring Jimbo's jibe. 'Look over there. See that cave with the sangar wall in front of it? There are four guys guarding it and there's a faint hint of smoke over the entrance. I think there might be more people inside.'

They stayed in cover and kept the cave under observation. About an hour later, two men in clothes that were a cut above those an Afghan farmer would be wearing, stepped outside the cave to relieve themselves, then disappeared back inside. 'Did you see the weapons they were carrying?' Jimbo said, putting down his binoculars. 'Brand-new AK 74s, adapted for Russian SF use.'

Shepherd nodded. 'That and the guards posted outside suggest they are definitely not your average locals. I'd say they're Taliban Head Shed.'

'Yeah, you're right,' Geordie said, 'but the guys doing the firing are amateurs. Look, they're still hiding behind the rocks and holding their arms above their heads before pulling the trigger. They're shit scared of being fired at.

'So the guys in the cave are Taliban heavies using conscripted local labour to stir up the squaddies in the base, trying to tempt them to come out,' said Shepherd. 'If and when they do, the Taliban can set up an ambush and take on a much easier target than the base itself. And from up there they can see if the squaddies start preparing a fighting patrol, and that could happen at any time because they must be as frustrated as hell,' Shepherd said. 'Right, here's what we do. We haven't any grenades or heavy weapons, so we'll have to fall back on the good old grind. You three, take out any one outside of the cave, and provide me with covering fire while I circle round to the entrance. When I get there, it'll just be them inside against me. It's text book stuff, the reverse of what's happening at the base, so we'll see how much the Taliban like it.' He grinned. 'Not really a fair fight is it?'

'Don't get cocky,' Geordie said. 'There might be fifty blokes in that cave.'

'They must have bloody strong bladders then,' Jock said, 'because we've been here a couple of hours and only those two have come out for a piss.'

'Ah but not everyone's got prostate trouble like you, Jock,' Geordie said. 'Believe it or not, some people can actually last all night without having to take a piss.'

'Anyway,' Shepherd said. 'Even if there are a few more Taliban in that cave, I'd still back myself to take them down. Everything the Taliban do tends to be at long range. They don't get to practise Close Quarter Battle and I'm betting they won't have much appetite for it.'

'What about the locals firing on the camp?' Jimbo said.

Jock shrugged. 'As soon as we open up, they'll disappear like Geordie on bath night. They're here under duress anyway.'

While Shepherd slipped away between the rocks and began skirting around the hillside towards the cave, Jock, Geordie and Jimbo selected their first targets. It was a straightforward system, left man took the left target, right man the right, and the third man the left hand one of the two in the middle. When their own target was down, the first to fire would switch to the remaining target with the others providing additional fire if needed and also shooting up the entrance to the cave to prevent those inside either escaping or taking up firing positions from which they could target their attackers.

After the first few shots, the four Taliban guards outside the cave had been eliminated, with Jock putting two rounds into the fourth man even before his primary target had hit the ground, the back of his head blown off by the exit wounds from two rounds punching through his face either side of his nose. Geordie and Jimbo had already switched to firing into the cave mouth. There was a flurry of activity as the people inside tried to escape. When they found that the level and accuracy of the SAS men's fire made that impossible without being shot, they tried to return fire but were unable to locate the firing positions of their assailants.

Shepherd made his way undetected to the side of the cave entrance. His AK 47 was already loaded and cocked, and he had a further two magazines together, one facing up, one facing down. When he was ready, mentally and physically, he waved to the others to indicate he was going in, then took several deep breaths and leapt over the wall, firing his AK as he went. As he did so the cave erupted in fresh turmoil with Taliban in all directions diving for cover or scrambling to pick up their weapons, making it impossible for him to count the number of men inside. Unsure how to react, the Taliban were split between fight and flight, and in those moments of hesitation Shepherd had no difficulty in picking his targets. The ones who reacted to his presence fastest were the first to be taken out with smart double-taps.

All the time he was shooting, Shepherd was subconsciously counting the number of rounds he was firing, a skill learned over many hundreds of hours training in the "Killing House" at the SAS camp in Hereford. When he had taken out nine of the enemy, Shepherd did a fast roll to his right, hit the ground and did a simultaneous magazine change, before regaining his feet and repeating the manoeuvre to his left. When he had regained his feet for the second time, he was the only man left alive. He did a quick visual check of himself. A couple of rounds had nicked his belt kit and one had torn a hole in his clothing but he was unharmed. He shrugged carelessly, it had been no contest really, a professional against amateurs.

Once Shepherd disappeared inside the cave, the rest of the patrol began sprinting across the hillside to see if they could be of any help. By the time they arrived it was all over. 'Bit greedy of you not to leave us any,' Jock said, surveying the carnage inside the cave.

'Sorry,' Shepherd said. 'You can have first go next time.'

'Well, now that's all been taken care of,' Geordie said, 'perhaps we can make contact with the base down there and see about getting a lift back to Bagram.'

Before anyone could reply the air was split with gunfire. The reaction to the outburst of firing up on the hillside was for the Patrol Base to go on full stand-to. Up to now they had had little knowledge of who was doing the firing or where it was coming from, but the fire-fight in the cave had at last given them an identifiable target and they were now making up for lost time by targeting it with every small arm and support weapon they possessed. Rounds spat through the air around them.

'Quick, get back in the cave,' Shepherd shouted. 'The next thing is going to be an air strike.'

They sprinted into the cave entrance and almost before the words were out of his mouth, they heard the shriek of a fast-jet engine at full throttle, followed by the massive detonation of a high explosive bomb. Even though they were shielded by the rock walls from the full force of the blast, the shock waves knocked them off their feet and caused their eardrums to pop. They scrambled deeper into the cave as a series of bombs detonated around it, each one rocking the cave and causing torrents of dust. Small rocks and pebbles, shaken loose from the roof, rattled down around them. The aerial bombardment lasted for only a few minutes and was clearly random but it was then followed by an artillery barrage that lasted for much longer. But again, in the absence of visible targets for the spotters, it was only random fire. Just to be sure, the SAS men waited a good twenty minutes after the guns at last fell silent before coming out into the open once again.

'At least we know that if we go anywhere near that Patrol Base, they'll shoot first and ask questions later,' said Jock. 'But because of the artillery fire, we also know that there must be a support base not too far away. The maximum artillery range is up to forty kilometres but it'll be a lot less in this hilly terrain. The only problem is which direction?'

'The direction is east of south,' Shepherd said. 'While you heroes were hiding your heads up your arses I was taking note of the direction of fire. Mind you, I was shitting myself too, so I didn't take the time of flight of the shells and can't estimate the range they were firing from, but at least we know roughly

where they are. Our only problem now is working out
a way of getting into the base when we do find it.'

They left after dark but it took them two more
nights to reach the Fire Support Base. It was on a
wide, dusty plain with very little cover around it.
Shepherd and the team watched at first light as a
small group of local children approached the base.
The fence surrounding it was constructed of forty-
gallon drums, filled with sand and concrete, and
extending the full perimeter of the base. A small gap,
patrolled by a couple of sentries, had been left for
vehicles to enter and leave and this was the place that
the local children made for, to beg or perhaps steal
anything that was going.

The SAS men looked a motley bunch, dressed
in a raggedy assortment of well-worn oddments of
British military uniform and local Afghani dress.
As their uniforms had become torn from walking
through the wild thorn bushes that dotted the hills,
they had been replaced by local tribesmen's dress
filched from dhobi lines close to the villages at some
risk of discovery. Likewise, their military equipment
was a mixture of British and local, acquired on the
battlefield when their old kit was beyond repair. They
had each retained their regimental belt kit but had
swapped the military back packs for the locally manufactured ammo vests they had liberated from dead
enemy fighters.

From their position they could see the self-
propelled AS 90 artillery pieces on the base being

readied for firing. 'We've got to get down closer and then try to speak to the guards without being shot,' Shepherd said. 'If we spook them, they might just lower the barrels on the big guns and let us have it full blast.'

'If we can get within a couple of hundred yards I'll go forward and speak to them,' Jock said. 'They can't mistake my accent for anything else but Glaswegian. Anyone can speak English or Scottish but it takes a special person to talk Maryhill! Our problem is we all look as if we have just come out of the nearest Afghan village so I'll only have a few seconds to convince them that I'm the real thing.'

Using every bit of cover available they eventually reached a fold in the ground about 200 yards from the sentries. By now it was mid-afternoon and scorching hot. The kids had drifted away to find other sport, and the sentries were looking thoroughly bored and listless.

Jock got to his feet and held up his hands. He walked towards the gate, shouting that he was a British soldier. The first sentry, a Londoner, unslung and cocked his rifle, shouting to him not to come any closer. Jock ignored the warning, raised his hands even higher and continued to identify himself. By now the situation was critical and the first sentry had already released the safety catch on his rifle and was on the point of firing, when his mate, another Londoner, shouted 'Hang on! Stop! I think he's one of ours. I think he's a sweaty' – "Sweaty Sock" being the rhyming slang for Jock. 'Let him come a bit closer, so we can be sure.'

After a confusing half-hour, the patrol found themselves admitted to the base and given the first solid food they had eaten in a week, Before they were even half way through their meal they were interrogated by the artillery unit's commanding officer. He took some convincing that their tale was true, but eventually he contacted Bagram for orders. Within another half hour the patrol were on board a Puma for the short flight to Bagram.

CHAPTER 14

The noise in the Puma cabin was deafening, making conversation virtually impossible. The door gunner glanced briefly at the passengers before concentrating on what was happening outside the aircraft, but the loadmaster was trying to make them as comfortable as possible. There was always a very close affinity between the helicopter crews and the SAS, not least because all the crews knew that if their helicopter went down, it would be the guys from special forces who would be tasked with rescuing them.

The pilot looked back and indicated to the loadmaster to give Shepherd a set of headphones. 'I don't know what you guys have been up to,' the pilot said once Shepherd had them on, 'and I don't really care, but it's beginning to look as if you are in some deep shit, because I've been ordered to land at the secure LZ near the headquarters complex and there's a reception committee waiting for you. So it doesn't look good, does it? All I can do is wish you all the best.'

Coming in to land, the pilot deliberately put the Puma into a hover before setting down so that the

SAS men could get a good look at the people on the ground. They were not surprised to see a group of military policemen waiting for them, headed by the base Provost Marshal.

'I don't think the pilot was exaggerating,' Shepherd said.

'No, that's a lot of trench police for us four little ones,' Geordie said. 'It's nice to be wanted and welcomed back so warmly.'

As they were climbing down from the helicopter, the military policemen attempted to manhandle them towards an armoured personnel carrier. This nearly turned into a brawl when the hot-headed Jock took exception to this, and things only calmed down after Shepherd interceded.

'I hear what you're saying, Spider, but if they lay a fucking finger on me again I'll break it off and shove it up their fucking arse!' said Jock.

'They won't touch you again, Jock,' said Spider. 'If they do, they'll regret it.'

Their weapons and almost everything else they possessed was then taken from them on the LZ. Wearing only the clothes they stood up in, they were hustled into the APC and driven under escort to a deserted accommodation hut. There they were allowed to shower and change into tracksuits before being thrown into what passed for a jail – a khaki-coloured marquee without side panels, which left it fully open to the elements, surrounded by razor wire. There was a metal bucket with a dash of disinfectant in the bottom for a toilet and a *chatti* – a tall earthenware jar – for water. 'This is fucked up,' said Jock, shaking his head in disgust. 'This is seriously fucked up.'

Shortly afterwards they were given a cursory medical by a clearly embarrassed medical officer who declared them slightly malnourished but otherwise physically fit. They were then visited by the Provost Marshal, a tall, usually imposing figure who was somewhat diminished by what he had been ordered to do. Looking distinctly uncomfortable, he informed them that 'under direction of the Commanding General, you are to be charged with desertion, loss and misuse of military equipment and cowardice in the face of the enemy.' He used the various numbered sections of Queens Regulations to describe the charges, and was clearly embarrassed when Geordie asked him what the various sections meant. Since he did not know the detail of each section, to his further embarrassment he had to send for a copy of QR's before he could conclude the interview. He told them that as soon as a suitable aircraft was available they were to be transported back securely to the UK for court martial and in the meantime they were to be kept in isolation from all other troops to avoid what, avoiding their eyes, he described as 'any contamination of other units by your conduct'.

Their final visitor was the Officer Commanding SF in Afghanistan. Young for an officer holding the rank of major, he was on the accelerated officer promotion scheme. He had served with the Regiment for almost six years, three of those as a captain and three as a major, and during the whole of that time he had been on active service tours in Iraq, Afghanistan and on secret operations in other parts of the world. However, he knew he was now walking a tightrope because it was a results based career. One mistake could bring it crashing to the ground, and the situation he now found himself in could easily be the one that brought it all to an end. He knew that the greatest assets he had to help him on his way up the promotion ladder were the troops under his command, and the men in front of him had consistently provided the results to sustain and maintain his career. If he treated them right and with respect they would repay him tenfold, but if he lost their respect he might be out on his ear.

'Right guys,' he said. 'This is how it is. After you went missing, I sent a couple of patrols in the area to see what had happened. They found your radio and GPMG and followed your tracks a short way before losing them. We knew then at that stage you were okay. I signalled Hereford with a Sitrep and advised them to take no further action because I was certain you would eventually turn up safe and well. The situation we now find ourselves in regarding your current personal circumstances is deplorable. The problem, as you may have noticed yourselves, is that we are under the command of an arsehole who unfortunately has the power to do every one of us a great deal of damage. I'm sure you're aware that he hates SF with a passion.'

The officer took a long slow breath before continuing and Shepherd could see that he was choosing his words carefully. 'On the disciplinary side, the Commanding General wants your heads on a platter. He refuses to take any personal responsibility for the cock-ups on the operation, and attributes all the blame to your patrol and the other SF patrols for failing to give adequate warning of the presence of the enemy forces. The fact that you made an E and E across country rather than rejoining the main force, has allowed him to present this as desertion and cowardice. By all military rules, you should have gone to the RV, but for perfectly understandable reasons – in my eyes at least – you chose not to. However, he can use that to accuse you of deliberately disobeying orders and putting the op in jeopardy, though you and I would argue that you were acting to secure the op rather than jeopardise it. However, ignoring any evidence to the contrary, he has convinced himself of your guilt and is determined to press ahead with your court martial.

'I have tried very hard to reason with him and his staff, but to no avail. The good news is that his attempt to lay the blame for the failure of the operation on you is upsetting our bosses at home and in this regard, I feel he has bitten off considerably more than he can chew. In the end it will come back and bite him on the arse, but that will take time. Meanwhile, even though personally, I think the man is a prat, for now I am under his command, but if and when the court martial does come about, I promise you now that I will be there to give evidence on your behalf. I have outlined the situation to the Hereford and Northwood Head Sheds and they are working on it but for the time being, I'm afraid it's just a case of grin and bear it, and hopefully it will be all sorted out before you get back to the UK.'

'So our careers depend on whose head is farthest up the prime minister's arse?' Geordie said. 'Let's hope the Director SF gets there first and goes deepest then.'

'We've no option but to go along with it, I know,' Shepherd said, 'but to say we're not happy about it is the understatement of the century. If this does go wrong and your assessment proves to be too optimistic, we could easily end up in the slammer for a good number of years. The MOD is staffed by a vindictive shower of bastards who will do everything they can to protect themselves. However, let me make it clear: if we are going to go down because our chiefs lose a political arse-kicking contest, we won't just lie back and think of England. As long as everyone involved is aware of that, we will let it ride for now, but you had better make everyone involved aware of what I've just said. We won't go quietly, I promise you that.'

The OC nodded, and satisfied that everybody understood their positions, he hurried back to the comms centre to send yet another "flash" message to Hereford.

During the rest of the day Shepherd and his mates were fed at regular intervals by a clearly sympathetic cook. After dark a sentry patrolled around the wire but he did not interfere when a couple of squaddies who had clearly taken a drop or two of beer strolled up to the nick and threw a couple of packs of cigarettes over the wire. The word had spread that Shepherd and his patrol were being held and the other troops were indicating where their sympathies lay. They didn't need the cigarettes themselves – none of them smoked, even Jock had given up under pressure from both his wife and his patrol mates – but they appreciated the gesture. Jimbo scraped back the pebbles on the floor of the tent and stashed away the cigarettes for whoever occupied the place after them, then they all lay back and gathered their strength for whatever lay ahead.

CHAPTER 15

The atmosphere on board the Royal Air Force Hawker Siddeley 125 executive jet was frigid as the aircraft flew north-west across the Mediterranean towards Heraklion on the island of Crete. The various factions on board the aircraft were barely on speaking terms. The fact that the interior of the aircraft was little larger than the inside of a Transit van did nothing to ease the strain between them because there was literally no place to go to get away from each other. Even the toilet door at the rear of the plane had been wired open.

The catalyst for the ill feeling were the four gaunt, poorly dressed individuals, looking very out of place in the luxury cabin of the jet. They were seated at two of the tables in the middle of the cabin, alternately dozing or communicating silently to each other by means of hand signals. Occasionally one of them would raise an eyebrow or a finger to the Master Air Load Master, Aimee, who also doubled as Cabin Steward, and she would unhesitatingly bring them a coffee or a cold drink from the tiny galley near the front door of the plane. The way she fussed over them while ignoring the other occupants of the cabin left little doubt about whose side she was on.

Behind those four, sitting with their backs against the rear bulkhead, were two burly men who were obviously military despite their civilian clothes. They were occasionally shooting nervous glances at each other, but studiously avoiding looking at the scruffy individuals seated in front of them. Sandwiched between the two groups was an individual in khaki-coloured, cavalry twill trousers and polo shirt, who could not have been anything other than an army cavalry officer. The fact that his name was Rupert was almost too perfect for the four men he was nominally commanding. 'Finally my dreams have come true,' Jock said to his mates as they boarded the aircraft. 'A Rupert who's actually called Rupert. Do you think that makes him doubly useless?'

Like the RAF policemen, Rupert could barely bring himself to look at the scruffy group in front of him, but when he did so, his lip curled in disdain. Beyond the cockpit door the pilot and his co-pilot were also barely on speaking terms. As he piloted the plane, Wing Commander Norman Chamberlain was red-faced, still struggling to control his anger. His rank was equivalent to an Army Colonel, but he was a time-serving non-achiever who had wangled his way on to the RAF VIP Flight based at Northolt near the A40 on the outskirts of London. He spent his working hours flying high-ranking government officials and civil servants all over the continent and the rest of the world, but deep down he knew he was little more than the airborne equivalent of a cab driver. He bolstered his ego by namedropping the details of various well-known figures that he had 'in the back of my plane'. He knew his fellow pilots ridiculed him behind his back but that only served to make him even more pompous and irascible.

He had been delighted when a few days previously he had been briefed by the station Operations Officer that he was to fly a special cargo to Bagram Airbase in Afghanistan. The passengers were four senior members of a foreign aid organisation plus two escorts supplied by the RAF Police. Their cargo consisted of five metal ammunition boxes. Although officially the Wing Commander was not supposed to know what was in the boxes, he inferred from what the Ops Officer had said that, using the Government foreign aid budget as cover, they would contain several million US dollars for distribution to the American-allied tribes among the multitude of warring factions in Afghanistan. He was to fly the normal route, overnighting at the RAF base at Akrotiri in Cyprus, then transiting over Turkey to the Arabian Gulf, and overnighting again in Qatar, before flying the final leg into the Bagram Air Base in Afghanistan. At each stop the police detachment were responsible for securing the aircraft and cargo, even sleeping on the plane if necessary.

The crew were then to recover to Northolt on the reverse route, but this time carrying no passengers or cargo. This suited the Wingco down to the ground. He planned to get back to Akrotiri and then call a mechanical defect on the aircraft, enabling him to spend a couple of days topping up his tan and buying a few demijohns of local wine and Metaxa brandy so he was set up for the summer barbecue season in the UK.

However, a trip that had started so promisingly a few days ago had now turned to dust. The flight out had been uneventful, but it all began going seriously wrong at Bagram. After landing and taxiing to the secure unloading area for the cargo to be removed, he went to the flight control centre to file the first sector of his return trip to the UK. However, he was surprised to be given a message to report to the Base Senior RAF officer immediately. The CO then told him to forget his original orders. 'You are to carry out the delicate mission of repatriating a small group of Special Forces soldiers to the UK, using a non-standard flight route. These troops are not considered especially dangerous but they are to be kept under guard and monitored the whole way. They are not to mix with the public and especially not with members of the press or other media organisations, hence the need for a non-standard route to keep them well away from prying eyes and ears. Clear?'

Seeing his jolly to Akrotiri disappearing before his eyes, the Wingco vehemently objected, but was overruled and when he persisted in his complaints, the CO fixed him with a cold eye. 'Are you refusing to transport these men, Wing Commander? If so, I can arrange for someone else to make the flight and transfer you to a Chinook Squadron which is flying hazardous re-supply and casevac missions to the up-country Fire Bases. No? Then you have your orders. Carry them out.'

Subdued but inwardly seething, the Wingco had left in a sulk and then taken his bad temper out on his hapless co-pilot and loadmaster. The occupant of the right-hand seat in the cockpit was no happier. The co-pilot was a superbly qualified RAF pilot, having passed out from Cranwell near the top of his class. He had then flown several thousand hours on fast jets before transferring onto the HS 125 fleet so that he could spend more time at home with his new family. However, instead of the glamorous and exciting working life he had envisaged, he now found himself doing mundane taxi runs while being abused by the Wingco.

While scanning the aircraft dials and looking for any passing traffic out of the cockpit windows, the co-pilot was mentally going through his options, drafting his letter of resignation from the RAF and his application to one of the several executive jet companies based at Luton airport. All of them flew variations of the 125 and he was confident that when they received his application he would not be short of offers. 'If I have to work with divas,' he thought, 'I might as well work with the real thing and at least get well paid for it.' He knew he had to keep his head down in the meantime because the captain was looking for any target he could find.

In the back of the plane, Aimee was also furious, but with herself as much as the pilot. She was in a rubbish job but knew she only had herself to blame. She had started her career in the RAF as a junior entrant when she was a teenager, qualifying first as a physical training instructor and from there, desperate to become part of the aircrew fraternity, she had trained as a parachute jumping instructor. She was fortunate that she was able to take part in several mass parachute drops before the Ministry of Defence took a machete to the Army's airborne forces. Even now her blood tingled when she remembered the sight of a couple of squadrons of Hercules transports flying in V-formation, line astern, and the air full of parachutes. She felt protective towards the jumpers, because those supposed hard cases had invariably treated her as an equal and always with the utmost respect. She knew they relied on her expertise to get them safely out of the aircraft and she reciprocated by being meticulously professional.

After a few years when the number of parachute drops had dwindled to a trickle, she was transferred to the Special Forces Hercules Squadron at RAF Lyneham. There she first came into contact with the guys from the SAS Regiment, often despatching them from the aircraft to minute DZ's in the remotest regions, where only the pilot and co-pilot knew the location. Although the size of the patrols were small, seldom exceeding four men, they would decide for themselves how they would exit the aircraft, some preferring to go through the door, others from the tailgate, sometimes using static line, often with free-fall chutes.

She was particularly drawn to those guys, as they sat quietly in the aircraft, waiting for the signal to jump, and either pretending to sleep or communicating with each other by facial expressions or hand signals over the deafening noise of the Hercules engines. Occasionally she would notice one of their hands making an involuntary move to squeeze something in a pocket or a pouch as if to seek assurance from the contents. Her past experience told her that the four guys in the cabin now were also SAS but she didn't know what they had done to be in their current situation.

The two RAF policemen, known universally throughout the armed services as "Snowdrops" because of the white peaked caps they wore on duty, sat lower in their seats. The outward leg of this trip had been a doddle, looking after five ammo boxes, but the return journey was a nightmare. At first the skipper had demanded that the Snowdrops should physically restrain the four prisoners using either handcuffs or cable ties, but he was overruled by Aimee on safety grounds in case there was a flight emergency. He had also insisted that the toilet door was kept open for the duration of the flight, regardless of who needed to use it. Although both of the policemen were big burly guys, well over six feet in height, if push came to shove neither of them felt confident that the four men in their charge would not walk all over them. The prisoners said little or nothing to them, but exuded an air of quiet competence and menace. The Snowdrops normally relied on the threat of punishment and Queens Regulations to get others to do what they wanted but they had an uneasy feeling that none of that would count with these four. The Snowdrops knew they were on their own and they did not like it.

Meanwhile the cavalry officer, Rupert, surveyed the backs of the four heads in front of him and sighed deeply. He knew he had been rumbled. He had decided to join the SAS to improve his standing with the hunting, shooting and debutant circles in which he moved. By a mixture of luck and influence he passed the Selection course and thought that his problems were over. In fact they were just beginning. Before he knew what was happening, he had been posted to Afghanistan on a six month tour with the Active Service Squadron.

The thought of going into action with the insolent troopers he was supposed to be leading had gripped him with terror, so much so that prior to deploying to a Fire Base up country, when they were all zeroing their weapons on the range at Bagram, he put a pistol round through his left forearm. He swore it was an accident but the opinions of the spectators on the range was equally split between those who thought it might have been a genuine accident and those who insisted he had shot himself on purpose. Those who did that in the First World War found themselves in front of a firing squad *pour encourager les autres* but, patched up by the medics in country, he was casevaced back to the UK instead. There he used his contacts inside and outside the SAS to wangle a post as a liaison officer at the Permanent Joint Headquarters in Northwood.

His job was to carry hard copy dispatches to and from Bagram and he was able to use his frequent journeys to the Middle East, coupled with his connection to the SAS, to enhance his standing. The added bonus for him was that he hoped to be able to qualify for the Afghanistan campaign medals by accumulated service, without having to go within miles of any actual combat. His few days here and a few days there would eventually add up to sufficient days for him to be awarded the medal, unlike the combat troops who had to qualify by being in country in one continuous stretch. Although his skin was as thick as rhinoceros hide, he had mentally cringed when he first met the four guys now sitting in front of him and their contemptuous looks had chilled him to the core.

CHAPTER 16

In the cloudless, late-afternoon sky, the small jet began descending from its cruise altitude. 'Where are we landing?' Jimbo asked, squinting out of the window at the island they were circling. 'I don't recognise it.'

Aimee overheard him as she bustled about making everything safe for the landing. 'It's Heraklion in Crete.'

'Bloody hell,' Geordie said, 'talk about taking the scenic route. We'll be a week in transit at this rate.'

Jock nodded. 'And that's no coincidence. There'll be a shitstorm raging in Hereford about this, with the Head Shed and sycophants versus the rest of the Regiment. Therefore we're not going to be shipped back there anytime soon, because whoever gets there first gets in the first blow and controls the narrative. I've seen it before.'

Before anyone could reply, the noise in the cabin increased as the pilots engaged the air brakes and flaps to slow the aircraft, making conversation difficult. As they prepared themselves for the landing, tightening their seat belts and pushing further back into their seats, the intercom light went on. Shepherd could see Aimee's lips moving but not hear what she was saying, though her face was showing increasing irritation. As she replaced the telephone in its cradle, she gave it a fierce V-sign to vent her frustration. She made her way back towards the passengers, automatically tidying up as she went. 'A problem?' Shepherd asked.

'Only for you. Him Upfront has arranged for you and your team to be held in detention cells overnight. He says that in Bagram he was ordered to transport you back to the UK securely, and that is what he intends to do. Technically, I am in charge of the passengers and cargo and he is in charge of me, so he has ordered me to make sure that you are held securely overnight, while he and the co-pilot are ensconced in a suite at one of the airport hotels, wining and dining at the taxpayers' expense. Oh, and he emphasised that I was responsible for the security arrangements and you must have no chance of escape. As if!'

She focused her wrath on the two Snowdrops, who were vainly attempting to avoid her gaze. 'And don't think you two are getting away with it. I may know nothing about security arrangements but I do know about delegating, so when we leave the aircraft you're coming with us and you can do the guarding throughout the night while I go off and get some much-needed sleep, like the rest of the crew.'

She turned back to Shepherd. 'By the way, I have some spare food boxes I'll let you have, just in case there's nothing to eat where you're going.'

'I was wondering why there was no hot food on the flight,' Shepherd said. ''You've got the galley, an oven and a microwave, and I would have thought at least the crew would be eating proper meals.'

She smiled. 'The arsehole up front wanted hot food, but only for the crew, so I ordered cold food boxes all round. On my flights we all eat hot or we all eat cold. He went berserk when he found out, so with a little bit of luck he'll have a coronary.'

She disappeared into the galley and brought back a stack of white boxes filled with picnic-type food. 'These should keep you going overnight if there's nothing else available.'

To her astonishment, after thanking her they immediately tore open the boxes and devoured the contents. 'We'll eat now and drink now,' Jock said, intercepting her puzzled look, 'because we never know what's around the corner, but whatever it is, at least we'll have full bellies when we encounter it.'

The heat of the day had caused thermals to ascend from the mountains in the centre of the island, causing a steady offshore wind to blow around the airfield. There was an increase in tension on board the aircraft as it circled close to the high ground surrounding the runway, buffeted by the turbulence, before landing in a puff of blue smoke from the tyres.

At that time of day the airport was quiet, with a lull between the morning flocks of tourist aircraft and the equally large number of evening arrivals. The 125 taxied on its small, nitrogen-filled wheels over to the general aviation area of the airfield, where, on disembarkation, a clearly disinterested customs and immigration official gave their passports a cursory glance and then waved them through.

While the captain, the co-pilot and the cavalry officer headed straight to the hotel in the crew bus, the SAS men, Aimee and the Snowdrops were hustled on to an airport minibus driven by a local policeman. Unshaven and bulging out of his uniform, he was clearly disgruntled at having his extended lunch interrupted. He drove them at top speed to a decrepit, isolated cinder-block building near the perimeter of the airfield and deposited them outside the only door, which was broken and dangling from one hinge. He was about to drive away when Aimee stopped him by standing in front of the vehicle. 'You were supposed to take us to the detention centre, so what is this place?'

'It is detention centre,' the policeman said, his English as broken as the door.

She kept her temper with an effort. 'It can't be the detention centre. You wouldn't keep pigs in a place like this.'

'Is old detention centre, new detention centre is in port – new building, very busy place, full with immigrants.'

'Well why don't you take us there then?'

He shrugged. 'Bus only for airfield. No can go to port. Is not possible.

'Well how do we get there?'

Another shrug. 'Taxi maybe.'

''We can't take a fucking taxi when we are supposed to be escorting prisoners!' she snapped. 'Anyway, you said it was full. So what do we do?'

'Stay here. Is very quiet and is only few hours.' With that he revved up and roared off through the heat haze, back towards the airport buildings.

They peered cautiously through the doorway. The building contained a single room and the only furniture was a couple of metal bunk beds without mattresses, but it looked surprisingly clean.

'We've been in worse places,' Shepherd said, 'so if you don't mind, we don't.'

'But there's no lock on the door, what's to stop them from escaping?' one of the Snowdrops protested to Aimee.

She spread her hands, palms up. 'Why ask me? That's your job, isn't it? So you'll have to work that out for yourselves, but I'd say you'll have to take it in turns to stay awake through the night, just to make sure everyone is still here in the morning.'

'We're not going anywhere,' Shepherd said to the military cops. 'Go to the hotel with the rest of the crew if you like and collect us when you're ready in the morning.'

The Snowdrop's expression showed he was tempted but overcome with a sense of duty, his mate said sharply, 'No. If we have to stag it, we will, we'll find a chair somewhere and prop it against the door and if you try to get out, we'll be there to stop you.'

Jock gave a broad smile. 'Look my friend, if we want to go, we'll go. We outnumber you two to one, but even if we were outnumbered ten to one, we'd still win.'

The Snowdrop suddenly found that his mouth had gone dry.

'Right, I'm off then,' Aimee said, hiding a smile. 'I'll leave you all to it. But make sure you're still here in the morning, please, otherwise my already poor career prospects will really be down the pan.' She winked at Shepherd and walked off towards the airport terminal.

The six guys sat down in the dust, their backs against the crumbling wall of the jail, gazing up at the star-lit evening sky or watching the tourist aircraft taxiing on and departing from the main runway. They kept up a desultory conversation as the Snowdrops tried to make sense of the situation they'd found themselves in.

'So who is in charge of you lot?' one of the Snowdrops eventually said.

'Sergeant Shepherd nominally,' Jock said, 'but we work as a team, equal in position and responsibility.'

'Well what rank are you then?'

'Actually we have three ranks,' said Jock. 'Firstly, we have the rank we hold in our permanent regiment, which we relinquish when we pass the SF selection course. Then we have the rank we hold within the SAS Regiment, though that doesn't necessarily reflect our position or our role; for instance, a badged SAS corporal outweighs an attached arms warrant officer in position and role, but not in rank. And then there is the rank we assume when dealing with bodies outside of SF, which can vary greatly. If we need to be a commissioned officer to get something done, we will promote ourselves.'

'But that's anarchy, it's against all army rules and regulations.' Jock grinned. 'Maybe so, but the requirements of the Regiment are to get things done in a hurry and not be bound by petty rules put in place by bureaucratic officers and civil servants to protect their careers and pensions.'

They were interrupted by the headlights of an approaching minibus. It turned out to be the same bus and police driver that had deposited them a couple of hours before, but his new passenger was a small, wiry, dark-faced man, who got down from the bus and said in good English, 'Hey, what's going on here? Who's in charge?'

One Snowdrop looked around at the rest and said, 'I suppose it's me.'

'Then tell me what's going on. Why have you put these people in my jail?'

As the Snowdrop tried to stammer out a reply, Shepherd stood up, a big grin on his face. 'Bloody hell! Hello, Simos, what the hell are you doing in Crete?'

Simos spun around, beaming. 'Spider my friend! I could ask you the same question. What is happening?' He stepped forward and hugged him, his head barely reaching Shepherd's shoulders. What is it they say? You are a sight for sore eyes.'

'Right back at you Simos. We need a friendly face around here. Anyway, you remember Jock, of course, and this is Jimbo and Geordie.' He turned to his mates. 'We met at a counter-terrorist seminar in London a few years ago. Simos was the newly elected Athens Police counter-terrorist team leader when Greece was playing catch-up with the rest of the counter-terrorist world and desperate to acquire the latest equipment and techniques available. Every country was keen to give them free equipment: Germany, H&K rifles; the US, automatic pistols; the UK, flash bangs and method-of-entry kit. But only the UK offered them expertise and training as well. Me and Jock were on the training team that travelled to Greece, and we became mates with Simos.'

'My colleague here,' Simos said, indicating the driver, 'told me that there were English soldiers being put into the jail. I could not believe that could be happening, so I had to come and see for myself. And who do I find here – none other than the famous Spider Shepherd.'

'Like I said, it's a long story, Simos, so I'll bring you up to speed later, but you haven't told me what you're doing in Crete?'

'You must understand, Spider, I am Cretan first and Greek second. My cousin's uncle was the legendary Mitsotakis from the Cretan resistance in the Second World War. He worked with the British, fighting the Germans in Crete. He told me that it was easy, because every Cretan knows how to shoot a weapon from the cradle, and they also do not like interference from the authorities because that way they have to pay taxes. Many years afterwards he was in charge of the New Democracy party, which won an election and threw out the Socialists. Because I am related and he trusts me, and also because he knows I am clever, he put me in charge of the counter-terrorist team in Athens. They were good times and with your help, and the help of many others, we built a very good team. Then the Socialists won the next election and I was out on my ear, along with every policeman and government worker who supported New Democracy. I was sent to Crete to keep an eye on the immigrants coming from the Middle East. There are many terrorists coming to our country that way and no one helps us.'

'A waste of your talents though,' Shepherd said.

He shrugged. 'No worries. When the Socialists get kicked out, I will go back. It is the same for all government workers, when the bosses change, we all change.'

'How good are the people in charge now? Are they competent?'

Simos smiled. 'The short answer to that, my friend, is no, but they are in power now. All the equipment we were given is back in boxes and in storage, and the people in charge are too proud and too stubborn to ask for help from anyone. No other country thinks that Greece needs help now, because it has all been done. Besides, we are Europeans now.'

'But why was the whole team fired?' Jock said

'I know, it's madness, but that is how my country does things. We are now in Europe, so we are Europeans with supposedly European standards and prosperity, but we have no standards and we certainly have no prosperity.' He paused. 'Anyway, now we go, guys.'

'We can't, we're under arrest and in jail.'

'Who's keeping you in jail?'

Shepherd pointed to the Snowdrops. 'These two gentlemen are Royal Air Force policemen and they are responsible for keeping us safe and secure.'

Simos gave them an old-fashioned look. 'OK. They come too.'

'Where are we going?' Jock said.

'To my house. I have a housekeeper because my wife is still in Athens with our kids, who are at school, waiting for me to come back. My housekeeper is an excellent cook and I have lots of food and drink, so let's go!' He gave the Snowdrops a menacing stare. 'And if the RAF police are not happy, I will put them into their own jail.'

'Right guys,' Shepherd said. 'You had better come with us. Simos is serious and if you find yourself under arrest you might miss tomorrow's flight.'

They all piled into the bus and spent the rest of the evening at Simos's small house. Even though Shepherd and his team had already eaten the contents of several of the food boxes, they ate the dinner his housekeeper prepared for them and drank more wine than they usually would. The head Snowdrop was impressed. 'Where the hell do you put it all?'

'The golden rule is to eat and drink when you can,' Jock said. 'Because you never know where your next meal is coming from.'

Just as they started the post-meal craic, normal for military types the world over, they were interrupted by the shrill ringing of the telephone. When Simos returned from answering it, his face was thunderous. 'I'm sorry but I will have to leave you. My cousin Angeli is in a standoff with the police in his village up in the mountains. They say he has a gun for shooting at aircraft.'

'What? He wouldn't really have an anti-aircraft gun, would he?' Shepherd said.

'Of course, why not? Every family in the mountains has a machinegun, so why not an anti-aircraft gun? We Cretans are like the English, we have a horror of being invaded. The last time was in the war with the Germans, when we were defenceless. We swore then that it would not happen again, but it has. The Germans then were Nazis; now they're called Europeans, but to Cretans they're still Nazis. This is why my cousin is in trouble, because the Germans are trying to force us to pay higher taxes before we can be good Europeans and Angeli is refusing. I repeat, we Cretans are not Greeks, or Europeans. We are Cretans first, second and last—.' He broke off as they heard a police car with siren wailing, screech to a halt outside the house. 'Now I must go and get my cousin out of trouble.'

'Whoa, not so fast, Simos,' Shepherd said. 'If you don't mind, we'll come with you. If we leave our air force friends here, we can squeeze in with you and see if we can help. Any problem with that?' he said, turning to the Snowdrops. They exchanged glances and then shook their heads.

Simos got into the front with the driver while Spider and his team piled into the back, squashed in like sardines. They roared off up the road, Simos and the driver shouting a conversation between them, the driver smoking and gesticulating wildly, occasionally flicking ash out of his open window and all the while looking sideways at Simos and only occasionally at the road. Soon they left the tarmac and started to climb steeply up into the mountains on a graded track.

As they climbed higher, the track became narrower and bumpier until it was barely wide enough for the police car, with a steep cliff on one side and a precipice on the other. By now it was dark down in the valley, but the sky grew lighter the higher they climbed. Still chatting away to Simos, the driver was throwing the car around the bends, the wheels spinning in the gravel at the roadside millimetres from the cliff's edge.

Eventually, Shepherd could take no more. 'Stop! Stop! Stop!' he said. 'Stop the car now, and turn off that bloody siren.'

Puzzled, the driver brought the vehicle to a halt, switched off the siren and gave Simos a questioning glance before turning around to look at Shepherd.

'Look guys,' Shepherd said. 'I can accept losing my life in combat – that's just a risk that goes with the job. I can't accept being killed in some stupid accident because the guy driving the vehicle misjudged a corner and sent us over the edge of a bloody mountain. We want to get where we're going in one piece with our nerves relatively intact. So, we will drive calmly the rest of the way, we will arrive calmly, and we will deal with the situation, whatever it is, calmly. Understood?'

The Cretans exchanged another glance but then nodded in unison, and the driver set off again at a funereal speed. 'It's not too far now, Spider,' Simos said, 'only a couple more kilometres and we'll be there.'

Just as he finished speaking they heard a loud burst of automatic fire from further up the mountain. 'Bloody hell, that wasn't just any machine gun, was it?' Jock said. 'That was something much heavier.'

'Well, we don't need to go quite this slow,' Shepherd said to the driver. 'You can speed up a bit, just don't drive us off the bloody mountain.'

A few minutes later, they reached a point high on the mountain where the track did a loop before descending back the way they had just come. Inside the loop, a straggle of dirty, once whitewashed, single-storey buildings were surrounded by heaps of goat droppings and the rusted and neglected wrecks of worn-out tractors and pickup trucks.

'Natural causes?' Jimbo said, gesturing to the wrecks.

'More like kamikaze drivers, if this one's anything to go by,' Jock said.

A group of villagers were standing in the open in the middle of the village, smoking, chatting and taking occasional gulps from bottles of beer and a bottle of retsina they were passing around. Peering around the sides of the buildings were a posse of policemen in ill-fitting uniforms. Their pistols were drawn and their eyes were focused on a squat, ramshackle building with ancient wooden double doors. Hiding behind the policemen were two well-shaven, well-dressed individuals, presumably the hated taxmen, who were gesticulating wildly, exhorting the police to solve the problem by attacking the building, though they seemed to have little appetite for it.

Just when it appeared that they might actually be about to muster enough courage to carry out an assault, the wooden doors suddenly opened, revealing what Jock at once identified as a Soviet-era SU-23 anti-aircraft cannon. It was widely used by the Russian military and its many allies, and just as widely available on the black market in the years following the collapse of the Soviet Union, when soldiers in the former Soviet satellite or client states often took the opportunity to augment their miserable or non-existent wages by flogging off their equipment.

There was an ear-shattering burst as the gun opened up, sending five rounds flashing overhead and tearing away across the darkening sky, their course easily tracked by the burning tracer at the base of each round. Any notion that the police might have had about carrying out an assault on the building immediately evaporated. The doors slammed shut again with a resounding thud.

'Where the hell did he get that thing?' Shepherd said.

Simos shrugged. 'I think it came from Libya.'

'But what the bloody hell does he want it for, apart from shooting taxmen, that is? The thing's a beast. It's belt-fed and can fire about four hundred rounds a minute. Never mind the taxmen – with enough ammo he could demolish the whole island.' He paused. 'So, how much ammo do you think he has in there?'

'Oh he has lots, Spider. He bought a lot with the gun because it was cheap. The Libyans will sell any-thing to anybody.'

Shepherd thought for a moment. 'So what hap-pens if he comes out?'

'Well if the police get to him, he'll get twenty years in jail on the mainland, with no remission. But if he gets a few metres head start on them, then he can vanish into the high mountains and return here in a few weeks' time as a hero. The police will not dare to come back again after this.'

'Right then, we'd better get him out of there. The question is how?'

'We could do it with a flashbang if we had one,' Jock said.

'Which we don't,' Shepherd said. 'But we might be able to improvise one if we can lay our hands on some PE and det cord, and a few other bits and pieces.' He turned to Simos. 'Is there a quarry or a big construction site somewhere near here where they use explosives?'

'I don't think so, but I will ask the villagers. They may have something lying around. I told you every family has a machine gun, but every village also has a cache of other stuff hidden away, just in case.'

Simos walked over to the group of villagers, who had been staring at the SAS men with a mixture of curiosity and hostility. A loud argument ensued with much shouting, arm-waving, shoulder-shrugging and pointing. This went on for several minutes and it was only because Shepherd was watching the group intently that he spotted a couple of the villagers using the cover of the commotion to quietly slip away from the back of the group and disappear down the mountain.

The argument then petered out and Simos came back to join the SAS men, but within ten minutes the two men who had slipped away were back, struggling under the weight of a wooden crate with rope handles. They dropped it unceremoniously in front of them and went to rejoin their friends. The crate was painted a fading, dull brown colour with stencilled writing across the top and sides.

'Bloody hell,' Jock said. 'Do you see those markings? This is a World War Two Wehrmacht ammunition box. Look, it's even got the Nazi eagle on it. These things are rarer than hens' teeth because once the squaddies emptied them, they used the crates as fuel to cook their rations. Open it quick – it might be full of Nazi gold!'

Shepherd lifted the lid to find not gold, but a staggering range of weaponry and hardware from various countries and eras. Lying on the top was a Second World War Schmeisser machine pistol, and alongside it a Luger 9mm pistol from the same era, both lightly oiled and looking in pristine condition. They removed the contents, item by item, and lower down the crate found a British Mk I Sten gun that had been disassembled, probably to ease the pressure on the main spring. There were magazines for each of the weapons, kept empty so as not to damage the mechanism, with ammunition rolling loose around the bottom of the box.

Shepherd also uncovered a couple of No 36 grenades – the grooved and pineapple-shaped hand grenades that were the British Army's standard issue from the 1930s right through to the 1970s. To check whether they were primed or not, he unscrewed the base plates and was relieved to find that the timing fuses were not in place. He had almost reached the bottom of the crate and was beginning to wonder whether there was any explosive material there at all, when he found a silver tin with a screw top at either end. He recognised it immediately as a detonator-carrying tin, designed to safely house electric detonators at one end and non-electric ones at the other. There were no markings on the tin, so he unscrewed one end to discover that it was empty, but when he unscrewed the other end, he was delighted to find six of the No 27 detonators that had been issued to the British Army for decades. Right at the bottom of the crate he also found a loose coil of what looked like grey rope – safety fuse for use with the detonators – and then the holy grail: a long coil that looked just like a plastic clothes line, but was in fact detonating cord.

He grinned at the others. 'Right guys, we've got all the makings of an initiation set. Let's see if we can improvise a flash-bang with it. We need fuel, oxygen and ignition, so something that will burn slowly and give off a lot of smoke, an accelerant that we can prime with the initiation set, and a container to put everything in, because we'll have to restrict the amount of oxygen to give us smoke and not flame. Any ideas?'

Geordie glanced around them. 'We can use rags soaked in the sump oil from those wrecks dotted around the village and there must be a tin or a plastic bottle lying around to put it all in.'

'What about the brake fluid from the same wrecks as the accelerant?' Jock said.

'Brilliant!' Shepherd said. 'You two sort out the sump oil and the brake fluid, and Jimbo, you scout around and see what you can find in the way of rags and a container while I test the fuse to make sure it's not been affected by damp.'

Just as they were about to separate to carry out their tasks, they heard the faint sound of singing from Angeli's house. 'Dear God, it sounds like he's started drinking ouzo,' Simos said. 'Can it get any worse?'

'Oh things can always get worse, Simos,' Shepherd said.

While the other men were foraging around the village outbuildings, Shepherd discarded the first twelve inches of the safety fuse, in case it had been penetrated by damp. He then cut off the next twelve, chamfered one end and lit it with a match, timing its burning rate. Satisfied that it burned within the safety limits of twenty-seven to thirty-three seconds, he then began to prepare the initiation set. He cut off the next twelve inches of fuse and placed the non-chamfered end into the opening at the top of one of the detonators. Using surgical plaster from his personal medical kit, he taped the detonator on to a short length of det cord, tied a couple of knots in the end of the cord furthest from the detonator, and the initiation set was ready.

The others arrived back shortly afterwards, carrying two rusting paint tins they'd found in one of the outbuildings. One was nearly full with sump oil and the other contained brake fluid that they had drained from one of the wrecked vehicles. Jimbo was also carrying a discarded T-shirt, which he proceeded to rip into strips. 'There's a thick layer of dried paint at the bottom of the tin with the brake fluid in,' Jock said, 'so that would be the best one to use.'

Shepherd nodded and poured some of the sump oil into it, stirring it with a stick to form a solution with the brake fluid, and then added the rags, pushing them down into the mixture with the stick. He made a hole in the lid of the tin with the point of his combat knife and threaded the det cord through it, then jammed the lid back on. The improvised flash bang was now ready to go.

'Will it work?' Simos said.

'Only one way to find out,' Shepherd said, 'but it had better do, because we don't have a Plan B if it doesn't.'

By now it was almost completely dark. Fuelled by the prodigious amounts of booze they were drinking, the villagers were getting increasingly noisy and restless, making the police and taxmen even jumpier. However, when Shepherd, Simos and the others approached Angeli's house, the police made no attempt to stop them.

The singing inside the house had grown louder and Simos began hammering on the door, shouting, 'Angeli, it's me, Simos, open the door!' Shepherd stood to one side, ready to ignite the safety fuse on the flash bang. There was more shouting between Simos and Angeli before the doors were finally opened a few inches. Shepherd immediately lit the safety fuse and slid the flash bang along the floor through the narrow gap.

Angeli yelled in anger, throwing the doors wide open and firing another burst from his anti-aircraft cannon. Everyone hit the deck and the rounds flashed over their heads, etching hot white streaks across the night sky. The doors were suddenly slammed shut again, the noise almost masking the sound of a small bang from inside. There was a pause of a few seconds when nothing appeared to be happening inside, then wisps of oily black smoke began escaping around the door and they heard a loud bout of coughing from within. Shortly afterwards the doors were thrown back and Angeli staggered out, still coughing and gasping for breath, his face blackened and his clothing singed.

Shepherd, Simos and the others at once formed a line, keeping themselves between Angeli and the police while he recovered his breath. Simos yelled at him in the local dialect and began trying to hurry him away as the police, now recovered from their surprise and emboldened by the sight of their target in the open, began advancing to make the arrest. Seeing this, the villagers ran to block them.

After a few seconds Angeli had recovered sufficiently to realise what was going on. He quickly shook Simos by the hand and kissed him on both cheeks, then did the same with Shepherd and the others, treating each of them to a blast of second-hand garlic, ouzo and Metaxa fumes before disappearing into the dusk and heading up the mountainside like an inebriated mountain goat. Any remaining enthusiasm the police had for pursuing him was ended by the hostile stares that the villagers and the SAS men were directing at them. The police jumped into their cars and, with sirens wailing, disappeared back down the track towards civilisation, taking the taxmen with them.

After sharing a few celebratory toasts in beer, retsina and ouzo, Shepherd and the others eventually managed to extricate themselves from the boozy embraces of the villagers, who now seemed to have adopted them as honorary Cretans. Waving their farewells, they jumped into their car and followed the dust of the police convoy back down the mountain. When they arrived back at Simos's place, they shared a last nightcap with Simos and the two Snowdrops, and then crashed out on chairs and settees around the house.

CHAPTER 17

The tourist coach pulled up at the bottom of the short incline leading to the entrance of the Parthenon. It was early and the coach was one of the first of the day's arrivals, but the heat was already rising in shimmering waves from the ancient stones. Tourists poured off the coach, the Koreans, Chinese and Japanese photographing everything that moved, the clicking of their camera shutters a mechanical echo of the dry choruses of the cicadas in the dusty trees at the foot of the slope.

An elderly American couple, Hank and Leanne, were the last to climb down from the coach. Hank was fussing over Leanne, who was visibly exhausted and limping slightly from an attack of sciatica. By contrast, even though there were also lines of fatigue around his eyes, her husband kept his back rigidly upright – the posture of a veteran military man. An ammunition technical expert, he had served more years than he cared to remember, first in uniform and then, after retiring from the military, with the Department of Defense until it became obvious to everyone, even Hank, that he finally had to go.

During his long and distinguished career, he had watched many thousands of pieces of ordnance being fired, detonated or sent into orbit, and in fact had probably witnessed more gunfire and explosions than the most hard-bitten combat veteran. And yet, too young for Vietnam, too old for the Gulf War, he had never once heard a shot fired in anger. Indeed, it was his proud boast that he had never – till now – even left the continental United States. It was his job to monitor and assess the effectiveness of weapons and ammunition and, where necessary, to order the destruction or recycling of items that had reached the end of their shelf life. Consequently, he was able to identify every piece of ordnance equipment and ammunition used by the US military since the end of the Second World War.

A lifelong bachelor, on retirement he had moved to Florida and bought a condo close to Tarpon Springs – 'Sponge Capital of the World'. To his and everyone else's amazement he then met, fell in love with and married a local widow – Leanne – to whom he became devoted. With extra time on his hands after his retirement, he was able to indulge his hobby of attending military parades. It was a hobby that had started in November 1963, when he had been taken by his father to the funeral parade of John F. Kennedy at Arlington National Cemetery in Virginia. Too young to have been more than dimly aware of JFK as president, the raw atmosphere of grief and shock, just three days after Kennedy's assassination, made less impact on Hank than the pageantry of the funeral procession. The horse-drawn gun carriage carrying the coffin, the riding boots placed backwards in the stirrups of the President's riderless charger, the troops and sailors with their rifles reversed, the muffled rumble of drums, the rhythmic tread of slow-marching feet, all were to leave an indelible impression upon him. Ever since then, even the sound of a military bugle would stir his blood.

His last posting, at the Naval Air Station in Pensacola, had given him access to innumerable graduation and passing-out parades, always accompanied by a fly-past of naval jets and helicopters, with ground troops carrying the chevrons and unit flags and shouting out the cadences so loved by the American military. However, he had also read and seen so much about the different military traditions in Europe that he became determined to break the habit of a lifetime and travel outside the United States to see as many parades as possible. He persuaded his new wife to take a tour of European capitals with him; he would indulge his hobby while she could either tag along or shop to her heart's content while he was doing so. The tour they booked was for London and Paris, but they insisted on adding Athens to the itinerary, mainly so they could talk about it afterwards with their Greek neighbours in Tarpon Springs.

The military spectacles they saw far exceeded his expectations, with the Queen's Guards in London and the Republican Guards in Paris particularly delighting him. Although tired and fed up with living out of suitcases, he knew he would not be disappointed by their visit to the Greek capital either. Before arriving at the Parthenon, they had visited Syntagma Square to watch the changing of the guard there. Hank was tickled pink and could not wait to get back to Florida to have some gentle fun with his neighbours about the Greek Army uniform of tasselled fez, white skirt and ladies' stockings, and shoes with pompoms on.

By the time they had struggled down from the coach at the Parthenon, the tour guide had already set off, leading the rest of the party up the slope. Hank cast around anxiously for a moment before spotting them, but was puzzled to see that five or six strange individuals, dressed in steel-grey, loose-fitting, pyjama-like clothing, were now mingling with the tourists. 'Where did those guys come from?' he said to Leanne. 'They sure as heck weren't on the coach with us.'

The next moment, he felt a vicious blow to his kidneys and crashed to the floor. His wife fell next to him. He heard a volley of small-arms fire ring out and from his prone position, with the ingrained habits of a lifetime and even as he saw several people fall to the ground, he thought to himself: *Small arms, probably 9mm, but not US manufacture.* A shadow fell across his face and he looked up, squinting in the harsh sunlight. One of the strangely dressed individuals was standing over him, pointing a pistol at his head. Still not getting it, his last-ever conscious thought was, *Why is this guy wearing gloves on such a hot day? And why would he be wearing a det-cord necklace?*

CHAPTER 18

After an early breakfast, Simos had the SAS men and their Snowdrop guards back at the temporary jail by the time Aimee arrived to pick them up. 'I feel a bit guilty guys,' she said. 'Did you have a terrible night?'

'We've had worse,' Jock said, giving Shepherd the ghost of a wink.

After another cursory customs and immigration check at the plane steps, they climbed back on board the 125 and settled themselves for the next long sector, from Heraklion to the aircraft's home base at Northolt. Wing Commander Norman Chamberlain still appeared smug and condescending to his passengers, but seemed to be in a better mood, his outlook possibly enhanced by Aimee's report of the conditions in their makeshift jail. With all checks completed, the aircraft was taxiing for take-off when a call came from the airfield tower, ordering it back to its stand and demanding that Shepherd be put on the radio. The caller proved to be Simos, who was shouting incoherently down the line.

'For God's sake, Simos,' Shepherd said. 'Calm down. Your cousin's not back on the anti-aircraft gun again, is he?'

'No Spider, it's worse – much worse – than that. There's a terrorist situation in Athens. I'm going straight away, can you come with me? I think they will need our help.'

Laid-back and dozing just seconds before, Shepherd at once switched into action mode. 'Right, we'll go there on the 125, so get yourself out here as quickly as you can, and I'll have things sorted out by the time you get here.'

Only Shepherd's patrol mates showed no surprise at the transformation with him in the space of that brief call. In a tone that brooked no argument, he began giving orders to Chamberlain. 'Right, go to the crew room now and get on the radio to Northwood, the MOD or whichever HQ you prefer, and inform them that this aircraft and everyone aboard is now diverting to Athens. Explain that there is a terrorist incident there, and tell them that we are going there under the Protocol of International Observers. For your information, that means that if there is a terrorist situation, observers from other nations can attend without prior invitation. In other words, we can just turn up. If you can get through to Northwood headquarters, they will give you the go-ahead immediately. But don't pay any attention to anything that Northolt Ops says, because if they object, they'll be overruled. While you're doing that, get your co-pilot to file a flight plan for Athens with an immediate take-off time. We have stacks of fuel, so we can go as soon as Simos gets here. If there are any problems, he can get us priority take-off and landing slots.'

At first, Chamberlain had bristled at being given orders by someone he outranked. His mouth gaped open and closed, like a fish out of water, as he tried to object. However, Shepherd's air of absolute confidence and authority persuaded him to do as he was told. The two pilots rushed to do Shepherd's bidding. A short while later, they returned with Simos in tow.

Right,' Shepherd said. 'Let's go.'

'But we're still waiting for clearance from the UK to proceed,' said Chamberlain.

'Did you not speak to Northwood operations?'

'Er... no. I went through Northolt.'

'I told you how to do it and you still managed to cock it up,' Shepherd said, 'but it's not a problem, because we're going anyway. Simos, speak to the tower, explain the situation and tell them we're flying to Athens.' He turned back to the pilot. 'And we'll get your precious authorisation while we're in transit. Trust me on this, if there's any comeback, I'll carry the can.'

The Wingco was still dumbfounded. 'But you're only an "other rank",' he said. 'What has your officer got to say about this?'

Rupert opened his mouth to say something, but Shepherd spoke over him, drowning him out. 'First of all, he's not our officer.'

'And secondly,' Jock said getting in on the act, 'we're the SAS, not some half-arsed infantry unit, and in situations like this, it's not rank that counts but position. There's a terrorist incident, so we are any rank we need to be to get there and if necessary, get the job done. So if it makes your life any easier, then you can take it that we're generals, group captains, air commodores or air vice marshals – anything you like, as long as you get this bloody aircraft moving now!'

Chamberlain's mouth opened and closed soundlessly one more time and then he disappeared into his cockpit. A moment later they heard the whine as the jets began to fire up, the noise rapidly deepening to a roar as the aircraft began to taxi towards the runway.

The flight took a little over an hour and during it, as Shepherd had predicted, the flight authority came through from Northwood for them to proceed. Meanwhile, Simos was constantly on the radio, talking to his colleagues in Athens, then updating the SAS men with as much information as he had gleaned. 'It appears hostages are being held at the Parthenon,' he said, after coming off the line, 'but the situation is confused. At the moment the threat level is Amber, meaning there appears to be no immediate threat to the hostages, but nor have the terrorists made any demands – as far as we know, anyway. So it's just a stand-off.'

'What happened?' Geordie said. 'Was there no security?'

Simos grimaced. 'There was, but apparently they were distracted by some men in Arab dress acting suspiciously elsewhere on the Acropolis. They turned out to be innocent tourists'

'Or they were decoys,' Shepherd interrupted, 'drawing off the security guards while the terrorists had free rein.'

'Perhaps so,' Simos said, 'but anyway, the terrorists now control a large group of hostages and if they start killing them, it will be disastrous for the country's reputation and for the economy, which more than ever depends on tourism. The authorities in Athens know what ultimately needs to be done but they have no idea how to do it.'

'Brilliant,' Jock said. 'Tell us something we don't know.'

While Shepherd kept monitoring the comms traffic, the rest of the team put together a list of personal kit and weaponry for transmission to Athens, in the hope that Simos could get it for them from the authorities there.

'OK, Simos,' Geordie said, reading from his notepad. 'We need balaclavas, black, fireproof; coveralls, ditto; combat boots; gas masks; night-vision goggles; stabilised binoculars; British aircrew knives; personal medical kits; magazine waistcoats; cable ties for restraining prisoners; personal comms equipment. Weapons: Remington or Browning 9mm pistols with belt and holster; magazine gauges for the pistols, and either MP5s or MP-56Ks with close body slings and nine-mill ammunition, or HK G36s with 5.56 NATO ammunition.'

'And see if you can get me some tourist-type clothes as well, Simos,' Shepherd said. 'The more tasteless the better.'

Rupert, who had been taking a close interest while the list was being put together, now said: 'I'm not even going to ask about the tourist clothes but why the body slings?'

'We use them to clamp our weapons to our chests,' Geordie said, 'allowing us to have both hands free which is very useful when you're trying to gain entry or get over an obstacle.'

When sending the request, Simos had also asked for some time for them on a firing range to allow them to refamiliarise themselves with the weapons and zero them in, but he was told that the only range available was an old chain-mail one in a police barracks.

Jock was the first to voice his displeasure. 'That bloody range is dangerous. We used it when we were training you guys here before. There were ricochets all over the bloody place, so we're probably better off not using it.'

By now Shepherd was fully in control, with the others apparently happy to be led. 'OK,' he said, 'the final thing before touchdown is the skills inventory of all passengers and crew.' He called the Wingco through from the cockpit and the co-pilot took over the controls. 'So, everybody listen up, this is the sitrep: we are going into an unknown, possibly dangerous situation and we don't know how long it may last, so we need to know about every asset we have.'

He turned to Chamberlain. 'First up, you and your co-pilot will do what you do best: fly the kite. After landing, you need to ensure it is kept fully fuelled, so that if any of the bastards involved in this try to flee by air, we can follow them wherever they go. So keep an ear on the news channels, speak to the tower to keep abreast of things and don't go more than ten yards from the cockpit, because if we need to contact you, we will do it through the tower. Eat and sleep on the plane, and if the situation goes mobile we will get back to you ASAP. Understood?'

He waited for the pilot's nod of assent before turning to the others. 'Right, everybody else in turn, give me a short summary of any skills you have that may be useful to us. Start with your first name and keep it short.'

The loadmaster spoke up first. 'I'm Aimee, I'm a trained paramedic, and also trained in disaster management, specifically air crashes with multiple casualties. We carry an enhanced medical pack for the VIP passengers we sometimes have on board. I also have my aircrew knife. I always carry it on duty – force of habit,' she said with a self-deprecating smile.

'OK, you'll come with us. Bring the medical kit and your knife. Next,' he said, looking at the Snowdrops. 'I'm a … erm … my name is Charlie,' the first one said, nervous enough to stumble over his words. 'I'm a qualified marksmen with the service pistol and I am also qualified in arrest and restraint techniques. I also have a wide-ranging knowledge of Queen's regulations.'

'Next.'

'My name is David,' the other Snowdrop said, 'and I have the same skill set as Charlie.'

'Chas and Dave,' Jimbo said, chuckling, 'Perfect!'

'Okay,' Shepherd said, 'you two will come with us as well, but you can leave your knowledge of Queen's regulations behind. Whatever else we use, we won't be needing those.'

'Now you,' he said to the cavalry officer.

'I have basic British Army officer skills.'

'Don't you have any skills carried over from SAS continuation training?'

'I'm afraid not, no.'

Jock rolled his eyes heavenwards but managed to restrain himself from saying what was on his mind.

'Right,' Shepherd said, 'you'll come along too because we might find a use for you, but otherwise keep out of the way. OK, to summarise: everyone but the pilots comes with us, if we can find enough transport, that is. Next, we need call signs and nicknames. Me, Jock, Geordie and Jimbo already have ours. Aimee, you will be Blondie, you three will be Chas, Dave and Sir, Simos will be Ouzo, and the pilots will be Wingco and Junior. Use these nicknames in all conversations, because you don't know who will be listening, not least the media. If you need to speak about locations use initials only, for Northwood for instance, November Delta, for Northolt, November Tango. Any questions?'

There were none and it became very quiet on the aircraft as everybody tried to prepare themselves for what lay ahead. As they went back to their seats Jock muttered an aside to Aimee. 'Keep close to Spider with your med kit. He's the one most likely to need your services, because he's inclined to be a little reckless.'

'I heard that,' Shepherd said. 'And it's a bit rich coming from the man whose hot head has already got him busted down to the ranks twice!'

While Shepherd had been briefing them, Simos was up in the cockpit, talking to Athens air traffic control, requesting permission to land at the old Athens International Airport, now decommissioned and slowly falling into disrepair, but much closer to the centre of the city than the new airport. To their surprise permission was granted, with the proviso that it would have to be a visual approach landing onto a runway that, while usable, was far from perfect.

The landing proved to be bumpy and noisy but uneventful. They then taxied to a holding area that had once been reserved for hijacked aircraft. 'Brings back memories, eh Simos?' Jock said, with a grin.

They were met there by a fleet of police cars, with sirens wailing and blue lights flashing. The weapons and equipment they had requested arrived separately in an armoured van that was normally used for transporting prisoners between the police cells and the courts. As Patrol Signaller, Jimbo made a quick examination of the radio sets that had been supplied. 'These are VVHF,' he said. 'Line of sight, single fixed channel sets and OK for us to talk to each other over short distances without being listened to, but we won't be able to hear or talk to anyone else.'

'Looks like they're trying to restrict our involvement,' Jock said. 'No worries, we can buy throwaway cell phones on the way into the city.'

'Right,' Shepherd said. 'Divide the kit between four of the police cars, one of my team will go in each car, the rest of you divide yourselves up between the other vehicles. Simos, dismiss all the other vehicles, then please ask them to turn off those sodding sirens. You and me will go in the lead car and unless it all kicks off at the Parthenon while we're on our way, we'll all go direct to the police barracks and the firing range. Ask the drivers to drive safely and not too fast, we need calm nerves from here on in.'

The range was in a dilapidated barracks on a headland overlooking the sea, to the south-east of the airport, a corrugated iron building as run-down as the rest of the camp. The barracks was almost deserted except for half a dozen caretakers, keeping their heads down and patiently waiting to be pensioned off.

After stripping, cleaning and checking their weapons, including the angles at the top of every magazine, the team were ready to start their range drills. The Greeks had supplied MP 5s, each of which had a choice of a laser red dot sighting system or a white light torch. Each of them independently chose to keep the torch sighting, because the authorities had not supplied the requested night vision goggles.

When they were ready Jock ran the shooting drill for Shepherd who was wearing full gear, including coveralls, balaclava and respirator. He started very close to the target, firing single shots until he had a grouping of less than the size of a thumbnail. He then increased the range and went on to fire double-taps, working back to longer ranges, initially hitting head shots and then eye shots, and neither man was satisfied until every round was going through either the left or right eye of the target.

Jock then set up a number of obstacles, which Shepherd had to negotiate, going either under, over or through the obstacle, all the while taking on the targets, carrying out magazine changes, clearing weapons stoppages as ordered by Jock, rolling magazine changes, changing weapons from MP 5 to pistol and back again and firing in reduced light, then firing left handed to simulate being wounded. Eventually even Jock was satisfied, and Shepherd lifted the respirator revealing a face dripping with sweat.

Shepherd and Jock swapped roles and the others then ran through similar drills. When they were all satisfied with their performance, they again cleaned and checked their weapons and refilled the magazines.

'Now for some action!' Geordie said.

When they reached the Acropolis, they pulled up beside a group of yellow, air-conditioned pantech-nicons, designed to fit together to form a modular Incident Management Centre. Nearby was a further vehicle for the technical assistance people, respon-sible for surveillance CCTV and listening devices. There were also numerous ambulances, engines run-ning, their crews casually smoking as they awaited developments.

Shepherd had now changed into the tourist clothes he'd requested. 'Blimey, they've excelled themselves,' Jimbo said, as he took in Shepherd's Hawaiian shirt, purple Bermuda shorts and floppy orange cotton sun-hat, with a sports bag containing his pistol slung over his shoulder. 'If there's a fancy dress contest, I doubt if you'll win a prize but I can guarantee that people will point you out!'

Shepherd flashed Jimbo a thin smile and set off to make a careful recce of the area. The top of the hill on which the Acropolis stood was like a giant construction yard. After centuries of neglect, many of the ancient stones and columns had been sorted into piles as part of the long overdue reconstruction of one of the most sacred sites in Greece. Those gave him ample cover, making the recce relatively easy as he climbed the hill and made his way around the holy sites. The grass underfoot had been burned brown by the relentless summer sun and the leaves on the trees lower down the hill had shrivelled in the heat.

Most of the action was centred on the Parthenon, where there was an uneasy stand-off between the terrorists, who had surrounded themselves with tourist hostages, using them as human shields, and the Greek riot police and paramilitaries – a couple of dozen men, dressed in steel grey pyjama type clothing, some armed with pistols – who were trying, without too much success, to maintain some semblance of control over the area.

It was a surreal sight, with concentric circles of armed terrorists, their hapless captives and the security forces, yet immediately beyond them, there were still groups of tourists in summer clothing, apparently unconcerned as they sat in the boiling sun. Some of the tourist guides' umbrellas were raised, showing the name of the tourist companies, and sightseers were still snapping pictures of the ruins. Even the people walking away towards safety were strolling along as if they didn't have a care in the world.

Shepherd ignored them, quickly identifying the police sniper positions before spending the bulk of his time studying the terrorists. He used his binoculars from the shade of a stone pillar, studying every detail of what they were wearing and the weapons and explosives they were carrying. He made his way back to the rest of the group and gave them a briefing. 'It's pretty ragged,' he said. 'Parts of the police cordon appear to be extremely porous, with people seemingly coming and going at will. It's more like a works outing or a picnic than a terrorist siege.'

'I got a good look at some of the bad guys and it is worrying. I put the glasses on them and they're acting like automatons, or zombies, almost as if they're already dead. Each of them is wearing a mask at all times, obscuring their faces, they seem to be communicating only by hand signals and they are all wearing a necklace and wristbands of det-cord, ready to be triggered by a hand-held detonator. So if they release the pressure either deliberately or involuntarily after being shot, the det-cord will blow off their head and hands, with the obvious intention of making identification virtually impossible. The only other notable point – if it is notable and not just a coincidence – is that almost all of the hostages appear to be Asians: Chinese, Japanese, or maybe Koreans.'

Simos, who had been talking to the police commanders on site, brought them up to speed with what he'd discovered. 'The automatic initial assumption was that they are al-Qaeda,' he said. 'But it's pure speculation because there's been no attempt to negotiate for the release of hostages and no one is claiming responsibility. And there's been almost no comms chatter at all. The terrorists are apparently acting on a one-way radio link from some unknown source, because they're wearing earpieces, but as far as we can tell there has been no communication to them as yet.'

Shepherd frowned. 'Are we absolutely sure there isn't some back-channel communication going on? If the government was trying to buy off the terrorists

with a ransom payment, they certainly wouldn't want
it known, both because it would merely increase the
chances of further hostage incidents and because all
NATO countries have made a solemn and binding
commitment that they will never pay ransoms in terrorist situations.'

Simos spread his hands. 'My friend, they may
be negotiating a ransom payment, but if so, it is not
being done through police or military channels, so
we'll only know about it afterwards... if then.'

They went inside the Incident Management
Centre, passing a communications room, an operations room and an intelligence centre. Across the
corridor was a small room for the negotiators,
linked by field telephone to the "business" area of
the Parthenon, though the terrorists had shown no
apparent interest in negotiating with them. That
room was next to the one housing the assault team
and between the two a wooden contraption, known
as "The Stress Indicator", had been mounted on the
wall. It consisted of a circular wooden disc about
the size of a bicycle wheel and was painted in three
coloured triangles to indicate the degree of tension
being shown by the hostage takers. Blue denoted
calm, amber heightened tension and red would indicate that the situation was spiralling out of control,
necessitating immediate action.

They wandered into the assault team room. In
passing, Shepherd directed a questioning glance at
the negotiators and received a quick shake of the

head in reply. The members of the assault team were sprawled around their area relaxing, with belts undone and coveralls unzipped.

Shepherd stopped to speak to one of the negotiators. 'Anything yet?'

'Nothing. We've tried everything we have to contact them but they're just not interested. So there's not a lot we can do until they decide to talk to us.'

'Strange, isn't it?' Shepherd said. 'They must be doing this for a reason. Maybe they're negotiating with someone else we don't know about.'

They followed Simos into the operations room. 'We don't know how long this is going to go on for, Simos,' Shepherd said. 'But I think we'd better prepare for the long haul. I've got three guys here who have nothing else to do but are perfectly capable of running the Control Point. That would free up your guys to do something else more important. What do you think?'

'Good plan,' Simos said.

Shepherd called Rupert, Chas and Dave together. 'Okay guys,' he said. 'This is the drill: the Control Point books everyone, and I mean everyone, in and out of the incident site. We need to know which of our people are on the site, what they are doing, how they are dressed, time on site and time off site, and all of this has got to be logged. From now on this is what you're going to do. Simos will introduce you to the guys who are doing it now, so you can sort out a takeover with them, and then you'll run it from here on in. If anyone tries to short-cut the system, let Simos know and he'll come down on them like a ton of bricks. And guys? This isn't fobbing you off with a "McJob". This system is absolutely central to the outcome of any incident. Any questions?'

As dusk turned to night, a strange calm settled over the city. Shepherd walked out onto the Acropolis and again skillfully used the cover of the ruins and the piles of stones awaiting restoration to work his way towards the groups of terrorists and hostages near the Parthenon. There was a surprising amount of light from the stars overhead and using his binoculars he was able to see the hostage-takers clearly. They were showing signs of agitation, some of them had unslung their weapons and they were pushing and prodding the hostages into a ragged line. Shepherd sensed at once that the situation had gone critical.

'Go! Go! Go!' he whispered into his radio, at the same time unstrapping the MP 5 from his chest. Emerging from cover, he began to walk towards the terrorists, just as they began to shoot the hostages.

As Shepherd approached the terrorists, who seemed to be firing at random into the hostage groups, he had flicked on his sighting torch and, firing from the hip, shot the nearest terrorist through the eye. A fraction of a second later there was a detonation and the head of the terrorist disappeared in a cloud of blood and brains. He switched his aim to the next terrorist and repeated the action with the same result: another explosion. It was only then that

the other terrorists became aware that he was there
and began to target him. Several rounds flicked his
equipment but such was his concentration that he
barely noticed. He advanced remorselessly, taking
out targets in the half light, always with the same
aftermath, the terrorist's head exploding and covering the surrounding area with blood, bone and
tissue.

Jock and Geordie had arrived at the Control
Point moments after Jimbo, with Aimee at his heels,
had started sprinting towards Shepherd. Without a
second's pause Jock and Geordie also dashed towards
the gunfire, guided by the muzzle-flashes from the
weapons. They could make out Shepherd's silhouette
from the light of the torch strapped to the barrel of
his MP 5 and reached him just in time to help him
deal with the remaining terrorists.

In his haste to help his friend, Jock tripped and
fell on the uneven surface just as Shepherd was dis-
patching yet another terrorist. An unstable partially
re-assembled stone column crashed down on Jock's
forearm, trapping it, crushing the bones and almost
severing it from his upper arm. Within seconds
Aimee was kneeling beside him, unzipping her medical pack.

Soon afterwards the area was a mass of bodies going through post-incident procedures, with
the assault team separating the hostages from the
dead terrorists and forcibly evacuating the site. The
ambulance crews worked on the wounded and began

transporting the most seriously injured to hospital while treating the minor wounds on site until ambulances were available to take them away.

While Aimee checked Jock's airway and tightened compression bandages around the wound in an attempt to stem the bleeding, his mates carefully lifted the stone column from his crushed arm. 'We've got to get him to hospital fast,' Geordie said, concern etched on his face.

Aimee nodded. 'The wound looks pretty bad, but it's not life-threatening. He's relatively young and fit and strong as an ox, so if we stop the bleeding and then monitor his vital signs for indications of any worsening in his condition he should be OK for now. If he goes to the hospital he'll only be left on a trolley in a corridor while the ERT guys work on the more serious cases, so as long as we look after him, there's no rush until the panic dies down. The first thing we need to do is a one hundred per cent check to make sure there are no other injuries that we've missed.'

As Patrol Medic, Geordie might easily have been peeved to see Aimee dealing with Jock's injury instead of him, but he had no ego where treating casualties was concerned. Having satisfied himself that her diagnosis and the treatment she was proposing were correct, he was content to work alongside her to treat his mate's injuries and ease his pain. While the two of them were dealing with their patient, Shepherd was deep in thought. 'It might be quicker if we can casevac him on the 125 back to the UK,' he said. 'Jimbo, get through to the Skipper, explain the situation and find out what the flying time is to the UK, will you? The best place for Jock to be would be the Centre for Defence Medicine at Birmingham but we must make him fit for travel before we can make a move. Ask the Skipper for his advice, but it might be best if we go direct to Brum International.'

A tense half-hour passed before Aimee and Geordie were able to report that all the major blood vessels in Jock's arm had been either tied or clamped off, and the bleeding from the minor blood vessels was being controlled by compression bandages. 'In my opinion,' she said, 'I think he's fit to travel but we can't hang around too long because the wound is filthy and there is a chance of gangrene setting in. If he starts to bleed again *en route* we will have to divert to the nearest airfield and hope that any hospital within range of it has the right type of blood.'

'Not a problem,' Geordie said. 'Spider and me are universal donors, both O Positive. As long as you have cannulas, we could donate almost one-to-one. So if he's okay to move, let's get him back to the Management Centre where he'll be more comfortable.'

Jock, who was ghost-white and had been drifting in and out of consciousness, was listening to the exchange and spoke through gritted teeth. 'Get me back to the UK. It's the best place for me to be if they are going to save my arm.'

CHAPTER 19

As soon as they reached cruising altitude after leaving Athens International, Chamberlain was able to speak with the operations team at RAF HQ Air Command in High Wycombe and he quickly outlined the situation. After a crisp 'Wait Out', a calm female voice came through the headphones. She identified herself as the officer in charge of repatriating patients back to the UK, asked Aimee about Jock's condition, congratulated her on how she and the patient were both doing and said she was handing them back to operations but would speak to them again in a few minutes.

Another calm voice, male this time, outlined to Chamberlain the contingency plans they had in place. Along the route there were pre-selected airfields and hospitals to which the 125 could be diverted in the event of any deterioration in the patient's condition. It was a tried and tested system that had been used frequently over the years to repatriate wounded service personnel from the Middle East. With the responsibility removed from his shoulders,

Chamberlain visibly relaxed, and even Shepherd, Geordie and Jimbo stopped looking so anxious.

Every ten minutes, as regular as clockwork, the casevac officer spoke to Aimee, who relayed Jock's vital signs and general overall condition. Jock meanwhile had gone into a self-induced semi-hypnotic state, something he had taught himself over the years.

The follow-up from the terrorist attack at the Parthenon came in an immediate statement from al-Qaeda claiming responsibility that was relayed to them on the aircraft. 'But that's got to be bullshit, hasn't it?' Jimbo said. 'Those guys weren't Arabs or Chechens or any of the usual al-Qaeda groups. What was left of them looked more like they were Chinese or Korean, or something.'

Shepherd shrugged. 'Maybe. I agree it didn't look like the normal al-Qaeda MO but there are Muslim minorities in China and a lot of other Asian countries, so you can't rule it out.'

As they transited over France they were updated on how Jock's situation would be managed on their arrival in the UK. 'London air traffic control will give you priority clearance through to RAF Northolt, where you will be met by a surgical team and a helicopter which will transport the patient to the Centre for Defence Medicine in Birmingham. This is a better option than the 125 flying direct to Birmingham International.'

In the event, everything worked as planned. As soon as the jet had landed, Chamberlain was ordered to stop on the main runway and a Chinook helicopter landed beside it. A group of medical personnel, dressed in green operating theatre overalls, flooded into the cabin of the 125 and after a very short examination, Jock was transferred on a stretcher into the Chinook. One of the newcomers asked who had been looking after Jock.

'I have,' Aimee said.

'We need to know everything that happened from when he sustained the injury until now.'

Once Aimee had updated them on Jock's injury and treatment, the Chinook took off in a storm of dust and the 125 then taxied to its stand, where it was met by a party of RAF policemen wearing their customary white peaked caps. One of them, obviously a senior NCO, stuck his head into the cabin and barked 'Right you lot, which ones are the prisoners?'

Shepherd looked at Jimbo and Geordie and gave a weary smile. 'What do you know? Here we go again ...'

While Jock was on his way to the Centre for Defence Medicine, the departure of the rest of this patrol mates from Northolt was almost comical. They were driven to the station helipad escorted by the posse of RAF policemen and the Snowdrops, clearly nervous, kept eyeing the SAS guys as if expecting them to erupt at any second, while Geordie eyed them up in return and did not try to hide his contempt.

A Lynx helicopter was sitting on the pad, with the engines already idling and blades slowly circling.

A crewman standing in the open door gestured to Shepherd. 'Right mate, get yourself and your oppos aboard.'

'How many more seats have you got?' the senior Snowdrop said, preparing to clamber in after them.

'None mate, we've only got room for three.'

'But they're on close arrest. They can't go without a police escort.'

The only reply was 'Mind your fingers, mate,' as the crewman slid the door shut.

They were soon flying low and fast, west across the Cotswolds, bypassing RAF Fairford and Brize Norton and swooping over the escarpment above Gloucester. From there they could see the whole of the plain spread out westwards towards the Welsh mountains. Looking between the shoulders of the two pilots, in the far distance Shepherd could just make out the array of satellite dishes and towering aerials located at the training base known to everyone in the Regiment as "PATA".

Dotted around the training area and dug into the side of the small hill at the centre of the area were a number of massive, bomb-proof bunkers that had been used to store cordite blocks that were manufactured during the Second World War at an ammunition factory on the outskirts of Hereford. Cordite was stored on the site into the 1960s, but when that came to an end, the area was offered to the Regiment. The unused cordite blocks were burned by the thousands of tons, and as the bunkers became vacant, they were converted into a wide variety of uses. These uses were never referred to by name but by the bunker number, so that even within the Regiment, if you hadn't been invited inside a bunker, you would have no way of knowing what activities went on there. The one exception was Bunker 10, which was used for the interrogation training that every badged SAS trooper had to go through as part of the Regiment's brutal Selection process.

PATA was included in the MOD's list of training areas and in theory was available for any army unit to use, but if any other unit tried to book it, PATA was never available. Although it was a secret base, the aerials couldn't be disguised even though they advertised its location and its importance, but they were indispensable if the Regiment was to be able to communicate worldwide at a moment's notice.

As the chopper went into the hover prior to landing, Shepherd was able to see the area across the hill from the bunkers. To the untrained eye, it looked like any other rural scene in England, with fields and copses of trees surrounding a small village nestled in the bowl of the hills. Only an expert eye like Shepherd's would have identified the sophisticated open air range, complete with sniper positions, and the newly built village used to simulate hostage situations, in which live rounds could be fired in a 360 degree arc, the only range of its type in Europe.

They landed on the grass outside Bunker 8, scattering geese and sheep as they landed. The geese were better guards than humans and the sheep kept the grass short, so that human maintenance was kept to a minimum. After they'd disembarked, the helicopter took off again while an escort in camouflaged uniform led them into the bunker. Shepherd and the others had been inside many times and knew that it was designated the Anti-Terrorist Cell, where all intelligence relating to past, present and possible future operations worldwide, was collated and pored over by a small, select staff, not all of them from the SF and not all of them British.

They were taken to a small room and were unsurprised to find the General who was Director, Special Forces, and a sharply dressed, middle-aged man with a rather patrician air were sitting behind desks, waiting for them. They shuffled into a semblance of standing to attention and said 'Morning, sir'.

'Morning boys,' was the affable reply. 'I'll let my guest introduce himself.'

'Take a seat, gentlemen,' the other man said. 'Make yourself comfortable, this may take a little while. You probably know who I am.'

'No, can't say I do,' Geordie said.

The man sat back sharply as if he'd been slapped. It was obvious that he was not used to being spoken to like this.

'Rein yourself in Mitchell,' the Director said. 'Remember His Lordship is my guest.'

His Lordship tried again. 'I apologise for dragging you all this way but it is almost impossible to have a meeting in London without it being leaked all over the bloody Daily Telegraph, whereas at least here everything is below the radar. I'm here as part of a Parliamentary delegation, so it was an easy matter to arrange to have you brought along. We have been able to keep your existence out of the press and I wished to meet you in person, firstly to thank you and secondly to ask for your further support. There is no need for names but I am a government minister and I sit in the House of Lords, not in the Commons. There is a reason for this…'

He hesitated and Shepherd finished his sentence for him. 'Yeah, it's so you are not subject to too much detailed questioning.'

His Lordship started to purse his lips in annoyance at another interruption, but then inclined his head in acknowledgement. 'Quite so, quite so. Now my remit to the government is the whole field of terrorism, both here and around the world. As you know, largely thanks to your expertise, we in the UK are considered the world leaders in the field. Our friends and allies look to us for guidance and when some new threat crops up, we are expected to be in the vanguard of the response to that threat. However, at the moment we are in something of a quandary. We are close to a lock-down situation in all the UK's major cities. Every armed policeman is out on the streets, although frankly we don't have the greatest confidence in their ability to contain major terrorist incidents; too many innocent people have been killed and injured by terrorists for us to be comfortable. Your own Regiment has been deployed as well but this is mainly to give politicians like me the confidence and the backbone to deal with a major terrorist situation if it arises. At the same time, we would like to offer support to our friends and allies wherever and whenever it is needed, and this is where you and your team come in. In short, we would like you gentlemen to be available to respond if or when there is another violent terrorist incident that affects our friends and allies, like the one in Athens that I gather you dealt with so capably. I realise it is a lot to ask when you have already been separated from your families for some time, but we cannot see any other viable solution. We simply do not have the manpower or assets to do it any other way.'

Shepherd glanced at the others. 'We might be willing to get involved,' he said, 'but for one small problem. We're on open arrest, awaiting court martial.'

His Lordship made a gesture with his hand as if flicking crumbs off his immaculately pressed trousers. 'I can't do anything about the court martial, I'm afraid, that is out of my hands.' He turned to look at the Director who shifted a little uncomfortably in his chair.

'You have been charged by an officer of General rank' the Director said, 'and I can't interfere with the judicial process. But strictly between us this is only internal MOD politics, someone trying to harm the Regiment. As you know, we have no shortage of friends in high places, so I guarantee it will all be sorted out when your Officer Commanding gets back to the UK from Afghanistan. Meanwhile, your being on open arrest will not be a problem. You can use the same resources that you used in Athens, including the escort.'

'Do we get to see our families first?' Geordie said.

'I'm afraid not. No one is to know that you are here and that includes your families. Is that clear?'

There was a brief hesitation before Geordie gave a reluctant nod.

'Right,' Shepherd said. 'We'll do it, of course, as you knew we would, but we need a full inventory of kit, weapons and ammo with full support for any other thing we ask for. If that's agreed, then we'll go.'

The Director nodded. 'You can request any support you think you might need through my office and I guarantee you will get it. Meanwhile, the heli is over at Credenhill being loaded as we speak. It will be back in a few minutes and you can then get your arses back to Northolt. In the meantime, you can wait outside.'

After they had filed out, His Lordship gave the Director a doubtful look. 'Can't you do anything about this court martial situation? It seems to me to be very unfair, asking them to possibly risk their lives with nothing in return.'

'Believe me, Your Lordship, it's just MOD politics, and it will get kicked into the long grass and then quietly forgotten.'

'But why do they do it, with so little reward?'

'As to their motivation, I think it's largely out of loyalty to the Regiment and the SAS hierarchy, including me, of course.'

'Strange that,' His Lordship said quietly. 'I got the distinct impression they thought you were a bit of a shit.'

CHAPTER 20

Shepherd, Geordie and Jimbo had barely landed back at Northolt when they saw Rupert hurrying towards them. The suppressed excitement on his face suggested he had big news for them. 'We're getting reports of an incident in Paris,' he said. 'Terrorists have forced their way into the Louvre and taken scores of hostages. They're now holed up in one of the galleries.'

'Fucking hell, it never rains but it pours,' Jimbo said. 'To think a few short weeks ago I was complaining about having nothing to do.'

Shepherd frowned. 'These incidents have got to be related. It's too much of a coincidence that two of the world's most famous tourist sites are hit by terrorists.'

'So who and what are we dealing with?' Rupert said.

'That's what we need to find out.'

The "heads up" on the incident in Paris had come from the anti-terrorist liaison officer in the British Embassy. The details were sparse, just people being held hostage and casualties in a terrorist incident at the Louvre. But that was enough for Shepherd and the rest to pile onto the 125. The same pilot and co-pilot were flying them and by now, his earlier hostility apparently forgotten, the Wingco was all smiles and greeting them like old friends. 'I think I preferred it when he hated us,' Geordie muttered as they took their seats.

They did a "hot take-off" through the crowded skies over London, heading for Le Bourget, and were able to cleave a pathway through the dense air traffic by preceding their call sign with Alpha Sierra, the call sign only allocated to flights of the highest priority. Also on board were the waterproof sports bags containing their equipment, arms and ammo. The bags were all closed with diplomatic seals, while the accompanying diplomatic carnets to get them through any customs without being opened or checked, were safely tucked in Shepherd's pocket.

The flight took just under an hour and during it they kept their ears glued to the radio news channels, though very few further details were forthcoming. The French government had imposed a news blackout about the incident and the gendarmerie had already arrested several news reporters, cameramen and photographers and confiscated their cameras. 'Shame they're not quite as efficient at arresting terrorists, isn't it?' Geordie said.

Whether or not they were connected to the main incident, there were also reports of riots breaking out among the disaffected young residents of Middle

Eastern origin or descent in the *arrondissements* to the south and east of Paris.

So intent were the passengers on what was coming over the headphones that when, on its final approach to Le Bourget, the Wingco threw the aircraft into a sharp turn to the left before leveling out again, they grabbed instinctively at the arms of their seats and looked around perplexed. After landing the Wingco looked back into the cabin. 'Sorry about that chaps, but the approach here means we have to aim as if we're landing at Charles de Gaulle airport and then at fairly low-level, we have to do a very quick adjustment to get onto this runway. A bit dramatic but perfectly safe.'

'Not a problem,' Shepherd said. 'Though a little advance warning wouldn't have hurt. Now, the four of us will head into Paris. 'You and your co-pilot stay here at Le Bourget and follow the same drill as in Athens, keeping abreast of events and the aircraft fully fuelled and ready to go.'

As they disembarked, Shepherd noticed a small jet with German Luftwaffe markings parked next to them on the apron. 'Looks like GSG 9 got here before us,' he said.

Jimbo intercepted Rupert's questioning look. 'It stands for *Grenzschutzgruppe 9 der Bundezpolizei*, the German police unit responsible for dealing with terrorist incidents,' he said.

'I expect Delta Force and the FBI won't be far behind either,' Geordie said, scanning the skies as if he expected them to appear out of the clouds at any moment.

'Then let's get there ahead of them.'

As they walked towards the terminal building, they spotted several helicopters parked around the airfield, used to transfer personnel to the heliport close to the Eiffel Tower or direct to the open areas near the Louvre, thus avoiding the heavy traffic between the airport and city centre. Among the helicopters were a couple of Super Pumas. 'Presumably they're keeping those in readiness for a heli assault if it all goes pear-shaped,' Jimbo said.

They completed their arrival formalities with the minimum of fuss and delay and were then directed to a police people carrier, with a pair of motorcycle outriders waiting alongside it. The four men jumped in to the people carrier and they sped off out of the airport. As the motorcycles, blue lights flashing and sirens going, carved their way expertly through the heavy traffic on the AutoRoute and Le Peripherique, quicker-witted drivers latched on behind the police people carrier, eventually forming a long convoy.

While they were driving, Shepherd was finally able to talk to Jock on the GCHQ secure satellite phone. Having checked that he was okay, Shepherd was about to bring him up to speed on the incident when he discovered that Jock had not been idle at the hospital and was well ahead of them.

Jock's room in the hospital in Birmingham had been transformed into a makeshift operations centre, complete with maps, computers and communications kit, receiving information from GCHQ at Cheltenham, Hereford, Northwood and the Ministry of Defence. Assisted by a couple of Intelligence Corps collators, Jock was sifting through the intelligence and trying to make sense of it all. He asked Shepherd to send as much information from the incident as he could, ideally anything on CCTV that showed the hostage takers.

The escort delivered Shepherd's group to a checkpoint in the inner cordon, from where they walked to an imposing building close to the Louvre. They were taken to the Incident Management Centre in a large, high-ceilinged room decorated with frescoes on the walls and ceiling showing scenes from Napoleon's victories.

A group of Germans from GSG 9 were already there, drinking coffee and looking expectantly at any new arrivals. Their lack of weapons and smug expressions suggested that they were regarding this trip as a no risk op. One of the Germans stood up and shook Shepherd's hand. 'Now the English have arrived, things will get done,' he said, beaming. 'We have been kept here waiting for half an hour, which is not usual. We expect to be treated with more respect by our friends at GIGN.'

'It's not like the old days any more,' said Shepherd. 'There's too much politicking now. In the past, the bosses of GSG 9, GIGN and the SAS dictated policy and co-operation, but now nothing is done unless the impact has already been calculated in advance by some politician. So don't expect GIGN to do anything until the French Prime Minister or President has assessed the political gains if the terrorists are taken out, and the political fall-out if the hostages are killed.'

'GIGN?' Rupert murmured, looking embarrassed. 'I'm sorry, but who or what are they?'

Jimbo sighed. '*Groupe d'Intervention de la Gendarmerie Nationale,*' he said, with exaggerated patience, as if teaching a slow learner the alphabet. 'Part of the French armed forces.'

'They were formed in 1973,' Shepherd said, 'just after the formation of the SAS counter-terrorist team and GSG 9. Those groups were responsible for some of the first successes in the early days of the fight against terrorism. GSG 9 cleared a hijacked Lufthansa jet at Mogadishu and GIGN did the same on an Air France jet at Marseille. The SAS were at both incidents as supposed observers but helped out with expertise and weaponry, particularly stun grenades. That set the tone for the informal co-operation that has continued up to the present day, though lately things have been less smooth and that's entirely down to political interference. Politicians do not trust military guys unless they think it will help their careers – think no further than Maggie Thatcher and the Iranian embassy.'

Just then a tall, well-built man entered the room. He was in civilian clothes – a dark blue three-piece suit – but his bearing marked him out as police or army. He glanced at the Germans, then walked over to the SAS team. 'I've come from the British Embassy,' he said. 'I'm the Anti-terrorist Liaison Officer seconded from the Metropolitan Police and I've been told to offer any assistance to you that I can.'

Shepherd looked up at him. 'Thanks, but assistance to us? Seriously? Such as?'

His smile faded. 'Erm- Well, I thought I might be able to help you on things like risk assessment. I know the army are not very good at such things.'

'Risk assessment? On us or the hostages?' Geordie said, making the question sound more like a declaration of war.

Shepherd smiled. 'I'm afraid you've had a wasted journey. We've already got everything we need for risk assessment right here,' he said, nudging the sports bag with his foot just hard enough for the weapons it contained to make a metallic sound.

The Liaison Officer's face flushed in a mixture of embarrassment and anger.

'Look,' Jimbo said, adopting a more kindly tone. 'I'm sure you mean well and we appreciate the offer, but we train relentlessly for just this kind of terrorist situation and we've dealt with at least a dozen actual incidents, as well as countless contacts with enemy forces all over the world. We're the most highly skilled and highly trained counter-terrorist force in the world so, with great respect and sugar on top, what could the Metropolitan Police possibly teach us that we don't already know?'

STEPHEN LEATHER

The policeman opened his mouth to speak again but then fell silent and sat down on the far side of the room. The ensuing silence was broken by the arrival of another newcomer, this time a man dressed in similar black coveralls to the ones the SAS wore, with a leather belt and cross-straps, and a rolled-up black balaclava on his head. He looked to be in his late twenties or early thirties, with short dark hair and bony, prominent features. An MP 5K was strapped across his chest and he had an automatic pistol holstered on his hip.

He took in the different groups in the room at a glance, then nodded to Shepherd and said in lightly accented English. 'I am Guy,' he said, pronouncing it the English way. 'You and your team come with me, please.'

The rest of the people in the room had stood up expectantly and the Met Liaison Officer said, 'What about me?'

Guy shook his head. 'These people have something I need. Everybody else stay here until someone comes for you.'

He ignored the glares that the Germans were directing at him and led the SAS men out of the room. As he did so, Shepherd heard Guy mutter to himself '*A bas les Boches.*'

They followed him down the corridor. 'What have we got that he needs?' Geordie whispered.

'Knowledge,' Shepherd said.

Guy led them into another room with a high vaulted ceiling, this time decorated with overblown

234

scenes from the life of Joan of Arc. A bank of TV screens half-covered one wall, some showing internal CCTV images of the hostage situation and the surrounding area, while other, larger screens were streaming news channels from countries across the world. A few more men in black coveralls were sitting in a semi-circle, talking quietly but with their gaze never leaving the CCTV images. Others in police uniform or civilian clothes were monitoring telephones and radio handsets. Everything had a calm, quiet, efficient and organised feel.

'Bit different from the chaos in Athens, isn't it?' Jimbo said as he looked around.

Guy turned to face them. 'I'm the GIGN assault group commander, and we're facing a very puzzling situation.' Shepherd knew that GIGN was the tactical unit of the French National Gendarmerie, tasked with counter-terrorism and hostage rescue. 'In all my years' experience I've not seen anything quite like it. As you'll have realised, the Louvre is one of our key sites, and we have reconnoitered, rehearsed and practised endlessly for just such an eventuality. We know every sniper position and entry point and my men have an Area of Exploitation almost within touching distance of the hostage takers. So if we're given the go-ahead, this would all be finished in a few seconds, but I'm getting pressure from my bosses not to do anything, Normally we would expect the hostage takers to be negotiating to get out of the building and probably out of the country, and we would be counter-negotiating to keep them bottled up. But there is no apparent attempt to negotiate and they have not asked for transport, food or water. In fact they have asked for nothing at all. Yet still our bosses want us to do nothing while the poor souls inside are terrified of being killed.'

'Perhaps your bosses are worried about the paintings,' Geordie said.

'Pah! That cannot be it. Everything on show is probably fake anyway.'

'Then perhaps your political masters are not giving you the whole picture,' Shepherd said. 'We had the same situation in Athens and the suspicion there was that, in clear breach of the counter-terrorist agreements that all our governments have signed up to, a ransom deal was being negotiated behind the scenes. Perhaps the same thing is happening here?'

Guy paused while he pondered that. 'Perhaps. Anyway, since you were involved in the Athens incident, which may well be connected to this, I'd be grateful for any input and help you can give us.' He smiled. 'And if an immediate action becomes necessary, perhaps you will feel a little less constrained by our government's caution than we are.'

While they were talking, Shepherd was intently studying the CCTV images of the terrorists. 'It looks like a carbon copy of Athens,' he said. 'And these guys have the same dead eyes.' He thought for a moment. 'Guy, our mate Jock would love to be able to see these pictures and he could give us some valuable input.

He was injured on a recent op, so he's in hospital in the UK, but while his body has taken a battering, his mind is still razor sharp, so if your people can fix a link to get the real time CCTV pictures to him, I'm sure he'll make a valuable contribution.'

Guy shrugged. 'That will not be a problem.' He called one of his communications specialists over, explained the problem and then left him and Rupert to sort out the mechanics of it.

'Do you think Rupert's up to it?' Geordie said.

'It doesn't involve combat or require too much in the way of brain power,' Shepherd said. 'So he should be all right.'

'Don't you need your bosses approval?' Jimbo said to Guy.

He grinned. 'If you'll excuse the Anglo-Saxon English, 'Fuck 'em!''

'So how does a Frenchman come to speak such fucking fluent Anglo-Saxon!' Shepherd said.

'Well, I'm only fifty per cent French. My mother is English and my father was a middle ranking French colonial officer. They met in Reunion when he had been posted there to administer to the indigenous people and she was back-packing around the world in her gap year. So I grew up bilingual. I spent my early years moving around the remaining colonial territories and attending a succession of mediocre schools but I had a close up view of the French state in action.' He gave a self-deprecating smile. 'Not always an uplifting experience, because the grandiose press releases and lofty mission statements produced by my father, among others, were often in sharp contrast to the harsh reality for the people we ruled. So, if you like, those experiences gave me a vocation to protect the underdog, and when I finished my patchy education I enlisted in the *Gendarmerie Nationale*. After pounding the beat for a couple of years, my knowledge of English got me seconded to GIGN. I soon realised that I wanted to be much more than just a liaison officer, so I applied for and passed Selection. After spending time in all the various sections of the Force, I found myself in the Assault Group, and luckily I'm now its boss.'

'I doubt that luck had much to with it,' Shepherd said with a smile. 'Unless things have changed a lot in recent years, GIGN team leaders are like SAS ones: chosen on merit.'

While they'd been talking, Shepherd, Geordie and Jimbo had been donning their assault gear and weapons, ready to go forward with Guy. As they fitted their MP 5Ks Shepherd glanced at the weapon across Guy's chest. 'One thing must have changed though, I thought you guys were "encouraged" only to use French manufactured weapons?'

Guy smiled. 'My political bosses don't have to do what I have to do. So my men and I smile and nod at them, and then go ahead and use the best available, wherever it might happen to come from, and if the top guys don't like it, well, they can come and do the job themselves!'

Every person who would be involved in the assault was issued with a radio and given a call sign which they wrote on small yellow patches worn on the chest, high up on both sleeves and on their backs. That allowed instant identification in the event of reduced visibility due to the use of smoke or gas, and told medics treating any man down their blood group and any other relevant medical information.

They were about to leave the Incident Control Centre and move forward through the Louvre when Shepherd's sat-phone rang and he heard a familiar Glaswegian accent. 'Spider, I'm starting to unravel a few things. First, just like Athens, these guys are walking IEDs – they're suicide bombers – but it looks as if they're wired up not to cause massive casualties but, again like Athens, to prevent them being captured alive and stop their bodies being ID'd. I'm certain they're holding pressure release switches in their hands so when they want to wipe themselves out or if they're shot, the hand automatically opens and detonates the charge, blowing their heads and hands apart and making identification much harder, if not impossible. I've also noticed that they never go far from the hostages, so we've got to find some way to prevent them from becoming collateral damage if these guys decide to off themselves. So you need weapons with enough kinetic energy to throw them back a few yards when they're hit.'

'I think I know what might do it,' Shepherd said. 'I'll get back to you. Out.' He broke the connection and turned to Guy. 'Have you got any baton rounds or solid shot 12-bore ammo in your armoury?'

'We have both. The baton rounds and launchers came from H & K, when we bought the MP 5's, and for the solid shot we have Remington 12-gauge which we've been using to blow locks and hinges off doors. We've also been experimenting to see if they would shatter an engine block and bring the vehicle to a halt. I'll get some brought up.' He unleashed a torrent of French into his throat-mic and within a couple of minutes another of the assault team arrived at a run, carrying two shotguns with bandoliers of ammunition, and two Heckler & Koch 104A plastic bullet launchers.

'Are these what you were thinking of?' Guy said.

'Just the job,' Shepherd said. 'Now let's run through the pros and cons and decide which of them will do the job best.'

After a brief discussion they plumped for the shotgun, purely on the grounds that it held seven rounds in the magazine and one in the chamber against the single shot of the H & K 104A.

They then divided into two pairs, Shepherd carried a Remington and was supported by Guy with an MP 5K, with Geordie taking the other Remington and Jimbo backing him with an MP 5K.

'If it all kicks off, remember to aim high,' Shepherd said to Geordie. 'Go for the forehead.'

Guy made a final quick check with the negotiators, who reported 'No change, they are still not talking.' The four men then signed themselves out of the Control Centre and left the building.

A police cordon had been thrown around the whole area, keeping spectators and media far enough back to remove any possibility of unauthorised live television pictures being seen by the terrorists or a look-out in the crowd alerting them. Unseen by anyone, Guy and the SAS men crossed the road, pulling their balaclavas down as they made their way down the ramp to the vehicle entrance to the museum. Another two members of the assault team were guarding the door, stationed there not so much to restrict access – the police cordon would do that – as to ensure that the terrorists remained contained.

Maintaining absolute silence, Guy led them through a series of galleries. In other circumstances they would have been stopping to stare at the priceless paintings, familiar from a thousand illustrations in magazines and on TV but, focused entirely on their task, they passed them with barely a glance. As they entered another gallery, they linked up with the GIGN advance team who were maintaining a watch on the terrorists from a surprisingly close position. Shepherd and the others crouched down and crawled into place alongside them. From there, they were able to see and confirm what Jock had told them: each of the terrorists was holding a pistol in one hand while the other one was clenched tightly in a fist.

Shepherd was concentrating so hard that Geordie had to nudge him twice to get his attention, before indicating with his thumb the portrait of the Mona Lisa hanging alongside them. 'For fuck's sake don't hit that,' he breathed, 'or we'll end up in the Bastille!' It took a great effort of will to concentrate on the human tragedy unfolding in front of them while one of the most priceless artifacts known to man was only feet away from them.

Shepherd spent a long time studying the faces of the terrorists through the high-powered, stabilised binoculars that gave much better detail in the dim light than he would get through passive night goggles. Eventually, he thought he had identified the leader of the terrorists, who appeared to be silently communicating with the others through a series of nods and glances. He would be Shepherd's first target if the op went live. He then turned his attention to the hostages who, just as in Athens, appeared to be mainly Asian. He was trying to see if there appeared to be any "sleepers" among them, who would have to be dealt with, if and when the situation turned hostile.

For no visible reason the terrorist boss suddenly lifted his head, put a hand to his ear, and then without saying a word to the others, calmly began to shoot the hostages closest to him. Taking the lead from their boss, the other terrorists at once began to do the same.

'We can't wait for your assault team, let's go!' Shepherd shouted to Guy.

'Oui! Allez! Allez,! Allez!' Guy said, reverting to French for a moment.

They immediately split into their pairs, sprinting forward until they were only a few yards from the terrorists. Firing from the hip, Shepherd hit the terrorist boss in the middle of the forehead with a solid shot slug, knocking him backwards by several yards. He was probably dead already but, mopping up in Shepherd's wake, Guy put a near-simultaneous double tap of nine millimetre rounds from his MP 5 into him. If he wasn't dead from the Remington slug, he was definitely dead now.

As the terrorist somersaulted backwards, his body jerking as Guy's two rounds ripped into it, his fist unclenched. His head and hands were instantly vaporised by the blast as the explosives he was wearing detonated. He was well away from the hostages and caused little or no damage to them. Shepherd and Guy had already switched to their next target and the next, while Geordie and Jimbo were doing the same with other targets. The surviving terrorists had now stopped killing their hostages and were trying to direct their fire at the special forces men, but unlike the hostages, these were not passive targets but lethal killers. They were never still for a second, diving and rolling across the polished floors but maintaining such deadly accuracy that every round they fired struck a target. In the space of a handful of seconds, the terrorists had all been eliminated.

Most of the terrified hostages, though even more bewildered and disorientated by the rapidity and ferocity of the assault, had suffered only minor cuts and bruises from shrapnel from the explosives. However, four of them, the ones shot without warning by the terrorists, lay on the floor. One sprawled in a spreading pool of blood, but his agonised cries showed that he at least was still alive. The other three were unmoving and almost certainly dead.

Shepherd felt sick to his guts at the sight and, as always when innocent people were killed or caught in the cross-fire, his first thoughts were about the families, waiting at home for their loved ones, just as Sue was waiting in Hereford for him. Those three hostages would now never be coming home. His next thoughts, following close on the first, were also always the same: 'Were we too slow to act? Was there anything we could have done that would have kept those people alive?'

CHAPTER 21

The silence was deafening after the carnage and the noise of the gunfire and explosions. Shepherd slowly became aware of what was happening around him. The rest of the GIGN assault team had arrived and immediately cordoned off the hostages before quickly body-searching them and then rough-handling them out into the open air under escort. There was no guarantee that there was not still one or more terrorist sleepers among them, so they were all kept off balance, pushed and shoved roughly along a human chain of GIGN men, while others kept their weapons trained, alert for any suspicious movement that might indicate a terrorist reaching for a concealed weapon or grenade.

Some of the hostages were already in the first stages of Stockholm Syndrome and quite happy to obey the instructions of anybody who shouted orders at them, others were so overcome with a mixture of shock and relief they had to be helped bodily away from the scene. Shepherd looked around the gallery. It was now splattered with blood and gore and he wondered which unfortunate employee of the Louvre would have the job of clearing it up.

As they put their weapons in safe mode and were starting to relax, Geordie nudged Shepherd. 'You know what we were saying on the way in? Take a look at her now.'

'Take a look at who?' Shepherd said, but then followed Geordie's gaze and saw that the armoured glass protecting the Mona Lisa was now starred and crazed where a bullet fired by one of the terrorists had struck it.

He grinned. 'Thank God it was an Italian painting, if it had been a French Impressionist, we'd all be facing the guillotine by now.'

'You still might,' Guy said with an answering smile. 'Thanks for your help, but now I suggest you get out of here quick before the big bosses arrive and start asking embarrassing questions. I must stay here to sort out this mess, but you can have your own debrief and inquest. It will save you several days of your time, being questioned by an examining magistrate, and I can assure you that they won't like it if they find out that their faces have been saved by the English again. So let me know the outcomes of your debrief, but now go!'

They changed back into their street clothes, packing their operational gear into the ubiquitous sports bags, then moved quickly through the chaotic scenes outside the Incident Management Centre, where there were dozens of ambulances, police vehicles and fire tenders, all with wailing sirens. TV crews and reporters were arguing, pushing and shoving as they tried to get closer to the action, and riot police were beating back the crowds of curious onlookers behind barriers that were too flimsy to contain them.

Unnoticed among the chaos, the SAS men quietly commandeered a police van to take them back to Le Bourget. Once they reached the General Aviation Terminal there, Shepherd got the whole team together in a conference room. Using the encrypted satellite phones, they again set up a direct line to Jock's hospital room back in the UK, where he had been watching the drama unfold via a CCTV link. They began trying to make sense of what had just happened in the Louvre.

'The French government first tried to impose a total news blackout on the incident,' Jock said. 'Talk about locking the stable door after the horse has bolted. That didn't last very long and they've now been pushed into admitting that there was an attempted terrorist attack at the Louvre, but they're claiming that it was thwarted, thanks to the vigilance of the GIGN and the *Gendarmerie*. They've said that the terrorists have all been killed or arrested but there has been no acknowledgement of any other casualties or any damage to the Louvre and its exhibits. So even by government standards, it's a pretty misleading statement.'

Geordie chuckled. 'Well, they don't want inconvenient facts getting in the way of the French tourist trade, now do they?'

Shepherd was still mulling over the incident, replaying every detail in his mind. 'I think the bad guys must have had some sort of comms set-up, possibly receive only,' he said. 'Because just before the boss bloke started firing, he put his hand up to his ear as if he was listening to somebody. Why would he suddenly start firing for no apparent reason, unless someone had given him the order to do so?'

'It might have been intended to serve notice on other countries that these new kids on the terrorist block are to be taken very seriously, so don't try to spin out negotiations. Pay up and pay up quick and we might go away. I think both of these situations were set up as ransom demands. If you wanted to extort money in Europe, where would you go and have a fair chance of success? I think Greece and France would be pretty near the top of the list. Don't forget the lessons we learned years ago: terrorists and criminals need money just to exist. In Germany, for instance, the Red Army Faction was bankrolled by the East Germans – the DDR – but they still robbed banks to support their reign of terror. It's exactly the same for any terrorist group, they must have cash, because without it, they're toast.'

'Granted all that,' Shepherd said, 'but if so, why start killing the hostages? No one is going to pay a ransom if the hostages are already dead.'

'I've also found a backlog of emails,' Jock said. 'They were cached under UTS – Ultra Top Secret – so obviously not intended for our eyes, but they show that a few weeks before the Acropolis incident, a news agency in Athens received a call saying there would be a terrorist incident in Greece, nothing specific, but leaving a code word. So far, so normal. The agency informed the Greek government and luckily for us, they also informed their head office in London, who in turn notified Anti-terrorist Command in Scotland Yard so the UK could keep an eye on any developments. A few days later they received a second call, complete with the same code word, saying that they were serious and that there would be a deadly attack within 48 hours. Before the end of the deadline there was a shooting on a ferry between Piraeus and one of the Greek islands in which a couple of gunmen shot and killed a number of Greek citizens before throwing themselves into the sea. The killers' bodies were not recovered so there was no positive ID. Fortunately for the Greek authorities they were able to blame the killings on their domestic terrorist organisation, November 17, and that's how things stood until the atrocity at the Acropolis, but to me, all the indications are that the Greeks coughed up a ransom payment and were still left with a pile of bodies. Shades of Danegeld.'

'Dane-which?' Geordie said.

'Danegeld – what the Anglo Saxon kings paid the Vikings to go away. The Vikings took the money and then attacked anyway.'

'And if the ransom had already been paid when the firing started,' Jimbo said, 'then it's a win-win for the terrorists: take the cash and then kill them anyway.' He paused. 'But hang on, if that's what had happened in Athens, the French government would know, and they wouldn't pay a ransom knowing what the consequences were going to be anyway.'

'Call me cynical if you like,' Shepherd said, 'but if the Greek government had paid a ransom, in defiance of every anti-terrorist agreement between EU and Nato countries, they'd be keeping pretty quiet about it, wouldn't they? So maybe the French had no idea what had gone down in Athens and thought that by paying a ransom, they were actually making sure it didn't happen in Paris.'

'Maybe,' Jock said, 'or maybe, the terrorists who carried out the attacks had already been paid...by al-Qaeda. By all accounts they aren't short of funds so maybe they've started using hired guns to carry out some of their attacks. That would tie in with intercepts picked up by GCHQ. Just prior to everything kicking off, Cheltenham picked up a load of chatter emanating from Switzerland, much of it regarding the transfer of funds into and out of the country. When they looked back through their records, they found that just before the Athens thing kicked off, the same thing happened there. So it looks like some Swiss banker has been playing dirty.'

'Well, if you can persuade Northwood, Hereford and Cheltenham to support us,' Shepherd said, 'it sounds like the next stop should be Switzerland, but there's no point in going unless they provide us with

enough intelligence and back-up to achieve something when we get there.'

Such was the concern about the incidents in
Whitehall that the SAS team got the go ahead to
proceed to Switzerland within two hours and GCHQ
gave them the name of a bank in Zurich, the *Bank of
Commerz and Privat*, which they suspected was being
used in the transfers. That gave them a real chance
of identifying a suspect by mounting a surveillance
operation, because although it was much easier to
deal on the edge of illegality with Swiss banks than
any other banks in Europe, to comply with Swiss law,
the initial transfer paperwork always had to be done
in person. However, because of Swiss government
sensitivities, the SAS men's surveillance operation
would need to be carried out covertly. If the operation was compromised, the Swiss would not hesitate
to arrest and imprison anyone they suspected of ille-
gal activity on their sovereign territory.

The pilots went off to file a flight plan to Zürich,
only to return within a few minutes to report that
their request had been delayed by the Swiss because
it was a military flight. Depending on what part of the
country they came from, Swiss people spoke German,
French and Italian, and many of them also spoke
the language of international finance – English.
But when it came down to it, the only language that
really counted there was cold, hard cash. Neutrality
had proved very lucrative for the Swiss in two world
wars and they were fanatical about avoiding even

the appearance that they were favouring any foreign country over the rest. So they were never keen to allow foreign military aircraft access to their airports. The Wingco had therefore contacted the British Embassy in Switzerland to expedite their flight plan and had been told that the resident Military Attaché was working on the problem and expected to have it resolved within a few hours.

In the meantime, after downloading a map of downtown Zurich on to his laptop, Shepherd outlined a plan to the others, including Rupert, Chas and Dave, and Aimee. 'This is going to be a straight-forward surveillance operation, a total shot in the dark. We have nothing else to go on but Jock says there has been a lot of internet activity, so it is worth a try. However the only ones who know anything about surveillance are me and my two oppos here. So we are going to have to improvise. The hardest part of any surveillance operation is the pick-up – the starting point of the operation. This is when the subjects are at their highest state of alertness, because they know they are vulnerable at that stage and that is when they would expect any surveillance to begin. If they have any outside help, it's where those resources would be deployed. However, we have some resources of our own – yourselves – and the most important of them is you Aimee. You don't look like a cop or a soldier, so you will be able to stay in one place, even at the pick-up, either alone or with a bloke, whereas a man would stand out like a sore thumb. We also

have a start point, the *Bank of Commerz and Privat.*
We can pinpoint it on the map and, given five minutes on arrival, we can stake it out using you guys
to keep watch while we – the followers – keep out
of sight until there is any activity. So Aimee and the
rest of you will be the watchers and Jimbo, Geordie
and I will do the follow. Keep rotating your positions
and use the street furniture if any, such as telephone
boxes, street benches, bus stops and cafes. The more
natural your activities, the longer you will be able to
stay in situ, but come up with a good cover story just
in case you get into conversation. Keep it as near to
the truth as you can and only lie if you must. Change
your appearance slightly over time, take your jacket
off or put it on – and if it's a reversible one, so much
the better – and even a pair of sunglasses or a hat can
make a subtle but significant change to your appearance. Most importantly, act naturally, don't drama-
tise and don't over-act. Once you have identified any
possible subject, hand him or her over to us and we
will do the rest. We'll use the traditional surveillance
method, the A, B, C system, but we will only be able
to follow the subject if he walks or uses public transport. If he uses a car we have no chance. And since
we have no comms, we will have to use discreet hand
signals. We will have an emergency RV: in front of the
main Bahnhof. As soon as the pick-up is complete
and we've taken over, the watchers – you – should
make your way there and wait for us. If during the follow any of us get burned – spotted by the subject – we

will make our way to the same RV. At the end of the operation we will all meet there and make our way back to General Aviation at the airport, where we will link up with the aircraft and crew. So, all good?'

He was faced with a row of nodding heads.

'Right, from the moment we leave here, we don't talk to each other, walk or stand next to each other, or even look at each other, except with the most casual of glances. Remember, the scale of this operation is limited and just because we are there ready to do surveillance, does not mean that there will be anyone for us to carry out surveillance on. We are probably looking for a subject or subjects of Chinese or Asian appearance and that is all I can tell you. Finally, and most importantly, do not take risks; there will always be another opportunity.'

As the meeting was breaking up, the Wingco stuck his head into the room, gave a thumbs up and said 'The flight plan's been approved. We're on our way.'

After the short flight from Paris, they landed at Zurich Airport, where they were directed to a parking slot in General Aviation, taxiing in among scores of private jets belonging to seriously rich individuals and, no doubt, a few African dictators. The plane was immediately placed under a police guard and the passengers and crew were directed to a private room in the General Aviation terminal, where they were met by a red-faced British military attaché, an army colonel, and his deputy, a Senior NCO from the Intelligence Corps.

'I have been told to liaise with the person in charge and offer every support I can, so which of you is in charge?'

Rupert looked expectantly at Shepherd, but Shepherd ignored him, remaining silent and expressionless. Eventually Rupert muttered, 'Well, I suppose that's me technically.'

The attaché gave him a baffled look. 'What do you mean technically? Either you're in charge or you're not.'

Shepherd stepped in. 'We're grateful for your offer of support, Colonel, but what we would like you to do is to go back to your office, sit by the phone and tune in to the local news channel. If we call for help, we'd like you to keep us out of jail. There's no need for you to know the details of what we're going to be involved in – need to know and all that – but suffice to say that we are here and we are going to attempt a little operation in downtown Zurich that may be a bit risky.'

As the Colonel began to stutter a protest, Shepherd held up his hand. 'We have the highest possible authority for this operation, so if you don't want to spend the rest of your career in the Outer Hebrides, it would probably be wisest to fully co-operate with us. Thank you.'

The attaché's facial colour moved another couple of shades towards the purple end of the spectrum but he swallowed whatever he was about to say and then stormed out, venting his anger by barking at his deputy for being slow to follow his lead.

The watchers and the followers boarded separate trains and made their way to Zurich where they spent a couple of hours doing a ground recce in the area around the bank, before meeting again at the RV in front of the Bahnhof. They found a fast food restaurant a few streets away, where they discussed their positions for the stake-out around the bank. When everyone was satisfied that the plan they had was workable, they were about to leave to start the surveillance operation, when Geordie sounded a note of caution. 'I don't like it, Spider, I can't put my finger on it but something doesn't feel quite right.'

'I know what you mean,' said Shepherd. 'I've had the same feeling all day but I can't pin it down. It just feels off, doesn't it? But we've learned to trust our instincts over the years and sometimes it has saved lives, so everyone needs to be one hundred per cent alert. You know what we're looking for, but if you're not happy for the least reason at any time, just ditch the operation and make your way to the RV.'

The team spent the rest of that day adjusting their positions around the entrance to the bank and refining their visual signalling techniques. They were able to discontinue the operation when the bank finally closed and locked its doors for the night and, after a short debrief, during which Jock relayed a report from GCHQ that there had again been suspicious internet chatter centring on the *Bank of Commerz and Privat*, the team split up. They spent the night in various modest guesthouses around the city before taking up their positions again the following morning, shortly before the bank opened, ready for another full day's work.

As soon as they hit the streets they were aware that something was different. In particular, there were a few Asian men wandering around the area near the bank, where the day before there had been none. They were dressed as tourists with the obligatory guidebooks in their hands and cameras around their necks, but they did not act like typical tourists, In any event, the quiet street lined with Swiss banks was not part of the usual tourist itinerary. The surveillance team immediately slipped into what was now becoming a familiar routine, with Aimee sipping a coffee in a café facing the bank, while Chas, Dave and Rupert strolled in and out of the shops, consulted the time-tables in bus shelters or sat on benches reading news-papers or consulting their phones.

About an hour after the bank opened its doors, Aimee noticed a powerfully-built Asian in a pin-striped business suit slip into the bank. She imme-diately gave a discreet, hand-signal to Shepherd who was in visual contact with her and he and the other two followers went on to maximum alert. Three quarters of an hour later, the same figure slipped out of the bank and began to walk away from them towards the end of the street. Against all Shepherd's instructions, Rupert could not contain himself. He got up from the bench where he had been sitting and with his gaze focused on the subject, began to move closer to him. He was immediately leapt upon by a man who, unseen by Rupert, had been tracking the subject and carrying out counter-surveillance. The man was bigger than the target, well-muscled with a wicked scar across one cheek. It was clear that Rupert was no match for him and as his attacker drew a knife, Shepherd, Geordie and Jimbo were forced to break cover and intervene to save him from a wounding, or worse.

Jimbo grabbed the man's knife arm and forced it back against the joint until there was a cracking noise and, with a howl of pain from the man, the knife clattered to the pavement. Shepherd followed up with two savage punches, splintering the man's nose with the heel of his left hand and then following up with a straight right that crushed his Adam's apple. The assailant crumpled to the ground but the fight had drawn another four of the subject's protection team out of cover and within a few seconds a vicious street brawl was going on in the middle of the staid banking street.

The SAS men were still trying desperately to extricate Rupert when they heard the approaching sirens of a police car. The three of them kicked, punched and gouged the attackers to drive them back and then bodily lifting Rupert up and sprinted away with him. The battered attackers did not pursue them.

The team made their way quickly to the RV in front of the Bahnhof. Except for a few grazes and abrasions, everyone was unharmed, but Aimee was nowhere to be found. No one had seen her since the beginning of the fight.

'We'd have had that bastard if it hadn't been for this fucking idiot here,' Jimbo said, directing such a baleful glare at Rupert that he flushed and dropped his gaze. 'If you had just sat still, we'd have been all over the subject like flies. Instead you go and jump up and alert the minders, and we end up in a fucking punch-up with nothing to show for our efforts.'

'Leave it for now guys,' Shepherd said. 'The most important thing now is to find Aimee.' He sent Jimbo and Geordie to scour the area around the surveillance site, while he contacted the attaché at the embassy for any update.

'The Swiss police have already been in touch and are very keen to interview your group,' the attaché said, 'and they will be waiting at the airport when you return there.' He paused, enjoying his moment. 'So, you're not quite as professional as you think you are, are you?'

Shepherd broke the connection without bothering to reply. A couple more hours had passed without any sign of Aimee and they were on the point of leaving the RV area, when she suddenly emerged from the station.

'Where the hell have you been?' Shepherd said.

She smiled. 'Out to the airport. When I saw you lot rolling round on the ground, I thought at least one of us should follow the subject, so I stuck to him like glue. He came here and caught a train out to

the International terminal where he checked in for
a flight to Singapore. I was behind him all the time,
even in the check-in line. I followed him to the departure gates but then obviously I had to turn back as I
didn't have a boarding pass. I wasn't close enough
to see the name on his passport, but he's travelling
economy on Swissair.'

'Fantastic work, Aimee,' Shepherd said. 'You've
salvaged the op and shown us all up.' He paused.
'Well, one of us in particular.'

Once more Rupert flushed and looked away.

They retraced their steps to the airport and
General Aviation, where, as the attaché had predicted, they found half a dozen plain-clothed Swiss
policemen waiting to question them. Not liking the
vague answers he was being given, the senior officer
threatened them with arrest.

'On what charges?' Shepherd said.

The officer began ticking them off on his fingers.
'Assault, riot, affray. That enough for now?'

After a tense few minutes the stand-off was
brought to a head by Rupert who, in a voice just loud
enough to be overheard, muttered to himself 'Bloody
Swiss, only good for making money and cuckoo
clocks.'

The police inspector blew his top and gave Rupert
a multi-lingual mouthful, but instead of arresting
them, he then rounded on Shepherd. 'I want you
and all your thugs out of my country. Do not expect a
warm welcome if you ever return.'

'We'll need to file a flight plan,' the Wingco said, having watched the interrogation from the sidelines.

'Don't worry,' the policeman said. 'We have no desire to detain you further and I'll make sure your flight plan is filed without delay. Where are you travelling to?'

The Wingco gave Shepherd a quizzical look.

There was only one possible answer. 'Singapore.'

CHAPTER 22

The atmosphere inside the cabin of the 125 was tense. After an online discussion with Jock, the SAS team had left Zurich, but had then been forced to fly to the RAF base at Akrotiri in Cyprus. It was an unwelcome delay and diversion but they had to refuel because the 125 did not have the range to reach Singapore non-stop and it was also a chance to have the aircraft checked out by the RAF ground crews at the base.

While that was happening, the team had a heated discussion about the operation in Switzerland. Despite Shepherd reminding them that the aim of a debrief was always to 'highlight good points, highlight poor points and improve best practice in the future', it had nearly developed into an all-out punch up. Geordie in particular was still furious with Rupert, insisting that his stupidity and recklessness had placed Aimee in danger.

Apart from their irritation with him, another factor was making the team even more edgy: they were falling further and further behind their quarry.

They all knew that the 125 did not have the legs of a commercial aircraft; they were unable to fly as far and as fast as the guy they were chasing even though, after leaving Akrotiri, the Wingo and his co-pilot had deliberately ripped up the flight hours rule book and insisted that they could fly all the way to Singapore under Royal Air Force emergency regulations. This allowed them to fly more than the stipulated twelve hours maximum, if the situation was deemed to be "in pursuit of the mission". The Wingco, unrecognisable from the grumpy stickler for the rules they had first encountered just a few short weeks before, had decided to employ this interpretation with the proviso that as soon as they arrived in Singapore he and the co-pilot would have to crash out for at least twenty-four hours. That was also niggling at Shepherd because he didn't know whether everything would come to a head on the island or they would need to crack straight on from Singapore.

As the 125 was on finals in bound to Changi airport, Shepherd was staring out of a window on the right hand side of the aircraft. He could see the whole of the island of Singapore laid out below them, with hundreds of ships awaiting access to the docks and beyond them, the high-rise buildings occupied by the commercial enterprises that had made the tiny state "the Switzerland of the East". Countless other tower blocks housed the millions of workers needed to service the industries driving Singapore's remarkable success story. To the south, dozens of dredgers were at work, creating artificial reefs to increase the size of the island still more to accommodate the ever-growing population.

They were sandwiched in the long stack of pas-senger jets lining up to land at Changi, but unlike the civilian aircraft in front of and behind them, the 125 had been directed to the military side of the airport and once they had landed, they peeled away from the procession of jumbo jets making for the terminals and came to a halt alongside a row of Republic of Singapore Air Force F-15s.

During the flight Shepherd had had several dis-cussions with Jock back in the UK, who had been hav-ing a frustrating time trying to track down people to help them in Singapore. The fear that they all had was that without the help of the authorities there, their quarry could disappear without trace. 'There's no help to be had from this end,' Jock said, 'because it was made pretty clear to me that any assistance from the Foreign and Commonwealth office is out of the question. The focus there is purely on Europe these days, since the old colonialists with their "East of Suez" mind-set have long been pensioned off. I also drew a blank in the MoD, but then I remembered the name of an old ex-SAS officer – he was before your time, Spider – who also served with the Gurkha regiment in Brunei and the Gurkha contingent of the Singapore police. The old guy's long retired but still lives in Singapore, looked after by a couple of Gurkha orderlies, and he immediately offered his help when I contacted him. He still knows many of his old contacts and he's willing to meet you guys to see how he can help. However, any meeting has to be clandestine, away from official eyes. The population of Singapore is kept under very tight control – as you know, it's pretty close to being a police state – but the authorities are always prepared to do a deal with us, so long as it's not made public. So here's the plan, I've come up with, subject to your approval of course. The Crabs stay on base at Changi,' he said, using the traditional Army nickname for the RAF. The grease used on Navy gun breeches was called "crab fat" because it was the same blue colour as the ointment used to treat sailors for "crabs" – pubic lice. When the RAF began to be issued with uniforms of a similar colour, the nickname was transferred to them.

'They can use the facilities there to unwind,' Jock said, 'but you guys should get yourselves rooms at a decent hotel. You've roughed it enough, so now you can relax in some nice surroundings until you're contacted. Oh and by the way, remember the Squadron Boss in Afghanistan who said he was going to back us all the way? He's now saying "Sorry, but I'm afraid you're on your own", and by an amazing coincidence he's just got a DSO in the latest military honours list.'

The SAS team duly booked themselves into a luxury hotel on Orchard Road. Shepherd had just finished a few fast laps of the Olympic-size swimming pool and had joined the rest of the guys who were nursing Tiger beers at a poolside table, when a small, thin, extremely pale-skinned man approached them.

'Excuse me, I'm looking for a Dan Shepherd?' he hesitated. 'My name is Garry Winterburn. Garry with two Rs. Jock said I should ask for a Dan Shepherd.'

'That would be me,' Shepherd said. 'Though everyone calls me Spider. This is Geordie, this is Jimbo and this gentleman,' he said, gesturing towards Rupert, 'is our in-flight window-cleaner, better known as Rupert.'

The newcomer smiled. 'Yes, I suppose it's much better to keep things on a first name basis. It's almost impossible to keep anything a secret in Singapore, but let's give it a try.' He directed a shrewd glance at Rupert. 'I was in your position once and I made two mistakes when I joined the SAS. One was that I accepted a position without doing Selection and, quite rightly, this was held against me throughout my time there.'

Rupert shifted uncomfortably in his seat, having done exactly the same thing himself.

'My second mistake,' Garry said, 'was to think that the SAS were like the Gurkhas. In retrospect, although they share many of the warrior traits, the Gurkhas tend to follow orders faithfully and accept the plans that others formulate for them, even when they may lead to their deaths. From my experience the SAS do not accept any plan or course of action without thinking it through to see if it can be improved or indeed, if it is the right course of action which, I may add, is one of the things that makes the SAS Regiment so successful and unique. Anyway, enough of my reminiscences, tell me how I may be able to help you?'

Shepherd outlined the situation regarding their quarry, and how they knew when and how he had arrived in Singapore. 'We've had no assistance from the FCO or the Singapore Authorities and we are very keen to discover our subject's whereabouts, and whether he is still on the island, or has disappeared into the Malay Peninsula or Indonesia, or indeed whether he just caught another flight out of Changi.'

'I think I may be able to help you there,' Garry said. 'During my time with the Brunei Gurkhas and the Gurkha Contingent of the Singapore Police, I liaised closely with the Singaporean security authorities.' He flashed a bleak smile. 'There are many people in Singapore and abroad who think that the Gurkha contingent is nothing more or less than a counter-coup force, in case the Singapore armed forces ever try to flex their muscles and oust the President, but of course I couldn't possibly comment on that. However I can arrange for someone to contact you who will have access to the information that you require. I realise the matter is urgent, so please do not wander far from the hotel until he makes contact. There will of course be a price to pay and the Singaporeans do tend to drive a hard bargain. I suspect that it will take the form of a request for training in the UK for a number of the Singaporean police. The

Singaporeans place education and expertise at the top of their requirements, believing that it is the only way for them to stay ahead of their neighbours. Don't forget, they are surrounded by hundreds of millions of people living on the breadline, and Singapore's wealth attracts a lot of envy. The only thing that has stopped them from being swallowed up is the ability of their people to keep ahead of the game.'

'No problem,' Shepherd said. 'If the British Government receives a request for training or indeed anything else from Singapore, I give you my word that the request will be honoured.'

'Very well,' Garry said. 'It's been a pleasure meeting you but I don't think it will be necessary for us to meet again. I hope the colleague I send to you will be able to solve your problem. I think he can.'

They watched his slight figure pick his way back through the hotel and out into the furnace heat and humidity of the street.

Shortly after dusk that day the telephone in Shepherd's room buzzed. 'Mr Spider?' a voice with a strong Chinese accent said, when he picked up the phone. 'This is Mr Garry's friend. Can you meet me in the lobby?'

Shepherd gathered the others and they took the lift down to the lobby where a small, round-faced and beaming Singaporean was waiting for them. 'Hello Sirs,' he said. 'My name is Chee, shall we go for dinner?'

He led them out of the hotel and they piled into a couple of taxis. If the drivers thought they had picked up another party of gullible tourists they could fleece, they were soon disabused of the idea by Mr Chee. After he had machine-gunned instructions at them in Chinese, they began driving as quickly as they could through the thick rush-hour traffic.

Mr Chee sat in the back of the lead taxi next to Shepherd. 'I hope you have no particular preference for what you eat, because I am going to take you to my favourite restaurant. The food exactly resembles the people of Singapore: Chinese, Indian, and Malay, though if you prefer European food, that is also available. The surroundings are a little basic but, believe me, the food is excellent.'

They eventually arrived at the base of one of the huge tower blocks that housed the worker bees of the Singapore economy. While Mr Chee paid off the taxi drivers, Shepherd took in their surroundings and was surprised to see that, around and between the concrete and steel pillars holding up the skyscraper, there were metal dining tables covered with checked, oilcloth covers, surrounding a number of stalls that were cooking delicious-smelling food.

'Gentlemen, let me explain,' Mr Chee said. 'The stalls selling food here are run by the old hawkers who used to sell street food on every corner in Singapore. To clean up our image for the tourists, the government moved the hawkers to where they were needed, closer to the people who bought the food. This not only increased the hawkers' turnover but also the quality of the food. Now, this is how the system works: we select a table, a waitress will take our drinks order and then we go to the food area and order what we want to eat. When it is ready, the waitress will bring it to us, and when we are finished, we pay the bill and the waitress in turn pays the hawkers. A very simple system, don't you agree? You may order for yourselves or ..."

'Why don't you order for us, Mr Chee?' Shepherd said. 'You know what's good and there's nothing we don't eat.'

He did so and then joined them at their table. 'While we are waiting for our food to arrive, gentlemen,' Mr Chee said, 'to business. The person you are interested in arrived at Changi approximately thirty hours ago on a Singapore Airlines flight from Zürich. He passed through immigration using a Republic of China passport issued in Hong Kong. He was waved through customs and left the airport by taxi. He travelled to a branch of the *Commerz and Privat Bank* in downtown Singapore. When he emerged from the bank, he changed taxis and travelled over the causeway to Johore Bahru in Malaysia. Three hours later he returned to Singapore using the same passport, and went straight to Changi. Using a bank card issued by the same Swiss bank, he bought a ticket on a flight to Hong Kong and departed a few hours later. When his luggage was searched on departure he had only a few hundred dollars in his possession, and yes, in case you were wondering, all luggage, including hold baggage, is searched at check-in.'

He put the tips of his fingers together and leaned forward, lowering his voice. 'Now for our analysis. When the gentleman arrived in Singapore he came as just another tourist or businessman. It wasn't until you alerted us to his real status that we reviewed all the information we were able to turn up on him. We now believe that he came here to withdraw a very substantial sum in Singapore dollars from his personal account, then took it across to Malaysia to pay off a person or persons unknown for as yet unknown reasons. I'm sorry that this tells you so little, but I can reassure you that he did nothing suspicious during his time in Singapore. We are a very highly regulated society, we can draw on numerous sources of intelligence, including CCTV cameras and other means of surveillance, and there is nothing to indicate any activity other than what I've already described.'

Shepherd and the others asked a few questions but there was clearly nothing more to be discovered about their target and they turned their attention to the plates of food that the waitress kept putting in front of them. After they'd eaten, Shepherd insisted on paying the bill. This caused Mr Chee to explode in amusement. 'Okay, dear chap,' he said. 'Go ahead, I will not be offended, even though I am your host.' Shepherd signalled to the waitress and was presented with a bill written on a sheet torn from a school exercise book, demanding the princely sum of sixteen Singapore dollars, including tip – less than ten pounds sterling.

CHAPTER 23

The news that their target had already flown to Hong Kong caused disquiet in the team. They had no leads on their quarry, and he would find it easy to disappear into the teeming streets of one of the most densely populated cities in the world. They shared the feeling that they might have hit a dead end, but before cutting and running back to the UK, they investigated all their options. Over an open line to Jock on the sat-phone they discussed whether the Singapore Special Branch could be wrong about the target having headed for Hong Kong.

'The intelligence services in Singapore are as good as any in the region,' Jock said, 'so it is most unlikely that they would make a mistake.'

'But why Hong Kong?' Shepherd said. 'If he is connected to Chinese dissidents, as we suspect, he couldn't have chosen a more dangerous destination.'

'If his documents stood up to scrutiny in Singapore, they'd pass anywhere,' Jock said, 'and as to why he'd head for Hong Kong, I suspect he'd go there for money. For him to achieve anything he needs hard cash. He can't do anything with a bank card or bankers drafts, he must have the folding stuff. He has to pay for his manpower, and all the day to day mundane things like food, lodging and travel for the team he's assembling to carry out his next attack – and there will be another one, that's for sure. He will also have to buy his logistic support, weaponry, explosives etc., and everything costs money. The problem he has is that it is difficult to physically take cash in large sums through airports and sea ports – he'd never have been allowed to fly out of Changi with an unexplained pile of cash, for example, so he has to find another way. We know that he has money in the Swiss bank from the Greek and French jobs, and the bank has branches in Hong Kong, Shanghai and Macau, as well as Singapore.'

'But assuming he can get his hands on the money, how does he get it out of China?'

'Since he arrived in Hong Kong, GCHQ have had no intercepts on him, he's just disappeared. He might be staying in China or may be going underground on the refugee trail, so it's difficult to anticipate where his next target might be. Apart from China itself, the region from the Philippines to Australia is a hotbed of people with grievances. He is playing a high risk strategy by going into China, but if he had been picked up or arrested we would have heard about it by now. The question is what do we do now? We can't have you waiting around for ever, and it won't be long before the Singaporeans start itching for you to move on. So, where do you want to wait and for how long?'

Shepherd thought for a few moments. 'How about Swanbourne with the Aussie SAS? None of us have been there but I've heard the training facilities are excellent so while we are waiting to catch a lucky break, we can get up to training speed and our kit can be checked over. A few days training in the sun won't do us any harm.'

'Okay,' Jock said, 'but we'll have to set a time limit, otherwise I can't see the brass authorising the plan. Let's say three weeks tops before you have to haul your arses back here. I think I can swing it because Whitehall are kicking the Frogs' arses about paying a ransom. But one word of warning: you won't find the Aussie SAS the same as here, I've been there and they are much more regimental than we are. They pretty much follow the book and although you might find it hard to believe, they frown on mavericks, so keep your neck wound in. If you're still up for it, I'll try to swing it through Northwood; they have a liaison officer in SF group headquarters who can be leaned on. I will get back to you ASAP with either authorisation or a return ticket to Blighty.'

The authorisation to move to the Australian SAS camp a few kilometres north of Perth was a couple of days coming through, because Jock had a difficult time persuading the various Head Sheds, until he pointed out that if Shepherd's team were recalled to the UK and something kicked off in the Far East, it could prove to be very embarrassing should the facts ever hit the media. 'Not that I was threatening anyone you understand,' he said with his trademark growl, 'I was just giving them the facts.'

The final couple of days waiting in Singapore before they were cleared to fly to Western Australia had been almost too much for the Wingco. The military at Changi were suspicious of what might be in the aircraft and made several surreptitious attempts to gain access, so much so that the Wingco made the Snowdrops, Chas and Dave, sleep on the locked aircraft. 'It's breaking the Royal Air Force health and safety SOPs,' he said, 'but better than the Singapore's Military Intelligence crawling all over everything.'

They eventually got clearance but when they arrived at Swanbourne, things didn't get off to a good start. While Spider and the others were ignored, Rupert was hauled off to an interview with the Adjutant. As they waited for him, Geordie glanced around, taking in the neat, single-storey buildings and the starched uniformed soldiers marching past. 'Not much like the big H is it?'

Shepherd nodded. 'They seem to like the rank structure and things neat and tidy, but they're supposed to be good squaddies. Lets just hope they let us get on and do what we want to do.'

Rupert arrived back from his meeting soon afterwards, red faced with embarrassment. 'That was damn difficult,' he said. 'They seem to think we're a band of ruffians. I had to promise, on pain of expulsion, that we would stick to every rule and regulation that applies to their camp and their Regiment.'

'You can stick to what you like mate,' Geordie said, 'but we're here to get ourselves back up to speed, ready to finish what we started in Athens, so if you want to stick to rules and regs, that's up to you, but don't count me in.'

They were interrupted by the approach of a uniformed soldier wearing a short sleeved shirt, and a small crown on his wrist, the badge of rank of a warrant officer. His hair, bleached by the sun, was flecked with grey and his face bore lines that might have been stress or the advancing years catching up with him, but his gaze was keen and when he shook hands, his grip was like steel.

He had been studying them as he walked over and, ignoring Rupert, he spoke directly to Shepherd. 'G'day mate, my name's Ronnie and I'm the senior guy here, except for the bloody Adjutant, who doesn't really count. The rest of the guys on the camp are either REMF's or admin, because all the bayonets are over in the East in CT – Capital Territory – or Sydney. Something big is brewing and because we are a small unit we sometimes get stretched and we are certainly stretched now. Anyway, I spent a couple of years with 22 in the UK on secondment and I was treated like a gent, in fact I would have stayed only the pension rights here are better. So if there's anything you want, you've got it, and if anyone gets in your way or tries to obstruct you, let me know, and I'll tramp all over them. Do me a favour, mate, though: in front of any of the officers or other ranks, call me Sir, would you? We both know it means nothing but it keeps the bastards off my back. I've put the Tiffy – the Weapons Artificer – and the Ammunition Technical Officer on standby so they can check over your hardware. I suspect it's been bounced around a bit and needs a bit of TLC.'

'Thanks Ronnie,' Shepherd said. 'We prefer to do our own maintenance and checks but your two techies are more than welcome to give us a hand.'

Having arranged to meet them for a beer that evening, Ronnie left them to it and Shepherd allocated tasks to everyone. 'Geordie, you and Jimbo get down and see the Tiffy in his workshop. I want you to go over every weapon we have in minute detail, checking every part, every spring tension, and paying particular attention to the springs in the magazines. Get him to run his measuring gauges over everything and by the time you're finished I expect every weapon to be 100% perfect. While you're doing that, I'll work with the ATO to check every piece of ordnance that we own. We'll test the electrical resistance in every fuse, check the powder weight of a sample of ammo and at the end I will have him issue a new hazardous aircraft cargo certificate for the whole nine yards. When that lot's done, and it will take three or four hours, we will then write a new aircraft manifest for hazardous air cargo. That will mean re-boxing and re-packing everything we own, weighing the individual boxes and writing the manifest. I know it's a balls-ache but it's got to be done, because the Aussie customs are the worst bureaucrats in the world and we don't want to be held up at the airport on our way out, if and when the shit hits the fan.'

'What would you like me to do Spider?' Rupert said.

'I want you to go and see if Ronnie will lend you a Ute – a pick-up – for a couple of hours. Then drive down to Fremantle or Perth, find a surf shack that rents wet and dry suits to surfers. I want you to buy at least ten of their discarded stock. I don't care whether they are wet or dry material as long as they are one-piece body suits, and it doesn't matter what state they're in because nobody is going to be diving in them.'

Rupert gave him a puzzled smile and started to turn away.

'Hang on,' Shepherd said. 'There's more. When you've got your hands on the suits, I want you to go to the nearest recycling site and buy as many old rags as you can get your hands on. When you've done that, come back here and spend the rest of the day stuffing the rags into the dry suits. When you've finished, I want them to be the same size and weight as a human.'

'But what will we use them for?'

'We?' Shepherd said, with a smile. 'We use them to practice our CQB moves. With the Aussies' fixation on health and safety, if we want to grapple man on man we'll have to wear padded head- and body-guards which are totally unrealistic and make the training artificial. But with our dummies we can get stuck in and do the moves, bend the limbs, stab them and so on, and it's just the same as fighting man on man. And when we are finished fighting them, we can take them on the ranges and shoot the shit out of them. They are virtually indestructible and will last for as long as we need them.'

'Yeah and another thing about them,' Geordie said, 'is that we don't need to patch them up like ordinary plywood targets. The bullets go straight through and the neoprene seals itself, so they save a lot of time on the range and you can get on with the shooting sequences you want to practice without having to stop and paste up the holes. It saves hours and gives better continuity.'

The team and the two Aussie technicians spent the rest of the day and most of the night checking and testing their equipment and finally, just before dawn, the last piece of paperwork was written and checked. The technicians were happy to contribute because of the team's appreciation of their skills and their own willingness to put in the hours.

After a short nap, Shepherd, Geordie and Jimbo were up at first light and decided to work-out in the open air. They began their fitness and skills updating. Because they were unsure if or when their quarry would resurface, they focused first on the parts of the anatomy that he felt required the most attention: the fingers, hands, arms and shoulders, and then the abdominals.

They concentrated first on the suppleness of the joints and muscles, then exercises that increased their strength and mobility, then repeated the same exercises with weights. They kept this up for several hours until they were drenched in sweat and Shepherd called a halt.

By the time they finished they had attracted an audience of Aussie squaddies who looked on in awe at the work-out. When the training resumed in the late afternoon the audience had increased in size and included the Adjutant and Ronnie the Warrant Officer, who was watching eagerly.

In the following morning's session Shepherd added some interval training for the lower body, sprinting 400 yards, jogging 100 yards, sprinting another 400 yards, continuing until the guys were almost exhausted, and then they repeated the previous day's upper body exercises but with extra weight and increased repetitions.

That evening they started weapon training, first doing dry practices, stripping and assembling different types of weapons blindfolded, loading and unloading, changing magazines and running through the range of weapons stoppages, all the while never standing still but rolling, changing positions, seeking cover, making it as difficult as possible for any potential adversary to take them on. Despite the West Australian heat, all this was done in full combat gear, fireproof coveralls, magazine vest and webbing. Finally they went through the full range of weapon training again but this time wearing respirators.

'It's good to be back in harness Spider,' Jimbo said, as they staggered off to the showers afterwards, 'and doing the hard yards, I'm feeling better already.'

'Yeah, I don't think we were that much out of condition, but it's good to get rid of the kinks in the body and get the mind sharp again. Tomorrow we go shooting.'

On the range the following morning they started by using the instinctive method of pistol shooting, using one hand to grip the pistol and the other to steady the weapon, sighting on the target with both eyes. They fired double taps, always counting the rounds fired, never having an empty magazine and rolling and using cover while changing magazines. This method had the advantage that the team could use the supporting hand to assist when they had to move through, under, over and around obstacles that they placed in the shooting area.

They started by shooting twelve round groups, and when the grouping was the size of a postage stamp, they moved back to a longer range, remaining there until the grouping was again acceptably small and then moving to a longer range still, repeating the exercise again and again. Never bored, they set themselves seemingly impossible aims, facing the target, turning right and left, and from the rear, then walking and firing, always practising until they had achieved their goals.

When they had reached about the twenty yard mark, the grouping spread and became unacceptably large, and they then changed to an adapted version of the Weaver method of shooting, an American technique, where the shooter holds the weapon in both hands and sights on the target using the pistol's iron sights, while keeping one arm slightly bent. Effective at longer ranges, it was cumbersome if there were obstacles to cross and not entirely trusted by Shepherd and the others to get the job done.

Once they were satisfied with the results of the pistol shooting, they progressed on to the H&Ks. These came with a selection of optical and laser sighting systems but Shepherd had dispensed with all of them, including the factory fitted iron sights, preferring a smooth clean weapon which would not snag when in a Close Quarter Battle environment. The drills were a repeat of the pistol drills with the emphasis on targets at longer ranges though they proved to be more exhausting because of the extra weight of the weapons and ammunition, but the guys still went to bed happy that night.

Things changed after the following morning's work-out session on the indoor and outdoor ranges. Ronnie was waiting for Shepherd as he left the ranges. 'The Adj wants to see you, mate,' he said with a half-smile on his face. 'But don't worry, a miracle has happened! A lot has changed in the last few days and now he thinks he needs your help, he's much more amenable.'

As Shepherd entered the office, he noticed Rupert sitting in the corner looking uncomfortable, which was fast becoming his default setting. 'Come in Spider, if I may call you that,' the Adjutant said, with a big shit-eating smile. 'I have a slight problem that I think you might be able to help me with. The bulk of the Regiment, along with all the training staff, have been sent to the East Coast to deal with a potential terrorist threat and I've been left with guys who were not deemed suitable or good enough to travel with them. This has caused a crisis in the morale of the guys left behind and somehow I have to create a viable strategic fighting reserve from them to deal with any other threat that might arise in Australia's area of interest. I couldn't help noticing how impressed my guys were when they were watching you and your team train. Is there anything you could do to help get them motivated and better trained?'

'I'm flattered to be asked,' Shepherd said, 'but my qualifications are UK-based. However, I'm sure Ronnie and I could do something together. He could be the lead trainer and I would support him, provided we can work around our own training times and commitments, always remembering that my team are still putting in twelve radio schedules a day back to our mate in the UK, and if the shit hits the fan at any point, whatever stage of the training we've reached, we'll simply have to cut and run. Anyway,

Ronnie and I will sort out a training schedule and content and then, since we don't know how long we'll be here, I suggest we make a start first thing tomorrow. I assume that you and Rupert will also be joining in, but as this is intended to be a morale building exercise for the rankers, don't expect any favours.'

Although he had suggested that Ronnie would be running the training, in fact Shepherd took the lead. He quickly outlined a programme concentrating on the main weapon of the Aussie SASR, the M-16, with a short course on the pistol as a support weapon. Like their own training, each session started with some fitness and mobility exercises followed by dry practices, and when the trainees were at an acceptable level, they moved on to the live firing ranges. After just a few short sessions the results had improved to such an extent that the Adjutant, whose own expertise had also been greatly enhanced, was delighted. He was discussing with Ronnie and Shepherd what the next step should be, when Jimbo came dashing onto the range. 'We've got an OP Immediate from Jock, our guy is on the move!'

'Sorry gents,' Shepherd said, 'looks like you'll have to handle the training yourselves from here on in.'

He and Jimbo hurried to join Geordie who was keeping the sat-phone link to Jock open, mainly by taking the piss out of him and his injuries. 'I hope the arm's not too weak, Jock,' he was saying as Shepherd hurried in, 'because that's the one you hold the porn magazine with while the other one's busy isn't it?'

'We're all here, Jock,' Shepherd said, before he could come up with a suitably witty reply. 'Bring us up to date.'

'Well our wee friend's been having a little vacation in Macau,' he said, 'laundering his money at the tables in one of the casinos. He then slipped out of Macau on board a high roller's jet supplied by the casino, so we can assume he lost enough cash to keep them happy. As the Chinese always want the high rollers to come back and lose some more, those jets are not subject to the same immigration and customs checks as normal flights, so we only became aware of his movements when the intercepts by Cheltenham suddenly went off the scale.

'There are a bunch of his guys in Papua New Guinea – we know that because he started to chat to them just before landing at Port Moresby. So we can assume that he now has cash and manpower, and is looking to get his hands on the hardware necessary to carry out his task, whatever it is. The intercepts are more sporadic now – PNG is not ideal terrain for any form of communications more sophisticated than shouting or throwing spears – but it appears that he has moved location from Port Moresby to a place up-country. I'll send you the co-ordinates.'

'Why PNG?' Jimbo said.

'Why not? I can't think of many better places to carry out clandestine training. The government is about as corrupt as they come, the country is wild and semi-lawless, modern communications are almost non-existent away from the cities – there are no roads at all linking the north and south of the island – and the interior is so mountainous and jungle-smothered that tribes even a few miles apart speak completely different languages.'

'And is there any military hardware in PNG?' Jimbo said.

'Absolutely shedloads,' Jock said. 'A few years ago the neighbouring island of Bougainville tried to declare independence and take their enormous copper mine with them, so the PNG government took umbrage and set up a deal with a particularly nasty British/South African mercenary outfit to bring the rebels back under control. The mercs were paid a lot of money from the PNG education budget and they bought a load of Soviet-era weaponry including a couple of HIP helicopters, and were all set to fly into Bougainville, all guns blazing, and take control of the copper mine, until the Australian government got wind of what was happening and put a stop to it before there was any bloodshed.' HIP was the Nato reporting name of the M-8 Russian transport helicopter, which could also be fitted out as an airborne command post and an armed gunship. It was one of the most produced helicopters in the world but Shepherd wasn't a fan.

'A couple of the merc ringleaders were arrested and thrown in jail and then deported back to where they came from, but the hardware had already been bought and paid for, including a huge profit mark-up that went straight into the mercs' bank account. The helis are still operating in PNG, flown by a couple of Ukrainian pilots scraping a living, and most of the rest of the kit is in a warehouse in Port Moresby. No doubt some of it is on our target's shopping list, and by all accounts, you can get anything you want in PNG with enough cash. They won't just sell you their weapons, they'll sell you their whole goddam army if the price is right.'

'So if we move fast,' Shepherd said, 'we might catch the bad guys as they pick up their shopping.'

'You might,' Jock said, 'though there's a good chance they'll already have taken delivery of it, and in any case, I think we'll need to use a bit of diplomacy. The Aussies are very, very sensitive and don't like outsiders – especially Poms – sticking their noses into something that doesn't concern them, and they see PNG as their own backyard. So if you try to go on your own without Aussie support, they'll stop you stone dead, just like they did with the mercs. The best approach would be to sell it to them as a joint operation, with us supplying the expertise and knowledge of the enemy, and the Aussies providing the heavy back-up.'

'I think you're dead right, Jock,' Shepherd said. 'If you can start the diplomacy side between the UK and Canberra, I'll go and brief the adjutant here and see if we can formulate a plan that's agreeable to them and us. I'll keep you posted.'

CHAPTER 24

When his high roller's casino jet landed at Port Moresby, Sabit stepped out into the overpowering heat and humidity of mainland Papua New Guinea and his shirt was instantly soaked with sweat. A driver with a battered Toyota saloon was waiting for him on the other side of the rudimentary immigration control, watched over by two surly and indifferent Papuan police, their guts straining the buttons of their faded blue uniforms. Both of them were chewing betel nut and splashes of spit, like blood stains, littered the concrete floor around them.

As the driver took him in to Port Moresby, at Sabit's request he avoided the heavily policed dual carriageway from the airport and instead took the old coastal highway past the strangely named settlements – "9 Mile" and "5 Mile" – and the sprawling shantytowns built of scraps of corrugated iron, rotten wood and palm fronds. Any vehicle owner unlucky enough to break down or run out of fuel near them would be beaten and robbed of all his possessions, while his car or truck would be stripped of everything of even the slightest value in seconds; if he was doubly unlucky, he would also be raped or killed.

They drove into the city and turned into the underground car park beneath a hotel that catered mainly to expatriates and the Papuan government politicians and officials whose palms they greased and whose pockets they lined. Sabit was taken to the cocktail bar and introduced to two men, both Papuans. One wore a sharp business suit, the other had the gold braid and medals of a General in the Papuan Defence Force. While the Papuans downed the succession of whiskies he bought for them, Sabit sipped green tea and outlined his requirements: explosives, weapons including grenades, tear gas, AK47s and RPGs, and a fast ship to ferry himself, his men and his cargo across the Torres Straits in one week's time. Payment would be in dollars, one third in advance, the balance on safe delivery to the Australian coast. They haggled over terms for a few minutes, then shook hands on the deal.

Sabit left Port Moresby at first light the next morning, heading up country to rendezvous with his men and complete the training for the task he had set them. His obligations to al-Qaeda were now complete and the money their Arab backers had paid him was being put to good use. He had waited many years to take his revenge on the men who had killed his father and his brothers. Now the time was almost upon him.

CHAPTER 25

News of the presence of a well-funded and well-armed terrorist group in PNG had reached the Australian Ministry of Defence in Canberra and the Australian SASR on the West Coast. Before sending his report, the Adjutant had agreed a plan with Shepherd. The British SAS men would leave immediately on the HS 125, fly to Port Moresby and approach the target area on foot, acting as a reconnaissance group for the SASR. They would radio back intelligence on the terrorists' numbers, weaponry and defences, and identify a suitable Drop Zone that the Aussie Sabre Squadron – the attack troops – could parachute into.

The plan was readily agreed by the Australian MoD in Canberra with the proviso that the Australians, not the British, had operational control. Warrant Officer Ronnie supplied the patrol with the additional kit they needed from the Aussie armoury. Shepherd had asked for a satellite voice radio to communicate with the Aussie Head Shed, which Rupert would carry and operate. He also requested AR-16's for Rupert, Jimbo and Geordie, but not for himself. He asked Ronnie for something with a bit more punch.

Ronnie thought for a moment. 'We've a couple of FN's in the armoury. They're museum pieces really, we only keep them because some of the guys used them on operations in Vietnam. We've only a few hundred rounds to go with them but if that's what you want, you're very welcome, provided they're signed for, of course.'

Shepherd smiled to himself. You just couldn't beat military bureaucracy.

With Chas, Dave and Aimee in tow, the SAS team flew to Port Moresby that night, landing at dawn when there were unlikely to be any locals around to witness their arrival. When Shepherd checked in with Jock on the sat phone, he reported a problem. 'We have a time and distance issue with the Aussies. They've now decided to bring the job forward and no argument will convince them otherwise. I think the problem is that their Head Shed think they are dealing with a bunch of untrained head-hunters but according to the resident spook at our embassy in Port Moresby, the Ukrainians have already flown at least forty men who looked like ethnic Chinese up-country. There may be others who were there already or arrived by different means. So it's reasonable to assume that they are from one of China's separatist groups, possibly Uyghurs from the Xinjiang region in the far north-west of the country – the Taliban's Chinese cousins, if you like. They're Muslims who have been oppressed and sometimes terrorised by the Chinese government. They've carried out a number of purges and mass arrests of them, and a fair few deportations and executions too.'

'That would explain why the terrorists have been so careful to obscure their identities,' Shepherd said. 'They'd know that if they were identified, the Chinese wouldn't hesitate to carry out further reprisals on their families and people.' He paused, thinking hard. 'So if we're right about their identities, that suggests their ultimate target is to force concessions from the Chinese and they're going to have to do something more dramatic than kill a few tourists in Athens or Paris to do that.'

'True enough,' Jock said, 'but regrettable though it is to be giving the Beijing regime a helping hand, we've got a chance to wipe out the terrorist group. However you need to re-think how you're going to insert, because the Aussies have brought the para drop forward and it is now set for tomorrow night.'

Shepherd swore. 'Looks like we'll have to make use of the Ukrainians and their second-hand HIPs too; we'll not get in position quickly enough otherwise.'

'My thoughts exactly,' Jock said, 'so I took the liberty of getting the resident spook in Port Moresby to hire them. They're on standby and good to go as soon as you're ready.'

'Good work,' Shepherd said. 'We've still a little testing and training to do, but we'll then get up country as quickly as possible.'

Jock brought him up to date on the rest of the intel he'd gleaned and then Shepherd broke the connection and began to brief Jimbo, Geordie and Rupert. 'The village we think the bad guys are holed up in is at the head of a river valley. The terrain there is typical of the country: the valleys are all narrow and viciously steep, with the slopes smothered in dense primary and secondary jungle, so it will be a tight DZ, and if the jumpers are slow off the mark, they could end up in the wrong valley altogether. Also, if the Aussies jump in blind there could be problems with the locals as well as the terrain. We've advised them to jump in small sticks and from the map I estimate they can find primary jungle around the village that could give them an 850 yard run in. So that's five jumpers, taking one hundred and fifty yards each with a hundred yards margin of error. If they jump into trees that will be fine, the forest canopy will give them a soft landing and they can climb or abseil down. But if there are any stands of bamboo, that will be much more dangerous. As the SAS learned in Malaya way back in the 1950s, bamboo shatters when you land in it and leaves long, jagged slivers that are as deadly as knives; they can kill a jumper instantly. So we need to find them a safe DZ and I've suggested that they jump from combat height, five hundred feet, just time for the chute to deploy and get the weapon container away before hitting the trees.

'I told the Adj that the guys doing the drop should have a weapon to hand, when they leave the aircraft,

STEPHEN LEATHER

either a pistol on the belt or their Armalite. They usually pack their AR-16s into personal weapon containers but in this case the guys must have a weapon they can get their hands on, preferably the long weapon, because we don't know what might be waiting for them on the ground. It's not just the terrorists, the local tribes can be very feisty. I suggested they should jump with the rifle slung over the shoulder but it's down to the parachute training guys to make the decision.' He gave a weary shake of his head. 'And you know what? I'm 99% certain that this op is just too complicated and is going to end up in a glorious fuck up.'

Having briefed his patrol mates, he summoned Aimee, Chas, Dave and the pilots. 'It's time for a little concurrent activity,' he said, 'because we don't have long to get this right. We're going to be inserting by heli, so I need to know accurately how far away the HIP helicopters we'll be using can be heard in various situations. I need to know how far away it can be heard first in primary jungle – virgin jungle, in other words – then in secondary jungle, where the trees have been felled for slash and burn agriculture and the undergrowth has grown back up, and lastly how far away it can be heard along a river valley. The HIPs are on standby for us, so I need you guys to test it out. That will allow us to plan our insertion. The second part of the equation is how to stop the Ukrainians telling the guys upriver what we're up to, because it's quite possible the bad guys have paid them to report anyone on their track.'

'Er, but how are we going to communicate?' Dave said, clearly hoping he'd found a reason to cancel the exercise.

'In the aircraft rescue pack there are some metal heliographs – mirrors to you and me,' Aimee said. 'We can use them to reflect the sun when we hear the heli and the guys on board will be able to record the distance on the air chart. There are also some mini-flare packs, so we can each take one of those and when we hear the aircraft we can fire them and again the heli guys can record the distance.'

Shepherd nodded. 'Spot on, Aimee. Keep this up and we'll be promoting you in place of Rupert.'

'What about keeping the Ukrainians quiet, once we have been dropped off?' Jimbo said.

'Easy,' Aimee said, 'we'll keep them under lock and key until you get back. It's what Chas and Dave do best, right guys?'

While the rest of the group set about their task, heading across the airfield to where the Ukrainian pilots were waiting with the HIPs, Shepherd, Jimbo, Geordie and Rupert made for a patch of secondary jungle just beyond the airfield perimeter where they could practise their Immediate Action drills.

'Erm, Spider,' Rupert said, eyeing the jungle uneasily. 'Just one small problem, I'm afraid I'm not actually jungle trained. In fact I've never even been in the jungle.'

'You what?' Shepherd said. 'I thought you told us you were badged SAS?'

'I am, but I didn't do jungle training, I was fast tracked into SAS HQ as a badged officer.'

'You mean your friends in the Head Shed cut corners and badged you without you being properly trained or qualified,' Geordie said, 'thinking no bugger would know. But you've been found out now my friend, and I'll make sure everyone in the Regiment knows as well.'

'Well, jungle trained or not, you're coming with us,' Shepherd said. 'You're going to carry the radio set and be our voice link to the Aussies, so you'd better make sure you can use it. Right, we're going to practice our IA drills. In case it wasn't covered in the five minutes training you actually did, Rupert, IA stands for Immediate Action and drill means something that is practised until it becomes instinctive. Previously when we've had a contact with the enemy in the jungle, we've put down fire to keep their heads down and then pepper-potted backwards, covering each other, making for an RV which everyone in the patrol could find. Once the patrol was complete we would then find a way around the enemy. The rationale for that manoeuvre was that we knew we would always be outnumbered, so we would avoid taking casualties and our jungle craft would get us to the target even if we had to make a very long detour. And no, you can't use a GPS because the jungle canopy is too dense to let the signal through. Therefore we have to rely on a paper map and navigational skills. Now if we do our normal IA drills, they will be long gone before we get to the village, so we will have to modify them. I suggest that we try this: I'll go as lead scout, with Geordie behind me, then Rupert, and Jimbo as "Tail-end Charlie". When we hit the enemy, Geordie moves to my left, Rupert comes tight behind me – you should be almost touching me – and Jimbo goes to my right, so together we form a chevron shape, with Rupert tucked in the back where he should be safe enough and not have to worry about getting lost. The theory is, it's a bit like running guard in American football, and we'll go through the enemy like a dose of salts. If you think it's workable let's give it a try, and we can tweak it as we go.'

Rupert nodded but he was clearly uncomfortable.

One of the HIPs took off with a clatter of rotors and wheeled overhead as they found a stand of trees large enough for them to practise the drill and in a few minutes it was working like clockwork.

Shepherd handed out small plastic containers of pills. 'These are your anti-malaria tablets. The pink ones are taken weekly and the white ones daily. Take them until I tell you to stop. I'm not sure if they work because even though they took the tablets religiously, lots of the guys have twenty-four hour fevers with exactly the same symptoms as malaria, but better take them than be sorry. In the Army they have malaria pill parades, but here you're your own boss, so remembering to take them is your responsibility. Wear a hat and long trousers and long-sleeves, rolled down, and use Deet on all exposed skin. That way you shouldn't get bitten.'

The HIP helicopter returned with the others an hour or so later and they had the information that Shepherd had requested. He and Geordie studied their maps, pinpointing a site where the helicopter could drop them, far enough from the terrorists camp so the HIP would not be heard or seen, but close enough for the SAS patrol to reach it quickly. They took off in late afternoon. The flight, rising up the almost sheer wall of the mountains that separated the coastal strip from the interior, was spectacular. As they followed the course of a river, they saw large shoals of brilliantly coloured fish in the deep water pools and literally thousands of butterflies feeding on the minerals in the sandbanks by the river, rising in clouds as the helicopter passed over them.

They touched down on a sandbar in the middle of a relatively placid stretch of river, the Wingco in the co-pilot's seat navigating the helicopter, while the Ukrainian pilot skilfully avoided the overhanging branches from the trees on either side. Behind them in the cabin were the two RAF policeman ready to take control of the pilot when they arrived back at the helicopter base.

The patrol exited the HIP and had disappeared into the jungle even before the helicopter had risen from the sandbar and wheeled away back towards the coast. They were in light camouflage uniform, wearing shirts with the sleeves rolled down and long trousers tucked into US-issue jungle boots. They had their belt kit, ammunition and weapon, but were not carrying rations, only nuts and raisins and high energy bars.

As soon as they moved into the cover of the trees, leeches tried to attach themselves as the patrol filed past and swarms of mosquitoes clouded the air around them. Within seconds their uniforms and webbing were sodden from condensation and sweat, rendering the camouflage useless, and enormous flies buzzed around them, trying to feed on the salty sweat from their bodies.

The leaf mould of centuries made a thick, black, oozing swamp under their feet and the undergrowth was so dense that the lead scout, Shepherd, could not see more than ten yards in front of him. He moved forward slowly and stealthily, the barrel of his weapon tracking his gaze. He carefully positioned each foot-fall, gently easing the foliage aside and guiding it back into place so not a trace of sound or movement would be detectable even from a few yards away and there was no torn leaf or broken plant stem to betray them to a skilled tracker. The roots of the giant trees extended dozens of feet into the air, searching for water as the trees fought for light high in the forest canopy. There was plenty of animal sign on the ground, with the tracks of wild pig and deer, intermingled with those of other, smaller animals, but though the air was full of the sound of birdsong, the birds themselves were invisible in the canopy high above them.

Every few yards Shepherd held up his hand and stopped, remaining motionless as he listened, watched and scented the air, alert for the tiniest sign that an enemy might be lying in wait. The dense undergrowth appeared impenetrable but, like his patrol mates, he had learned to look through, rather than at the undergrowth. It could be a life-saving skill, revealing the shadowy outline of a figure in hiding beyond the fronds and leaves.

They settled into their jungle routine, familiar to everyone but Rupert, taking drinking water from the many streams they crossed, and marching for fifty minutes and resting for ten minutes in every hour, with the rest period mainly given over to burning off leeches with a cigarette lighter. They made good progress except when Rupert marched blindly into thorn bushes and attempted to force his way through, but was ripping his clothing, equipment and skin to pieces until Shepherd told him to stop. 'You have to relax if you get caught up in this and take a pace or two backwards to release yourself. We call it the "wait a minute vine", take your time and it's harmless, but fight it like you are doing and by last light you will be weak from loss of blood. If you look above your head you will also see how you are making the undergrowth move, that can be spotted miles away by a local or a jungle tracker, so take it easy, okay?'

Despite Rupert's problems, they arrived near the target village ahead of schedule and, leaving the others lying up, Shepherd went on a recce. He found a spot on the jungle edge from where he could see the village, its patchwork of crop fields and the surrounding jungle. A large communal building – the village longhouse – with palm leaf sides and a corrugated iron roof, was surrounded by several smaller family houses constructed from the same materials.

The sides of the large communal building were open to the elements and he could see clearly a large group of Asians, mainly men but with some women, carrying out weapons training. There were also groups of local women and children wandering about the village and pigs and dogs rummaging for titbits, but no men were visible. It did not take him long to spot them. The tribesmen were being used as sentries, but were clearly untrained.

As Shepherd scanned the jungle fringes, he caught the aroma of local tobacco on the breeze – wrapped in a dried leaf, it was smoked by many of the tribesmen. He looked along the line of the undergrowth and caught sight of a tell-tale plume of smoke less than fifty yards away.

As he was mentally running through his options, the faint smell of food came drifting from the village and suddenly the sentries started to make their way home, abandoning their posts, moving across a dry rice field, and vaulting over the burnt branches and tree trunks that had been felled to provide the fertiliser to produce the vital crop.

Shepherd waited until all the men had returned to the village, then made his way back to the rest of the patrol. 'Fire up the radio, Rupert, will you?' he said. 'I've got to get a signal off to Swanbourne.'

Rupert hesitated. 'I'm afraid I can't get a signal, Spider. The tree canopy is preventing the signal getting through and hitting the satellite dish.'

'Then why haven't you connected the end-feed aerial instead of the dish?' Shepherd said wearily.

'I'll sort him out, Spider,' Jimbo said. 'We haven't got a lot of time to waste.' He dug a hand into one of the pouches on his belt and pulled out a fishing weight and a reel of fishing line. 'Like everything in my belt-kit, Rupert,' he said, 'these things are multi-purpose. They're part of my escape kit and if I'm on the run, I can use them to catch fish, but if I need to put an aerial through the trees I can tie the fishing line to the weight, throw it through the branches and use the line to pull the aerial through. If you'd asked, I'd have sorted it out for you ages ago.'

Within minutes comms had been established and Spider was speaking to the Adjutant at Swanbourne. He brought him up to speed on the situation around the village and told him that the Herc doing the parachute drop should adjust its heading to avoid some obstacles on the ground. 'There's a probability that the drop will be opposed by the terrorists. We'll attempt to minimise that risk, and in the event of injuries among the parachutists we'll be able to provide first aid on the DZ.'

Immediately after ending the call, Shepherd briefed the others. 'Right guys, it will be dark soon and we need to get a move on. Jimbo, you take Rupert and sit on the edge of the tree-line where you can see the sentry positions of the tribesmen. When the drop starts, if the tribesmen try to interfere, put down suppressing fire. While you're doing that, Geordie and I will work our way across the rice field to get closer to the terrorists. That's where the serious opposition will be, but we have got to try to get our hands on the main man. We should have enough moonlight to find our way without making too much noise. It's a dangerous operation, and once the drop starts everyone will be on full alert, so we'll have to rely on a little bit of luck going our way.'

Shortly after first light the tribesmen on sentry duty went back to their posts around the rice field. Hours passed in almost total silence but then the village dogs suddenly started barking. They had heard the Herc in the distance. The innumerable times that Shepherd and his mates had been in cover waiting for a re-supply drop had attuned his ears to the unique sound. The tribesmen, whose ears were accustomed to filtering out the background noises of the jungle, also picked it up, though most of them were probably unaware of what the noise was.

The last people to hear it were the terrorists. First alerted by the noise of the dogs when they heard the rumble of the Herc's engine note growing louder as it approached, they came tumbling out of the communal hut. Many of them were carrying their weapons but others were unarmed, and rubbing the sleep from their eyes.

With a deafening roar the Herc, painted a light grey and with minimal RAAF markings, flew over the village at combat drop height, about 500 feet, with jumpers leaping off the open rear ramp. When five jumpers were in the air, the Herc did a tight bank to the left, turning hard to get back on track and continue the drop.

There were shouts from the terrorists and those with weapons spread out and started to shoot at the guys hanging below the parachutes. Shepherd and Geordie, comfortably lying across a half-burnt tree trunk began to take out the most dangerous of the terrorist shooters. Suddenly there was a burst of tracer that seared a blinding white track across the sky, moving closer and closer to one of the jumpers.

'There's a Light Machine Gun behind that tree over there,' Geordie said.

'He's mine,' Shepherd said, taking aim with his FN at the tree. He fired a couple of rounds which went straight through the trunk and the LMG operator staggered back and fell to the ground.

'Bloody hell, I knew the FN was powerful but I didn't realise it was that heavy duty,' Geordie said.

'It's the round that packs the real punch,' Shepherd said. 'It'll knock a hole through a brick wall.'

They kept picking targets from among the terrorists and in the background they could hear the sound of firing from Jimbo and Rupert, making sure the local sentries kept their heads down and stayed out of the fight.

In the air the jumpers were frantically pulling down hard on the parachute risers, making the chutes slide quickly sideways through the air, releasing just before hitting the trees for the landing in the tree canopy. Some of the jumpers were lucky enough to land in the rice field where they quickly got their kit together and joined in the battle.

After the Herc dropped its fifth and final stick of jumpers Shepherd spotted a couple who had become entangled in the forest canopy. Both dazed from the hard impact with the trees, they were hanging limply a couple of hundred feet from the ground. One of the terrorists had also noticed them. He drew his comrades attention to them with loud cries and a group of them began to shoot at the easy targets. Shepherd stood up in full view, shouted to gain their attention and draw their fire, then, with support from Geordie, began to pick off the terrorists one by one. Only when the sounds of battle began to die down did the two jumpers manage to lower themselves to the ground and were then given a quick medical check by Geordie.

It took well over an hour before all the paratroopers were accounted for, all of them safe and well except for minor scrapes and bruises. Even with small sticks of five, they had become scattered over a wide area and by the time they arrived at the RV with the British SAS men the fighting was almost over. Once the last terrorist had been killed, Shepherd and his men went through the bodies, but none of them was the man they had glimpsed in Zurich. The Adjutant was keen to carry out a search and sweep in an attempt to locate the terrorist leader, and Shepherd, though he suspected it would be a waste of time, reluctantly agreed.

The area around the village was littered with dead terrorists. The villagers had fled into the jungle. During the sweep, the patrol found the tracks of a group of terrorists heading away from the village into dense primary jungle. The Adjutant was keen to follow but Shepherd advised caution. 'They can travel quicker than we can because we have to find and follow their tracks and if we get too close, they can drop a guy or two off to ambush us and delay us even further.'

Shepherd summoned the HIP helicopter to fly them back to Port Moresby and on arrival he spoke to Jock on the sat phone to discuss their next move. 'We've taken out some of the terrorists,' Shepherd said, 'but not the leader and a few others, who all scarpered into the jungle as soon as the firefight started. And we don't know how many others, including previously trained men and sleepers, he'll also be able to call on.'

'We'll have to assume that he has enough men for the job he's planning,' Jock said. 'And I've got a fair idea what it might be. There is a Chinese state visit to Australia next week. Several of the head honchos, including the supreme leader, are involved. If you were an Uyghur terrorist looking for a spectacular, that would certainly provide it. Small scale stabbings, shootings and bombings are not going to affect things, but as the old saying goes, cut off the head and the body dies. They can't get to him in Beijing because the state is too powerful and too well organised, and they'd be betrayed or detected before they'd got within miles of him. So they need to do it on neutral territory and where better than a country that has never witnessed any major terrorist incidents, so its security forces are likely to be lax and complacent?'

'Anything from GCHQ?' Shepherd said.

'There was a bit of a flurry immediately after the firefight, but now it's all gone quiet. I reckon he's worked out that we're intercepting their comms and imposed radio silence on his men. We'll have to assume that they'll be reverting to old-style comms in future – with our luck that'll be handwritten notes and bloody carrier pigeons.'

'If we're right that Australia's the target will they be able to enter the country undetected?'

'What do you think?' Jock said. 'They can either fly in among some of the tens of thousands of Chinese tourists that arrive there every year, or they can ship out from Port Moresby or somewhere more discreet, either bribing someone in the Papuan Defence Force to use one of their patrol craft or on board a fishing boat or a tramp steamer. Port Moresby is only seventy-five kilometres from Cape York and the Torres Straits Treaty allows free movement of indigenous people without passports or visas between PNG and the Torres Strait Islands, for fishing, trading or family reunions, so local boats don't get much in the way of inspections. They could trans-ship to an Australian-registered boat on one of the islands in the Straits – there are plenty to choose from – and then sail into any port they like.'

'So, assuming getting into Australia is no problem, how do they guarantee being able to reach their target when they get there?'

'They'll already have identified some event that the Chinese leadership has to attend. We'll need to get the Chinese itinerary from the Aussies and identify likely targets from that. Oh, and from my preliminary conversations with them, the Aussies seem to be adamant that while they don't mind you guys advising and assisting them, no way do they want you directly involved if anything goes down. Personally I think that's down to the Aussie inferiority complex, but be careful not to tread too heavily on anybody's toes.'

Shepherd grinned. 'I don't know what you mean Jock. Me, treading on toes? As if.'

'Yeah, whatever,' Jock growled. 'Anyway they'll have plans for countering terrorist attacks on the major potential targets on the Chinese itinerary, so you need to see them and evaluate them. They will no doubt be comprehensive and expertly thought through, just like ours for the UK, but the question is whether the plans will stand up when the shit hits the fan. Everyone is always happy until plans are put to the test and then they start crapping themselves because they haven't given them enough attention.

I'll let you go in a minute, but one other thing, Spider. I had a call from the Yorkshire Skunkworks, you know that strange little factory that has come up with a lot of really useful bits of kit over the years. It's like something out of the nineteenth century: a small forge and all sorts of metal-working tools, I'd swear they've even got steam-hammers in there somewhere. They employ highly-skilled old guys who worked in the Sheffield steel industry in the days when there was such a thing, plus a couple of new-fangled techie guys who do all the computer stuff. They've come up with a prototype of a harpoon style device designed to penetrate through solid doors or single brick walls. It could be a useful method of entry device because it's air-powered, so there's no problem with explosive over-pressure damaging people inside the besieged building. However the Skunkworks emphasised that it is a prototype and hasn't had a lot of testing, so they're giving us a chance to run the rule over it. I thought the quickest way of getting it to you was by FedEx. It should be with you shortly so keep your eyes open for it. I suggest you get Geordie and Jimbo to test fire it a few times and see if it's any good.'

CHAPTER 26

Later that day the SAS team flew into RAAF Richmond, near Sydney – the base for the Australian Air Force Hercules fleet. Shepherd immediately set up a meeting with Captain Jake Handy, the Intelligence Officer of the Australian SAS counterterrorist team. They met in a windowless basement room beneath the control tower building, next door to the classified documents registry for the base. It was also the temporary repository for the top secret contingency plans for potential terrorist targets in Canberra and the Greater Sydney area – the only places the Chinese delegation would be visiting.

Handy spread a number of files on the table. They were dark red in colour with a large black "X" on the front and "TOP SECRET" in capital letters above it. 'It's bloody madness, Spider,' he said. 'I wrote the bloody files, I gave them the classification I thought they deserved and now I'm not allowed to take the bloody things out of this building. I can tell you word for word what is in each of them but, technically I can't let you see them. As I said, it's bloody madness.' He gave Shepherd a wink and pushed the files across the table. 'However, as the saying goes, What the eye doesn't see, the heart can't grieve over. Fill your boots, mate, and tell me what you think.'

Shepherd flicked idly through the files. Five had been marked for special attention: "Parliament Building, Canberra", "Chinese Consulate, Camperdown, Sydney", "Casino, Sydney", "Opera House, Sydney" and "Harbour Bridge, Sydney". 'I'll just get a general idea of what you've got on each of the potential targets,' he said, 'but then my team will do ground recces to get familiar with what's out there. It's difficult to assess which of the targets they might go for, but I think we'll have a much better idea once we've had a look on the ground. We know they are ruthless and well prepared, and I suspect they will be looking for maximum publicity for their cause. The death of the Chinese leader would guarantee that, but even more so if it happened in a really prominent place, so there's no chance of a news blackout being imposed so it's hushed up or ignored by the media. We saw it in the dry runs they carried out at the Acropolis and the Louvre, and if I'm right about that, it would make the Harbour Bridge or the Opera House the most likely sites.' He pushed the files to one side and glanced through the official itinerary. 'Is this subject to change?'

'No mate, set in stone. It's even been published in the bloody newspapers. Day One, CT – Capital Territory – Days Two and Three, Sydney. What haven't been published, obviously, are the security details – the search teams and cordons around the various targets, and so on. But anyone who knows their business will be able to work out what'll be going on in the background. Even the timings are in the public domain, so people can get to see him, though the only ones who will make the effort will probably be the demonstrators, for and against. I tell you what, mate, there's going to be plenty of riots and demos. It could get pretty ugly.'

Shepherd studied the itinerary again, then abruptly stood up. 'Like I said, we'll need to carry out a recce on the ground, but on paper, I would say that this is the most plausible site,' he said, tapping his finger on the last entry on the itinerary. "A gala performance by the Chinese State Opera at the Sydney Opera House". I presume security is too tight at the Australian Parliament to make that a realistic target?'

Handy nodded. 'Fort Knox without the gold, mate.'

'Then the Opera House is the one event you can absolutely guarantee Comrade Chou won't miss, and you couldn't have a more iconic place for an assassination.' He held Handy's gaze. 'How can we work together with you on this? As you know, we've got a lot of expertise and a lot of recent experience in dealing with his kind of scenario, but obviously we don't want to be barging in where we're not welcome.'

Handy spread his hands. 'Mate, I'd love for us to be double-teaming this, but our hands are tied. It's been made very clear by the politicos that we're here in support of the NSW Police and not the other way round. They're running the show and are responsible for the whole shebang: crowd control, searching, cordons, vetting and entry to the various events. It's going to be a right head banger of a situation, demos for and against, blood on the streets, the city in lockdown. The Chinese have even shipped in their own security teams, listed as embassy officials. They know something is going to happen and don't trust us to keep their man safe, and they may be right about that. But we will only get involved if it's something the cops can't handle, and they are very unlikely to admit to that... until it's too late. So there you are.'

Something about Handy's expression told Shepherd that it wasn't his last word on the subject. 'So if I'm reading you right,' he said, 'although your hands are tied, you wouldn't be totally upset if we were to see what we could do, providing we don't tread on any police toes in the process?'

Handy smiled. 'I couldn't possibly say that – or not on the record anyway. Off the record, someone needs to be on top of this and I'm not sure the boys in blue are up to it. Sydney's finest are complacent – some would say arrogant. The only protests they've had to deal with in years have been union marches and campaigns for aboriginal rights.'

'Is there any point in us talking to the police?' asked Shepherd.

'You can, but I guarantee that the only answer you'll get is "Thanks Pommie, now fuck off".'

'Fair enough,' Shepherd said, 'but I'm sure that there's going to be a major incident. And I want to be there when it kicks off because I've got a score or two to settle.'

'I probably shouldn't say this,' Handy said, 'but something we Aussies admire about the Pommie SAS is that you're more prepared to take risks than we are. We're much more tightly controlled by our political masters.'

Shepherd inclined his head. 'We take risks, yes, but we train and plan to the max beforehand, so that we understand the risks and have taken every possible step to minimise them.'

'All right mate, go for it, and if you need any help in what you're planning, just ask. We owe you for PNG.'

'But I suppose a copy of these files is out of the question?' Shepherd said.

'I'd like to help you, mate, but if I did that and it ever got out, it wouldn't just be my career and my pension, I'd be jailed for betraying state secrets. Anything else, you've got it.'

'I understand,' Shepherd said. 'Just give me a few more minutes to study them.' In the event he spent a further two hours there, making a forensic examination of the plans of the Opera House, including all possible access points, not just doors and windows, but manholes, drains, conduits and vents. He made frequent notes and a few sketch plans and drawings and when he'd finished he had a glimmer of an idea about how he could access Sydney's most iconic structure unseen.

While Shepherd had been talking to Handy and studying the files, Jimbo and Geordie were staring dubiously at the contents of the package that the Wingco had just delivered to them. It had arrived in a FedEx cardboard box and they had unpacked it and assembled it following the clear and concise instructions that came with it. They now had a squat oval cylinder about eighteen inches long with a gas cylinder at the rear and an arrowhead-shaped harpoon protruding from the front. The whole thing was made from titanium alloy and mounted on a small tripod.

Having charged the cylinder from an industrial-sized bottle of compressed air, they first dry-fired it without the harpoon attachment. When they were satisfied that it actually worked, they took it to an abandoned building dating back to World War II on the edge of the airfield where they could carry out a full-scale test fire. Now was the moment of truth, they aimed the device at one of the building's single-skin brick walls, and Jimbo held the firing lanyard while Geordie did the countdown. As he reached 'Zero!', Jimbo gave a tentative pull on the lanyard and then, not knowing what to expect, both of them pressed their fingers into their ears. In fact, there was no loud bang, just a fierce hiss of escaping air, but the harpoon was blasted forward at incredible speed, trailing a thin cable in its wake. It disappeared through the wall, dislodging enough bricks to leave a hole that a man could just about have squeezed through.

They walked over to inspect the damage. On the other side of the wall, the device had opened into a metal framework, like the frame of an umbrella, on the far side of the entry hole, about two and a half metres in diameter.

'Now I get it,' Jimbo said. 'If we pull on the trailing rope, it will make a hole big enough to run through. If we attached the rope to a vehicle or a winch it would make a hole in almost anything: windows, doors, walls, you name it. What a bit of kit! Even the rope is carbon fibre, so it's almost unbreakable. This is going to come in handy!'

Although Shepherd had assessed the Opera House as the most likely target, in the course of the next day and night, the three SAS men carried out ground recces of all the other potential sites. They eliminated them one by one: too secure, too complex, no access, no escape route. The more they studied the alternatives, the more convinced they all became that the terrorists had chosen the Opera House as the stage for their spectacular. To get the full picture they took a tourist tour of the building, their keen eyes missing nothing as the cameras of the holiday-makers clicked incessantly around them. At the end of the tour, they strolled around the perimeter of the building, pausing frequently, ostensibly to admire the views across the harbour or gaze up in wonder at the soaring "sails" that formed the roof.

Although the itinerary had been set in stone, there had been one change: the original plan had been to hold the gala performance in the main Concert Hall of the Opera House, which had the greatest seating capacity. However a boycott organised in protest at China's repressive policies and contempt for human rights had been so effective that tickets were being returned and apologies for absence received, almost faster than the organisers could cope with them. All attempts having failed to solve the problem, to avoid exposing the Chinese, not to mention their Australian hosts, to the embarrassment of having a gala performance in front of an auditorium that was only one-third full, at the last minute it had been switched to the Number Two space: the Opera Theatre. It was also a very impressive space, but with only about half the seats to fill.

'So if that's the target, Spider,' Geordie said. 'What are our options for gaining access?'

'It'll have to be covert,' Shepherd said. 'Because the state police are running the show and don't want any input from the Aussie SAS, let alone a bunch of Pommies like us. It also needs to be well in advance, before the security around the place is tightened, so it seems like tonight should be the night.'

'Right, that's the when and where,' Jimbo said, 'What about the how?'

Shepherd flipped through the pages of his notebook. 'There are a couple of small grilles set in the roof. We can't see them from down here but they're marked on the plans. They give access to the roof void and from there I should be able to abseil down onto the lighting gantry above the stage.'

'Should?' Geordie said.

Shepherd smiled. 'Did I say should? I meant will.'

Jimbo frowned. 'I dunno Spider, those roof tiles are ceramic, aren't they? They look bloody slippery.'

'And how will you access the roof anyway?' Geordie said. 'The gig's not for another forty-eight hours but they're already putting the barriers in place.' He gestured towards a group of police who were cordoning off the whole of the steps and terraces leading to the Opera House with steel barriers, while others had begun steering the tourists out of the building and the surrounding area.

'I thought a late night dip might be the way to go.' Shepherd pointed towards the Botanical Gardens stretching eastwards along the shore. 'I can slip into the water round there, and the ferries coming in and out of Circular Quay will churn up the water enough to hide me from the sight of anyone watching from the Opera House terrace.' He smiled. 'And if I can't slip across the terrace and climb the roof without being spotted by a couple of half-asleep local cops or bored security guards, I shouldn't be doing this job at all.'

'So where are we in all this?' Geordie said.

'I need you to liaise with the Aussie SAS, who'll be on standby in case they're needed. Get yourselves inside the outer security cordon on the big night, and then await developments, but be ready to force immediate entry if and when I give you the word over the radio.'

'Weapons?' Jimbo said.

'I think MP5s for all of us.'

Geordie nodded. 'And we'll bring that new piece of kit. It did a bloody good job on a brick wall so it might be a useful method of entry if the bad guys grab some hostages and barricade themselves in anywhere.'

CHAPTER 27

That afternoon, Shepherd assembled all his kit and weaponry. He dressed in a dry suit with a tight-fitting tracksuit underneath, in the NSW police force colours. He checked his equipment container for negative buoyancy and leaks in the base swimming pool and then checked his own negative buoyancy, adding weights to the belt around his dry suit until he had achieved a level that would allow him to swim just below the water, with only twenty-five percent of his body above the surface. In that position he would be virtually undetectable to above surface radar on the police boats patrolling the approaches from the harbour and would be mistaken for flotsam by any sub-surface detection devices.

He slipped into the water from a cove in the Botanical Gardens just before midnight. He was wearing a pair of super-sized fins on his feet to propel him through the water, and was also helped by the current flowing around the bay towards the Opera House. By swimming on his side he minimised his silhouette to just a few inches above the waterline, and the choppy water caused by the ferries, pleasure boats and police launches around Circular Quay and Bennelong Point made him virtually invisible in the darkness.

He had packed his waterproof equipment container meticulously. Inside were an MP 5K with four thirty-round magazines, a workman's belt with a steel wrecking bar and a range of other tools that might be needed, a pair of trainers and a towel because he had to be absolutely dry for where he was going after the swim. He had a fixed channel HF radio with a set of spare batteries and also, crucially there was an abseiling system, with the rope wound inside a canvas bag. The rope would only deploy as he descended, making it more covert than the normal abseiling system.

In a holster under his arm he carried a Glock 9mm pistol, the rounds in the magazine lightly covered in grease to protect them from the small amount of sea-water they would be exposed to, and a razor-sharp fighting knife was strapped to his leg.

The swim was physically arduous, with the small swells from the boat traffic in the harbour occasionally washing over him, trying to push him off course. However, after twenty minutes of hard swimming, he reached the concrete retaining wall beneath the harbour-side terrace of the Opera House.

He worked his way round to the bottom of the steps leading up from the water and then quickly unpacked his kit. He cut off the dry suit with his fighting knife, weighed it down with his diving belt and silently lowered it back into the water, watching it sink out of sight. He carefully dried himself then dropped the towel into the water as well and, alert for any noise or movement, he climbed the steps. The promenade would normally have been bustling with people but the police cordons had left it deserted. The police and security teams had obviously decided that the harbour was all the security that they needed at the rear of the Opera House and were keeping watch at the front with only an intermittent foot patrol passing right around the building. Clad in black from head to foot and with the night sky masked by cloud cover, Shepherd was able to remain invisible in the darkness near the top of the steps for the next hour, timing the patrols as they passed by. Professionals would have varied the gaps between patrols but he was pleased to note that the NSW police were creatures of habit, passing by at precisely fifteen minute intervals.

He waited until the patrol had again just passed him and then, every sense attuned for any signs of them returning, Shepherd moved swiftly across the terrace and into the shadows of the recessed area between the two wings of the building housing the Concert Hall and the Theatre. He used a small grapnel to help him climb the sheer, roughcast concrete wall and spent a couple more minutes making sure he was in the exact spot he needed, directly below the intersection of the two banks of soaring sails that formed the roof, before starting to climb.

The roof panels were four feet square and so smooth and shiny that he could get no purchase on them, and there were no fixing bolts or other projections he could grasp. However, there were narrow fissures above the interlocking flanges of each panel, and by jamming his fingers into the gaps and then locking them in place with his thumb – a technique he had learned from free rock climbers – and bracing the soles of his trainers against the tiles, he was able to haul himself up far enough to jam the fingers of his other hand into the next gap.

It was painfully slow progress and the drizzle that had begun to fall made the climb up the steeply sloping, curved roof even more lethally slippery. Twice his foot slipped and he dropped down until his wedged fingers jerked him to an agonising halt. Ignoring the pain from his fingers, he dragged himself back up and climbed on. He kept inching his way up the steeply sloping roof. At last his groping fingers found their first secure handhold – the ridge line of the roof. He heaved himself up and paused there a moment, straddling the ridge.

The lights of the harbour-side tower blocks cast a faint glow over the roof but even if anyone had been watching at that moment, they would have seen nothing but a momentary dark shape, almost invisible against the black of the night sky. A moment later it was gone, as Shepherd lowered himself over the other side of the ridge. The grille he was seeking was only a few feet below him, but descending the roof felt even more precarious than climbing it, and his heart was in his mouth as he inched his way down, groping with his feet for the reassuring feel of the steel frame. It had been painted to match the tile work and was invisible from the ground, but he knew from the plans he had studied that it was there. At last, when his forearms were trembling from the strain of bearing his weight, his foot touched something that was not yet another smooth roof tile. Two minutes later, he was holding on to the steel bars of the grille.

Using his left hand to cling to the roof tile alongside it, he groped in his pack for the wrecking bar and used it to prise open the grille. With a faint squeal of protesting metal, it swung open on its hinges and Shepherd pulled himself up and swung feet first through the gap. The structural panels supporting the roof were concrete frames with diagonal cross beams connecting to a central boss, but the gaps between them were just wide enough for him to squeeze through into the vast, timbered roof space of the Opera Theatre. Searching around him, he eventually located a trapdoor, and glancing through, he found himself high above the auditorium, directly above the main stage.

Looking down, he could see the steel gantry, the grid deck holding the lighting rigs, and the suspended stage sets that hung ready for a future performance. To either side, steel "cages", hidden behind the sides of the proscenium arch, encased thickets of cables, ropes and wires, and more cables were wound around huge steel drums and mechanical pulleys at either end of the gantry. There were so many dangling ropes, wires and cables that looking through them was like peering into a jungle. He climbed down to the gantry, found a strong belay point and tied off his abseil rope, then settled down and made himself comfortable; he had a long wait ahead of him. From his perch high up in the theatre, he would have a bird's-eye view of events as they unfolded.

For the remainder of the night he observed the watchmen going about their duties, checking the auditorium, punching their time-clocks and occasionally taking a seat to ease the strain on their feet. Each time they checked all the exit doors, but none ever raised their eyes to the roof high above them. Even if they had done so, Shepherd was invisible, hidden by the lights and equipment.

Eventually an army of cleaners appeared, vacuuming the carpets and dusting down the seats. A procession of officials, some in uniform, then came into the auditorium to check that everything was to their satisfaction, taking notes, ticking checklists and talking loudly among themselves. They also staged a run-through of the ceremonies that would be held in honour of the distinguished visitors, with an assortment of minions filling in for the principals, rehearsing the ushering, bowing and scraping that would accompany the arrival of the dignitaries.

At the end of the morning and for most of the afternoon there followed the final rehearsals for the big night. The show was to be a staging of an opera eulo-gising Chairman Mao's revolutionary Long March, performed by the Chinese National Opera in the original Chinese, something Shepherd was sure that the Australian great and good would be keenly look-ing forward to. As stagehands began scaling the steel staircase leading to the gantry, Shepherd retreated to the shadows behind one of the giant steel cages encas-ing wires and cables, and remained unseen as they rehearsed the set changes and lighting cues.

From his vantage point, Shepherd was still able to see and hear the chorus, dressed in khaki uniforms and carrying replica firearms, as they marched around the stage, singing revolutionary songs in Chinese. When rehearsals were finally over, the stagehands descended from the gantry and the opera house quickly emptied, with everything now set for the next day.

Standard Operating Procedures when on surveil-lance required SAS men to carry in everything they would need with them and remove it again after-wards, leaving no trace that they had ever been there. So Shepherd had brought two containers of drink-ing water in his pack. When he had emptied the first one, he began to refill it with his urine because, as their instructor had remarked during his first days of training with the Regiment, 'Not even SAS men can go forty-eight hours without taking a leak.'

During the following night things went along the by now familiar routine, the watchmen coming and going from an auditorium bathed in the ghostly glow of the emergency lighting. After dawn, activity increased dramatically, with the same army of cleaners blitzing the auditorium of dust, wiping down the seats and vacuuming the carpets, while workmen carrying stepladders dusted the wall lights and replaced dud bulbs, leaving the auditorium spotless.

Next came the PR people, unconsciously wiping down the seats again before placing embossed name cards on the VIP seats. They were followed by florists and flower arrangers placing huge bouquets of fresh flowers along the front of the orchestra pit and at strategic intervals around the theatre. Before anyone could leave, a man who was clearly the head of the event organisation arrived and fussily removed a few flower-heads and ran a finger along a couple of ledges ostentatiously looking for dust, before giving a curt nod, at which all of them left.

A group of men in coveralls were next to enter. They began a search of the area, moving slowly and methodically through the VIP seats, using detectors and probes. About halfway through the search a couple of sniffer dogs and their handlers turned up. A few minutes later, the area was given the all clear and they all left, leaving the auditorium deserted, save for a few uniformed security men who stationed themselves at the entry doors.

While Shepherd had been an interested observer inside the Opera House, Geordie and Jimbo were safely inside the intermediate cordon, furnished by

Ronnie the Warrant Officer with the correct security passes identifying them as part of the technical support group to the Aussie SAS counter-terrorist team. They had kept in touch with Shepherd since he had entered the Opera House using a non-verbal click system on the radio.

The Aussie SAS had brought explosive charges in case it was necessary to blow the doors, but Geordie rapidly disabused them of that idea. 'Have you not heard of explosive overpressure?' he said. 'If you detonate those charges on the doors, you'll kill more people than you save. If we need to blow the doors, we'll use this,' he said, pointing to the harpoon. He and Jimbo had already done all the recces they needed to do, pacing out the distance from the main entry doors to the point where they would place the harpoon and checking the towing shackle on the front of the 4x4 camouflaged Ute they had borrowed from the Aussies. They had even gone inside the Opera House to check distances and angles that might not have been apparent from the scale drawings they had been given.

The only slight worry was that Rupert would be driving the Ute while Geordie and Jimbo were poised to burst into the building. 'Whatever you do don't cock it up,' Geordie said to the officer. 'Reverse nice and steady if I give you the signal, and for fuck's sake, don't panic and stall it. Think you can manage that?'

Rupert gave a hesitant nod that did not inspire much confidence. 'Would you rather I got one of the Aussies to do it?' Geordie said.

Rupert gave a rather more vigorous shake head. 'No, it's fine, I'll do it.'

Inside the Opera House, things now began to unravel as Shepherd had suspected they would. Being a security guard at the Opera House usually involved nothing more arduous than ejecting the occasional person trying to get in to a performance without a ticket or drunks who had overstayed their welcome in the bars. The guards had inevitably become lazy and complacent and were thrown off balance by the sudden arrival of a small crowd of Chinese men, dressed in near-identical, off-the-peg shiny suits, demanding entry and growing angry when the security men tried to insist that they weren't allowed in.

The voices became angrier and louder but just when it looked like they might come to blows, an Australian official hurried over, overruled the security guards and allowed the Chinese in. Arrogantly they walked around checking everything that had already been checked and then left, but not before haranguing the security guards again.

'Round one to chaos,' Shepherd thought. He contacted Geordie on the radio and asked for an audio sitrep, abandoning the click system for a whispered verbal report. Geordie brought him up to speed, reporting that there had been violent demonstrations at key points around the city, the self-appointed Chinese security teams were creating havoc and several dozen of them had assembled outside the Opera House, and were verbally and physically clashing with the spectators who had already begun to assemble. 'It's got all the makings of a glorious cock-up,' Geordie said.

'Yeah, they're doing a good job, those guys,' Shepherd said. 'They've already cocked up the sterile area around the VIP seating. It should be searched again but that's not going to happen, because the Oz diplomatic people are too frightened of upsetting the Chinese.'

When he checked in with Geordie again an hour later, his fears were confirmed. The Chinese were disrupting the whole security operation, breaking cordons, breaching entry points and turning the focus of the security operation from watching for potential intruders and terrorists to minimising the chaos caused by the Chinese security teams.

Things continued in a similar vein throughout the day, with new groups of Chinese security, even more important than the previous ones, demanding and gaining entry. Event organisers higher and higher up the food chain also entered, looked around and, having made the point of how important they were, left again having done little and achieved nothing. Eventually the first of the distinguished guests began arriving, having run the discreet security gauntlet of magnetic barriers, facial recognition television, chemical sensors, odour sniffing devices, explosive swab detectors and handbag searches. 'Too bloody late, mate,' Shepherd thought. 'The fox will already be inside the coop.'

CHAPTER 28

The Chinese Premier frowned as he examined his reflection in the full-length mirror in his suite. He prided himself on his figure and his immaculate appearance and the bulky outline he saw in the mirror was not at all to his taste. However, for all the precautions they had taken, the Kevlar body armour concealed beneath his jacket was a very necessary safeguard; it did not always take a skilled assassin to topple a leader, one stray bullet could sometimes be enough.

Chou Zhenhua's path to the leadership had begun in the most humble circumstances, growing up in the provincial backwater of Xinjiang, far from Beijing and the centre of power. He joined the youth wing of the Communist Party and steadily worked his way up the hierarchy, always volunteering for the least glamorous jobs, willing to do the drudgery of writing minutes and compiling reports, that others were happy to hand to him.

When he graduated from the youth wing to the senior party, he ingratiated himself with potential patrons and allies in a similar way, while working behind the scenes to undermine rivals and enemies. There was never anything with his fingerprints on it, just a murmured comment in someone's ear, or an apparently bland memo, concealing a scorpion sting in the tail. He courted the old generals and senior politicians alike, always apparently no threat to anyone, just a stolid, bureaucratic, safe pair of hands who could be trusted to keep the local party or the ship of state heading steadily in the same direction.

He impressed the Beijing leadership with the ruthless way he crushed protests and rebellion by the native Uyghur population in the city of Turguan, imprisoning many of the protesters and publicly executing all the leaders. Summoned to Beijing as a result, but still only a middle-ranking Party functionary, his relentless rise continued and as his power grew, so his mask began to slip even more. He was cold, friendless and feared. He never raised his voice above a quiet monotone, but there was no longer any disguising his ambition, nor the sense of menace in his icy glance or sibilant speech. No matter how busy and involved in national politics he became, he always had time to take personal charge of any "necessary measures" against the Uyghurs in his home region.

He became deputy premier and then assumed the leadership when his rival was implicated in a major corruption scandal. Chou, like the rest of the politbureau, was no less corrupt but much more adept at covering his tracks. Nothing was in his name. His substantial and ever-growing wealth was apparently owned by relatives and nominees, and laundered through strings of obliging capitalist banks and shell companies, spread around the globe.

Now his power was absolute and his authority unchallenged, striding the world like a colossus. This engagement – the final, climactic event of his Australian state visit – had been planned with meticulous care, even including a "dress rehearsal" with the banqueting hall of the Chinese Embassy standing in for the Opera Theatre at the Sydney Opera House. Every eventuality appeared to have been catered for but there was always an element of doubt, no matter how slight, in case some unlikely but possible scenario had been overlooked.

With a final tug at his jacket, he turned away from the mirror. Waving away the aides who were clustered around him, he glanced at his watch, a Hublot. It was less ostentatious than a Patek Philippe, but still a rare, extravagant departure from his carefully cultivated image as a homespun man of the people. It perhaps indicated that he now saw his position as impregnable. Not that he would ever be complacent, because his own rise to power was a pathway that other men of equally ferocious ambition might one day seek to emulate.

Distracted by that thought, he was almost out of the door of his suite before an aide at last caught his attention and placed a hat into his hands. He normally went everywhere bare-headed and, lined with Kevlar, the hat was both heavy and a little ugly but, because of the known terrorist threat, his head of security had begged him to wear it and for once he had bowed to his wishes. Even so, he carried it in his hand rather than wearing it as he emerged from the hotel and, flanked by a phalanx of his own security men and New South Wales Police, walked the few steps to his waiting armoured limousine.

A battery of press photographers and camera crews recorded his departure, the sound of Nikon motor-drives and shouted questions from reporters not quite covering the shouts and jeers from the crowds of protestors, kept penned by the police at a safe distance from the hotel. China was by far Australia's biggest trading partner and nothing was going to be allowed to disrupt the Chinese head of state's triumphant progress through the city.

Chou's armoured limousine was sandwiched between the black 4x4s carrying his battery of armed bodyguards and the paramedics who accompanied him everywhere, ready for anything from a heart attack to an assassination attempt. Two vehicles carrying Australian Special Forces rode shotgun at the rear, and the column was flanked by a score of police outriders on motorbikes, riding ahead in pairs to block each intersection in turn, until Chou's motorcade had sped past. Policemen on foot, stationed at two metre intervals the length of the route, stood with their backs to the road, their gazes fixed on the crowds penned behind steel crash-barriers. They had orders to confiscate any flags or banners other than the paper Chinese flags issued in thousands by Chinese advance-men working the crowds before the motorcade passed by.

The drive to the Opera House through streets cleared of all other traffic took only a few minutes. A huge crowd of protesters once more bayed their impotent fury from the temporary compound where they had been herded, far from the steps of the Opera House. Their democratic right to protest had been maintained but nowhere in the constitution did it say that the right had to be maintained within ear-shot of the object of their protest.

The motorcade of limousines and their attendant heavy security was followed by a rather more prosaic convoy of minibuses ferrying officials from the Chinese embassy. Six minibuses had left the embassy compound late that afternoon, but seven of them arrived at the security cordon surrounding the Opera House and were waved through by the guards.

Watched by an honour guard of NSW police lining the steps, Chou's bodyguards had fanned out, their suspicious gazes flickering over every inch of the surrounding area. Chou emerged from his limousine at the head of the Chinese delegation, now wearing his hat. He was greeted by the Australian Prime Minister and the Premier of New South Wales and then escorted into the building by the Director of the Opera House.

Even though the event had been switched to the smaller Opera Theatre and despite issuing free tickets to city, state and government employees and their partners, it was little more than half full. The audience were all in their places, excluding the three front rows. Row One for the VIPs and the Chinese guest of honour, Row Two for senior members of the Diplomatic Corps and their consorts and Row Three for Secretaries, ADC's and bodyguard team leaders. Around the walls the Chinese security guards in their shiny suits stared suspiciously at the seated audience. The opera chorus and stars, most wearing green uniforms and high boots with weapons on their shoulders, then filed out of the wings and formed two ranks on the stage. A hush fell over the auditorium and everyone in the audience got to their feet, some looking expectantly over their shoulders. Applause broke out at the rear of the theatre and was picked up by those at the front as the great procession came through the doors. The members of the Diplomatic Corps led the way with the Prime Minister of Australia and the Guest of Honour, Comrade Chou, bringing up the rear.

However, instead of making for his seat, Chou's phalanx of bodyguards steered him towards a doorway at the side of the theatre. He disappeared inside, accompanied by his bodyguards, and the door clicked shut behind them.

When the Chinese Premier re-emerged a couple of minutes later, only the keenest-eyed observer would have noted that just half the number of body-guards were now accompanying him.

He was escorted to the place of honour, front and centre in the auditorium with the still puzzled Prime Minister on his right and the State Premier on his left. However he sat staring straight ahead, ignoring all their attempts to engage him in small talk. Bizarrely he was still wearing his hat and made no move to remove it as the house lights dimmed and the orchestra played both national anthems.

There was a short pause with everyone politely remaining standing until the VIPs in the first and second row had sat down, but suddenly there was a commotion on the stage. Several of the uniform chorus had unslung their weapons into the firing position and they at once began firing long bursts, trying to take out the bodyguards lining the walls and those seated behind the VIPs. Pandemonium broke out as diplomats and government ministers were sprayed with blood, while simultaneously the Chinese security guards returned fire and some members of the chorus on stage started to shoot each other.

Shepherd felt rather than heard the great main fire doors on the outside of the building slamming violently shut – part of the Opera House's standard security procedures in emergencies. The pressure change caused his ears to pop. He shouted into his radio to Geordie, 'Go! Go! Go!', glanced at his tie-off on the belay point and then threw himself into space above the stage. He controlled his descent with his left hand while he held his MP 5K, primed and ready to fire, in his right.

As the shooting started, the theatre erupted in panic with people scrambling over the seats, pushing, shoving and trampling others in their rush to escape, while others flattened themselves to the floor between the rows of seats and remained there, trembling with fright. The Australian Prime Minister's bodyguards hurled themselves upon him, almost burying him under their bodies and then, shielding him from all sides, they tried to hustle him out of the building and bundle him into his limousine. With all the doors and exits in automatic lockdown, they could get no further than the foyer.

As Shepherd abseiled downwards, out of the corner of his eye he caught sight of the Chinese leader, who in the midst of all the gunfire, carnage and panic, made no attempt to escape and merely hunched down in his seat. He remained motionless, staring at the floor in front of him from under the brim of his hat, while volleys of gunfire echoed around him as the bodyguards flanking him fired at the surviving terrorists.

Even as he slid down, Shepherd had already begun taking out the shooters on the stage and killed several before the others were even aware that he was there. Just as he was about to target them as well, the abseil rope feeding out of the bag on his leg snagged sharply on itself, causing him to jerk to a halt and then swing like a pendulum a few feet above the stage.

As soon as the main doors had slammed shut from the inside, Geordie fired the harpoon and it smashed through the steel-framed doors as if they were paper. As the steel "umbrella" frame deployed, Jimbo shouted 'Go!' and Rupert put the Ute into gear and pulled away. The carbon rope tautened and with a sound like a bomb going off, the doors were catapulted out of their frames. Even before the dust had cleared, Geordie and Jimbo were sprinting through the hole with the Aussie SAS assault team hot on their heels. As they burst into the auditorium they were confronted by a scene of confusion and chaos, with members of the on-stage chorus and the Chinese security teams apparently targeting each other. They glimpsed Shepherd on his abseil rope above the stage but then focused on their own tasks, methodically working their way up the theatre, taking out any terrorist targets that presented themselves as they ran.

Shepherd needed two hands to clear the rope and as one of the terrorists brought up his weapon to shoot him, Shepherd kicked out and sent the terrorist tumbling into the orchestra pit. As Shepherd swung back he heard fresh shooting and saw Geordie and Jimbo sprinting towards the stage, double-tapping targets as they ran.

Still swinging on the end of his abseil rope, Shepherd caught the last of the terrorists on the stage in a leg lock, clamping his legs around his neck so tightly that he slowly rendered him unconscious.

As the man collapsed, Shepherd released his hold and used his fighting knife to cut through the abseil rope. He dropped the last few feet onto the stage, ran to the edge and looked down into the orchestra pit, then double-tapped the terrorist he had knocked there, as the man frantically tried to bring his own weapon to bear.

CHAPTER 29

While his men had sprung into action, in line with the plan which he had waited so long to bring to fruition, Sabit hung back in the shadows at the side of the stage. Only when the Chinese security guards had been eliminated and Comrade Chou brought on stage at gunpoint, would Sabit emerge. Chou would then be forced to his knees, the charges against him read out while one of Sabit's men filmed him, and then Sabit would pronounce sentence – death – and carry it out, shooting Chou between the eyes, revenge at last for the thousands of Uyghurs he had imprisoned, exiled, tortured or executed. The video would flash around the world. China would be plunged into chaos and the Uyghur people would rise up and overthrow their oppressors. Whether Sabit survived to enjoy that moment was irrelevant. His fate did not matter, because he would already have fulfilled his vow and his life's aim.

But when the firing broke out, he was horrified to see some of his men turning their guns on each other and he realised that Chou's men had somehow

341

infiltrated his group and the operation had been betrayed. Even worse, although he had known about it in advance, Chou had allowed the attack to go ahead. His mind racing, Sabit saw with terrible clarity, the trap into which he, his men and the cause of Uyghur freedom had been led. Chou's aim was also to use the full glare of publicity, not to free the Uyghurs but to enslave them further. If he survived an assassination attempt, his prestige and status would be enhanced and he would also have the perfect excuse for the most brutal purge yet of the Uyghurs.

Sabit saw Chou, still in his seat, apparently unmoved by the shooting echoing around him. Burning with fear and rage, Sabit drew his weapon and, stepping over the body of one of his men, moved forward onto the blood-soaked stage, his gaze fixed on Chou. If he could not fulfil all his aims, he could at least take Chou to hell with him.

CHAPTER 30

Shepherd scanned the auditorium for any remaining threats when he saw Sabit, dressed in the green uniform of the chorus, striding forward, his gaze and the barrel of his AK 47 fixed on Chou. One of Chou's Chinese bodyguards had seen him and fired, but the rounds went wide and Sabit dropped him with a short burst, then swung his rifle back towards Chou and his finger again tightened on the trigger.

Shepherd took aim and fired. Two rounds smashed into Sabit's head. The first drilled into his skull half an inch above his ear, the second punched another hole half an inch above the first. The two rounds created a single exit wound, a gaping hole on the opposite side of his skull, through which Sabit's lifeblood and brains exploded. Clamped in his death grip, his own weapon sent out a burst of fire but Sabit's lifeless body was already slumping sideways and the rounds merely stitched a line of impacts up the theatre wall and into the ceiling above.

Shepherd had already turned his attention back to the auditorium, still scanning for further threats, but

Geordie, Jimbo and the Aussie SAS men had already eliminated the remaining terrorists and were now flexi-cuffing all the Chinese who were still standing for vetting and interrogation, before allowing the emergency services in to attend to the wounded. Last through the theatre doors came Rupert, elated that for once he had not cocked up the task he had been set.

As soon as the shooting ceased and silence fell, Shepherd saw the Chinese leader get to his feet and, flanked by his surviving bodyguards, he hurried to the door at the side of the theatre. As if passing through a revolving door, he emerged again only moments later and this time his full retinue of bodyguards was accompanying him. To Shepherd's bafflement, instead of leading him out of the theatre, they then returned him to his seat.

Shepherd moved quickly over to Geordie and Jimbo. 'Everyone okay?' he asked, but before they could reply they were interrupted by a British army colonel, who had been seated in the third row and whose full dress uniform and face were now covered in someone else's blood.

'Excellent job men,' he said, mopping at his face with a handkerchief. 'I'm the Military Attaché from the embassy and I know who you are, because my in-tray has been full of signals about you for the last few weeks, but the Chinese leader wants to thank you personally.'

Shepherd was about to demur but the Chinese leader had already risen from his seat and was being ushered towards them. The SAS men smiled through gritted teeth as the introductions were made, but when Chou, through his interpreter, said 'Thank you, you saved my life,' Shepherd couldn't stop himself from replying, 'Really? That's not what it looked like to me. I don't think you were in any danger at any point.'

The translator nervously relayed the statement to Chou. The Chinese leader's smile froze on his face and he directed a look of pure hatred at Shepherd before turning his back and walking away.

'There are going to be medals for this,' the Military Attaché said, blissfully unaware both of what Shepherd had just said and the permafrost in the atmosphere as Chou went back to his seat. 'Which of you chaps is in charge?'

Shepherd, Geordie and Jimbo all immediately pointed at Rupert and said in unison. 'He is.'

Police, paramedics, fire crews and flustered Australian officials were now pouring into the theatre. While the paramedics checked the bodies for signs of life and police began searching the wings and the backstage area for any surviving terrorists, officials crowded around the Chinese party, desperate to placate Chou, who appeared to be in surprisingly high spirits considering his narrow escape. He was smiling broadly as he at last made his way out of the theatre.

CHAPTER 31

Reunited with their RAF aircrew, the SAS team were soon in the 125 high above central Australia and heading west. They had been hustled out of the Opera House, and were then hustled out of Sydney, Richmond and Australia in rapid succession.

Shepherd and the others were reviewing CCTV footage of the incident at the Opera House on a laptop, while Jock watched from his hospital bed on the satellite link. 'We haven't really had chance for an after action debrief,' Shepherd said, 'because we've been too busy getting the bum's rush from Australia, but there were things going on in the Opera House that the powers that be definitely don't want made public.'

He ran the footage of Chou entering the theatre, disappearing into the side-room and then re-emerging, and then showed the sequence after the shooting had stopped when Chou again went in and out of the side-room.

'So what the hell was going on?' Jock said.

'It's simple, isn't it?' Shepherd said. 'Chou was using a double. Real Chou came out of his hotel,

346

joined the motorcade and did the meet and greet on the steps of the Opera House and then disappeared through the side door in the theatre. He then apparently re-emerged a few seconds later and took his seat, but that wasn't the real Chou. It was the double.'

He rewound the footage again. 'Notice how only half the bodyguard team are there when he comes out again? Why were the others not with him? Because they were guarding the real Chou in the side room. And how do we know the other is a fake? Well he doesn't address a single word to the Aussies, nor respond when they try to talk to him. I think the Chinese knew that there was going to be an attack and they made sure that the Chinese Premier was never in harm's way.'

'So,' Jock said, 'the overall conclusion is that the Chinese government agents had penetrated the terrorist organisation, knew in advance that the attack was going to happen and had taken steps to neutralise the threat but still used a body-double in case Chou was hit by a stray bullet or one of the terrorists got lucky?'

'But if they knew about it in advance, why did they allow it to happen,' Jimbo asked, 'rather than rounding up or eliminating them beforehand?'

'Because it suited China's agenda that way,' Shepherd said. 'And to hell with how many innocent people were killed and wounded in the process. What better pretext could there be for launching a final crackdown on Uyghur dissidents? And I'll bet that the Australian and British governments were aware of this too, but chose to keep it under wraps for their own political and economic purposes.'

While they had been discussing it, Aimee had been watching rolling news coverage of a press conference about the incident on her own laptop. 'Speaking of which,' she said, 'he really is a prime shit.' She turned her laptop round so they could see footage of Rupert, in dark glasses, being humble for the benefit of the world's media. Already he was being dubbed "The Opera House Hero" by reporters looking for an easy story, coupled with suggestions that he should be "awarded the Victoria Cross for his brave actions during the siege of the Sydney Opera House."

'You know what?' Geordie said. 'When I first saw Rupert I thought he was a bit of an arsehole. As I got to know him better, I still thought he was an arsehole, but now I really feel I know him and do you know what? He's definitely an arsehole.'

'That's one thing we can all agree on,' Shepherd said with a laugh. He reclined his seat and stretched out his legs. 'Now keep the noise down, will you. I need to catch up on my beauty sleep.'

EPILOGUE

City of Ghosts
By a Special Correspondent
Turguan, Xinjiang, 14 May

Turguan in the Chinese Autonomous Region of Xinjiang, has always been a place with one foot rooted firmly in the past. An oasis and caravanserai on the edge of the vast Taklamakan Desert in the days when the Silk Road was one of the world's principal arteries of trade, its native Uyghur people still weave their cloth in patterns that would have been familiar to Genghis Khan.

Turguan went into a long decline as the Silk Road's significance faded, but in recent years it had begun to thrive again. The discovery of oil turned it into a boom town and its importance grew as the Chinese drove the great China National Highway ever westwards, channelling their goods through Asia and the West. That brought much needed jobs to one of the poorest regions in the country, but also increased its strategic importance to Beijing, leading to repression of the fiercely independent Muslim Uyghurs.

Sporadic protests and rebellions were met by increasingly ferocious government crackdowns, but even twelve months ago Turguan remained a bustling frontier city. Now, following the attempt by Uyghur terrorists to assassinate the Chinese leader during his state visit to Australia, a draconian solution to the "Uyghur problem" has been enforced and Turguan has become a city of ghosts, its outskirts half-buried by the advancing sand dunes.

The only Uyghur people on the streets are old men and women. After the assassination attempt, in a final effort to subdue and control this fractious province, young Uyghur men were rounded up. Thousands were imprisoned and thousands more exiled to isolated forced labour camps near the Mongolian frontier. Young Uyghur women were offered the choice of exile or arranged marriage to some of the floods of ethnic Han Chinese being relocated – so many that the Uyghur have become a minority population in their own homeland. Children were taken from their parents and sent to orphanages or adopted by childless Han couples all over China.

Government edicts prohibit any gathering of three or more people and forbid women to wear the traditional veil and men to grow beards. All manifestations of Uyghur culture – language, customs, even their traditional textile patterns – have been banned.

Try to speak to one of the few Uyghur visible in the city and the usual reaction is a frightened glance up and down the street and a hurried 'I can't speak to you'. Chinese security men are everywhere, their mere presence an implicit threat to those who remain.

Only one old man was brave – or foolhardy – enough to speak to me. 'Look around you,' he said, the sweep of his extended arm taking in the town and the desert beyond. This was our homeland, granted to us by Allah. Neither Genghis Khan, nor Timur, nor any Chinese emperor could destroy us. Yet now we are broken. One man, who grew up among us, has destroyed us: Chou.' He spat into the dust as he uttered the name. 'In twenty years' time, our language, our culture, the Uyghur people ourselves, will have ceased to exist.'

He would have said more but my Chinese "escorts" who had been shadowing my every step, intervened and surrounded me. I was steered away towards the town's mayor, a functionary appointed by Beijing who could be trusted to parrot the party line. When I shrugged off my escort for a moment and looked back, I saw soldiers dragging the old man away.

ABOUT THE AUTHOR

Stephen Leather is one of the UK's most successful thriller writers, an eBook and *Sunday Times* bestseller and author of the critically acclaimed Dan "Spider" Shepherd series and the Jack Nightingale supernatural detective novels. Before becoming a novelist he was a journalist for more than ten years on newspapers such as *The Times*, the *Daily Mirror*, the *Glasgow Herald*, the *Daily Mail* and the *South China Morning Post* in Hong Kong. He is one of the country's most successful eBook authors and his eBooks have topped the Amazon Kindle charts in the UK and the US. *The Bookseller* magazine named him as one of the 100 most influential people in the UK publishing world.

Born in Manchester, he began writing full-time in 1992. His bestsellers have been translated into fifteen languages. He has also written for television shows such as *London's Burning*, *The Knock* and the BBC's *Murder in Mind* series, Two of his novels, *The Stretch* and *The Bombmaker*, were filmed for TV and *The Chinaman* is now a major motion picture starring Pierce Brosnan and Jackie Chan.

To find out more, you can visit his website at www.stephenleather.com.

TALL ORDER

Hodder and Stoughton have published fourteen books featuring Dan 'Spider' Shepherd written by *Sunday Times* bestselling author Stephen Leather. The fifteenth, *Tall Order*, will be published in July 2018.

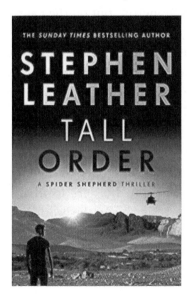

He is one of the world's most successful terrorists – codenamed Saladin. He plans and executes devastating terrorist attacks and then disappears, like a ghost.

Ten years ago he blew a plane out of the sky above New York, killing the wife and son of the US Defense Secretary, along with hundreds of innocent civilians.

CIA assassin Richard Yokely was sent to kill Saladin – but he failed. Now, ten years later, Saladin has struck again, killing dozens of fans at a London football match.

But one of the latest victims is related to someone who has the power to track down and kill Saladin, and Spider Shepherd is put on the case.

There is only one man who can identify Saladin – a psychologically-damaged former Navy SEAL called Dean Martin. But Yokely killed Martin ten years earlier. Or did he?

Shepherd has to track down Martin, make him a warrior again and take him back to the killing fields on the Afghan/Pakistan borders to identify and take long overdue revenge on the world's most wanted terrorist…

Printed in Great Britain
by Amazon

23406496R10209